PRAISE FOR RU

'Ruth Kelly is my go-to for destination thrillers'
Andrea Mara,
Sunday Times bestselling author of *No One Saw a Thing*

'Queen of the chilling thriller'
Veronica Henry,
Sunday Times bestselling author of *The Impulse Purchase*

'Deliciously addictive'
T. M. Logan,
Sunday Times bestselling author of *The Holiday*

'Hits the ground running and doesn't stop
until the final chapter'
John Marrs,
Sunday Times bestselling author of *Keep It in the Family*

'Sinister, atmospheric and deliciously chilling – with
a twist that made me gasp'
Mark Edwards,
Sunday Times bestselling author of *Here to Stay*

'A terrific page-turning thriller for dark winter nights'
B. P. Walter,
Sunday Times bestselling author of *The Dinner Guest*

THE AFTERPARTY

Ruth Kelly is a bestselling Richard & Judy Book Club author who writes pacy, twisty, 'up-all-night' psychological thrillers.

Holiday destinations feature heavily in Ruth's thrillers as she has spent most of her life travelling and exploring the world. Her family relocated to Papua New Guinea when she was seven years old and the travel bug hasn't let up since. The threat of what lies beneath the surface and the dichotomy of how paradise can also be hell fascinates Ruth. She lived in Amsterdam for many years and drew on the city's shadowy canals, winding backstreets and layered history as inspiration for *The Afterparty*.

Before she turned her hand to murderous plots, Ruth was a ghostwriter known for capturing authentic, compelling voices across a diverse spectrum – from celebrities and entrepreneurs to the unsung heroes of this world who have overcome profound adversity and trauma.

She's ghosted a string of *Sunday Times* top ten best-sellers – most recently *The Prison Doctor*, which sold more than 250,000 copies and is currently being adapted for television, and *The Governor*, the instant number one bestseller on Amazon Books.

Readers can follow Ruth on X and Instagram @ruthywriter

By Ruth Kelly

The Villa
The Escape
The Ice Retreat

THE
AFTERPARTY

RUTH KELLY

PAN BOOKS

First published 2025 by Pan Books
an imprint of Pan Macmillan
The Smithson, 6 Briset Street, London EC1M 5NR
EU representative: Macmillan Publishers Ireland Ltd, 1st Floor,
The Liffey Trust Centre, 117–126 Sheriff Street Upper,
Dublin 1 D01 YC43
Associated companies throughout the world

ISBN 978-1-0350-6396-3

1 3 5 7 9 8 6 4 2

A CIP catalogue record for this book is available from the British Library.

Typeset by Palimpsest Book Production Ltd, Falkirk, Stirlingshire
Printed and bound in the UK using 100% Renewable Electricity
by CPI Group (UK) Ltd

MIX
Paper | Supporting
responsible forestry
FSC
www.fsc.org
FSC® C116313

Visit **www.panmacmillan.com** to read more about all our books
and to buy them.

We're all one traumatic event away from the worst day of your life being reduced to your neighbour's favourite binge show.

Eric Perry

5 January

A cold mist drifts across the canals while the morning light breaks through. Everything is still, everything is calm. Hans inhales deeply; the cool crisp air clearing his lungs.

He pulls the cord several times, the motor splutters and then roars into life, the rumble of the boat's engine shaking the dawn.

Within minutes it settles down into something more rhythmical, idling in a gentle *chug chug chug*. The water quietly lapping against the hull, sluicing the sides clean in anticipation of their daily excursion into the city.

Hans has lived on the Amsterdam canals his entire life. His parents raised him on the water and he's carried on the tradition, although he must do so alone now his wife has passed.

Time is running away from him and it's frightening. He clings onto the past with both hands, keeping the memory of his beloved Anouk alive by honouring their traditions and daily rituals. Every morning, come rain or shine, Hans eases his creaking body into the small sky-blue boat moored to the side of his houseboat, in time to catch the sunrise. And this morning is promising something extraordinary.

The temperature plummeted last night and for the first time in years the canals have frozen. Frost sparkles across the surface like diamonds. Luckily, it's still just a thin skin of ice. He revs the motor, the rudder whirls and the ice cracks as he steers the nose of the boat out towards the Amstel River.

The noise of the ice breaking apart – the *chink chink* against the hull – it's immensely satisfying. Hans feels a rush of pride, for he's making his mark on the historic city, carving out the first inroad. Later, the tourist boats will arrive. Thousands of noisy weekenders choking up the canals with their rowdy behaviour and bad manners.

He feels a surge of anger. How things have changed since he was a boy. He does what he can, mostly fishing out rubbish and occasionally scrubbing off graffiti, but he's getting too old for this. His body is letting him down and he's uncertain how much longer he can go on.

It's better not to think about it. He boxes away his bitterness and focuses on what he does have – a glorious city at his feet. And the moment feels special.

So very special.

He moves the rudder. His wrist twinges. The arthritic joints are protesting, seizing up with the cold, but he pushes through because up ahead is the bridge that marks a junction, where the Keizersgracht ends and the Brouwers-gracht begins.

A seagull caws, circling above, coming to rest on a street lamp. Beady eyes, watching him, as he slows to make the turn. The purr of the engine, suddenly louder as he enters the tunnel. The noise rises up, echoing all around him. The dank smell of canal water, rushing to greet him.

The tunnel is shiny with damp. Moss and lichen feed off the brickwork. Someone has graffitied the wall with obscenities. His insides tremble with rage. How much more of this can he withstand?

He forces his attention back to the boat, for the ice is thicker here; he must be careful not to jam the motor. He slows the throttle, and then something up ahead catches his attention.

Something colourful beneath the ice.

'*Godverdomme!* Drunken tourists polluting my city with their stag weekends! They should be fined and punished, banned from my country,' Hans mutters under his breath and then kills the engine. He grabs hold of the pole he keeps handy for moments like this and lowers himself down, wincing as his knees make contact with the hard steel hull.

He lets out a groan as he swings the pole around, launching it into the canal. The wood bounces, skidding across the thick ice.

Gritting his teeth, he goes at it again, with more force. Jabbing. Poking. The boat rocks, but the ice behaves as stubbornly as him. If he loses his balance and falls overboard, the shock of the cold water will finish off his heart.

Clambering back onto his feet, he switches over hands. Gripping the pole like a javelin, Hans winches back his arm. He can hear his wife's voice in his head, *Hou op, het is niet veilig* – stop, it's not safe – as he throws his body weight into the stubborn ice.

The boat tilts.

Hans stumbles.

A loud crack. Echoing through the hallowed space, and sending a surprise shiver down his spine.

Then, nothing.

Hans sits back down heavily, defeated.

He hears a faint noise. A crackling. Like the sound of rustling paper. The ice splinters. Hairline fractures spread, reaching for him, and then all at once . . .

SNAP.

The ice breaks apart, water gushes up, like a breath it's been holding in. The trapped fabric balloons with water, working its way to the surface.

Hans pulls back a fraction, uncertain. What is it? Blood runs to his neck, a hot sensation suddenly crowding around his collarbone. He has a bad feeling about this.

He prods the material, hitting something hard beneath. *That's strange*. Fishing it out, he arcs it through the air, straining under the weight. Water pouring from it like an open wound.

Shaken free, the scarf lands inside the boat with a muted *thud*. Curled and twisted like a dead animal. Hans stares at the dull red fabric curiously for a moment, letting several beats pass. Then he shakes his head impatiently, places the pole where he found it and restarts the motor.

Chug chug chug.

The engine purrs with happiness as Hans carves a path out of the tunnel. The second he emerges into the bright morning light, he smiles at the new day and leaves his bad temper behind him.

And something else.

Chug chug chug.

The noise of the motor drowning out the quiet gurgling.

Chug chug.

Bubbles rising.

Chug.

Hidden in the dark water, trapped beneath the surface. Skin pale as frost. Eyes wide open and bulging, mouth gaping.

A face, pressed up against the ice.

THE FRIEND – BECCA

I can't hear a word they're saying. It's as if my head is being held underwater. A tangle of noise. A buzzing in my ear.

He's not the type to have an affair. Not my Nathan. My soulmate. He wouldn't, would he? The voice in my head is deafening, drowning out everyone around me.

I smile politely, make my excuses and peel away from the group.

My head is spinning, the heat in the room is making me dizzy. I stumble but quickly recover. It's these stupid high heels, I'm not used to wearing them and I can't wait to kick them off.

Carefully I pick my way through the crowd, weaving around the tables dressed in the finest white linen and polished silver. One of the waitresses shows me a tray of wafer-thin Iberico ham coiled around strips of ripe melon, sprinkled with lemon and rock salt. I take one, hoping the food will settle my stomach.

It doesn't.

A quick glance over my shoulder, making sure I'm not needed.

But nobody's even noticed I'm gone.

I'm relieved and upset. How can I be feeling both?

As I slide open the floor-to-ceiling glass door, the laughter and music, the clinking of champagne flutes fades, and I step into the December cold. I take in the icy air, my clammy skin finally cooling off while I look out over the canal and into the dark water. Without wind, it's as still as a mirror. Peaceful. So why do I feel so uneasy?

There's a sack of rocks in my stomach. I swallow, trying to clear the sensation.

It's still there.

Slipping off my heels, I let the chilled wood decking soothe my bare feet. I concentrate on my breathing, pulling air into my lungs, trying to calm myself with the relaxation techniques I've picked up from hours searching the internet for answers.

How to cure your anxiety. How to slow your racing thoughts.

Signs that your husband is having an affair.

I feel the prickle of tears. All the signs have been there. The grooming. Being protective of his phone. Working later than he needs to. Not wanting to spend time with me. Small things that individually could all be explained away, but when you stack them up . . .

There's a sudden swell of noise as the door slides open. Quickly I dry my eyes, hoping my make-up smudges won't give me away.

'What are you doing out here?' Nathan sounds surprised. I feel a sudden pressure, an arm sliding around my waist. Then lips brushing against my bare shoulder. But all I can focus on is his hand placed against my stomach and how desperately I want him to remove it.

'You feeling OK?' He kisses me again, his mouth working its way up my neck. Gently, he moves me around to face him. Eyes bright and blazing.

'I think it's going really well,' my husband says quietly, glancing back inside his restaurant where the investors are mingling for the soft launch of Muse. 'Jesus, my nerves are shredded.'

I follow his gaze, smiling weakly.

'I've persuaded Pieter de Jong into funding some extra seating for the terrace. We could start work as early as mid-January. Add some extra tables, outdoor heaters – a few more weeks to wait, that's all.' He steals the melon slice from my hand, taking a bite. 'How do you think it's going?' He searches my eyes.

Have I made a mistake? I watch Nathan, lit up from within, behaving lovingly and tenderly towards me, and my compass feels off again. I'm so confused.

'Tonight couldn't have gone better,' I reassure him.

'And after everything we've been through. I can't believe it.'

'It's all coming together, just like you said.'

'It's happening.' He exhales, and then frowns. 'Tell me, it's really happening?'

'It's happening.'

He takes my hand. 'Because I'm terrified. What if I wake up and this has all been . . .' He stops.

'All been what?'

'I don't know.' He shrugs. 'A crazy pipe dream that I've upended our lives for.'

'You've got to stop doubting yourself.'

'I worry about you, though. Moving abroad, taking you away from the village, your job, your friends. Dragging you with me on my mad adventure.'

I swallow the lump that's reappeared in my throat.

'You need to stop that.'

'What I've done, it's been a risk, I know that. But I can't go back; I can't. Working for Dad was killing me.'

'Nobody's forcing you to do anything,' I say calmly. Evenly.

'You're bloody wonderful. Have I told you that?' He kisses me. 'None of this would have been possible without you believing in me.'

'It was all you.'

'I've got so many ideas.' Nathan lights up.

'Which you need to tell them about.'

'And they're so impressed with the location.' His gaze lifts, sweeping up and down the canal. The Bloemgracht – one of the most picturesque canals in Amsterdam. He returns to the modern floating steel-and-chrome structure, its open-plan kitchen spilling into the marble-floored dining area. A sea of black granite, sharp-edged surfaces; simple, understated and expensive looking, with windows for walls. The whole place gleams in the moonlight.

'So what if it cost us more to build on the water? You have to stand out in this business, right? Seventy per cent of restaurants go bust in the first year. God! That's terrifying when you think about it.' He exhales, his eyebrows knitting together. 'The odds are stacked against us. So it was worth it, I think . . .' His eyes search mine again.

'It was the right thing to do.'

'And when the restaurant takes off, we'll be able to buy a place of our own.'

I nod gently.

'Somewhere on the canal, with lots of space for a family.' He spreads his hand across my tummy, running it over where my bump should be.

I fight to keep my smile in place. I can't bring myself to tell him what's happened. Now's not the time. And I'm not sure I've fully come to terms with it.

'All these people are here tonight because of *you*.' I change the subject.

'Are you coming through?'

'Give me a minute.'

'Everyone loves you, you know.' He kisses me again. He smells fresh from the shower, zesty, his hair still slightly damp.

I've made a mistake. I've misread the signs.

I iron out the crease in his shirt with my hand and kiss him back, feeling immensely proud of who he's becoming. It's been so long since I've seen Nathan this happy, this excited about anything. Living in the shadow of his dad almost destroyed him, and I must remind myself of that – how far we've come, how the sacrifices were worth it – whenever the loneliness creeps back in.

Our first Christmas away from home was bound to be difficult. But that's over now and there's the New Year celebrations to look forward to tomorrow. The firework displays in Amsterdam are world renowned and I can't wait to share it all with my Nathan.

There's a sudden noise from the party. Raised voices, then a rupture of applause and whistling. Nathan's attention is pulled from me to the woman who has taken centre stage.

'That must be Katya,' he says excitedly, releasing me.

Katya – Nathan's friend and now business partner. They met five years ago when she got a job as a chef in Nathan's dad's pub on her gap year abroad. She's the culinary talent behind Muse. She's the one who persuaded Nathan that Amsterdam was the next big thing; that the London restaurant scene was saturated and their idea wouldn't land in the same way in the UK as it would in her home city. She boasted about her connections to get the project off the ground. It was Katya who persuaded my husband to uproot our lives. And recently I've started to wonder whether the name of the restaurant – *Muse* – holds a deeper meaning than I first thought.

Circulating the party, she instantly takes up space despite her petite frame. Katya's everything you'd expect from a Dutch beauty – long blonde hair, a year-round golden tan.

How does she do it? How does she manage to turn heads even in shapeless chef's whites? Her cheeks are flushed from the heat of the ovens but she still looks stunning. She makes a slow turn, taking a bow to the crowd's applause.

'I'll see you in there,' Nathan says over his shoulder, already halfway to meet her.

I feel the sudden cold he's left behind. The emptiness is immediate and I search around for something to fill the void.

The large glass of wine I've been hiding from my husband.

More secrets.

I chase one gulp down with another, trying to flush away the insecurity, because that's what it is. I'm envious of how much time they're spending together, especially as Katya's attractive *and* slim. She's the cool girl all the boys want to hang out with; any woman in my shoes would feel insecure, wouldn't she? Especially seeing how Katya makes him light up.

I steal another glance, noticing her illuminating effect on the entire room. Heads are tipping back with laughter. Eyes are feasting on her. As if she can feel me watching, Katya looks up. Our eyes meet and she gives me a kind smile. I smile back, suddenly ashamed for mistrusting Nathan and Katya's relationship. And feeling even more guilty about what I did the other night.

It's the isolation. It's the loneliness of moving abroad. *Idle hands are the devil's tools.* Plus, all the hormones raging around my body aren't helping. I'm on a cocktail of prenatal vitamins and supplements – could that be ramping up my paranoia? And then there's what's happened. I bite my lip before I start crying. I've been doing that a lot recently: suddenly bursting into tears without any obvious trigger.

Jesus, calm down.

Breathe.

I need to pull myself together, go back inside and show these people I'm here for Nathan, that I'm fully behind my husband and his fine-dining experience. I must place my grief and insecurities to one side and stop being so bloody selfish.

I take a breath, and another, and then return to where I should be.

Next to the door is a table of drinks; one of the waitresses gives me a confused look as I pull the bottle of chilled champagne from the ice bucket. Breaking the seal, I pop the cork. The fizz spills out, running over my fingers and awakening my senses.

I can do this – put on a brave face. Play the charming hostess. It's one night, for heaven's sake.

Balancing a tray full of glasses in one hand, I move carefully in the direction of the crowd with a drawn-on smile. Taking care not to let my secret be known.

I'm the happy loyal wife. Who keeps secrets from her husband.

THE FRIEND – BECCA

Nathan's side of the bed is empty when I wake up.

I check my phone. It's 5.30 a.m. Oh God, he didn't come home.

Then I hear the flush of the toilet and feel a wave of relief. OK, stop now. Stop doing this to yourself, because it's a form of self-harm. All this stress, it can't be helping with getting pregnant. That's probably what caused *it*. Unable to subvocalize the actual word, I feel another wrench of guilt as my mind spins back to three nights ago when Nathan was away for work and I woke up to stabbing cramps and the feeling of ice-cold sheets wrapped around my legs.

The horror of turning on the bedside light to find the mattress soaked in blood haunts me now. So traumatic was my miscarriage that I reach for Nathan as soon as he's back under the duvet. He rolls over onto his side and I press my chest against his back, absorbing his warmth. He grunts and then moves away.

No, Becca, don't read into it; he still loves you, he's just exhausted. You're doing that thing again. When life is spiralling out of control, I cling on more tightly. Oh God, I have to stop these negative thoughts from taking over – it's becoming an obsession. And it's starting to show. I look awful – haunted, in fact – and I can't find the energy to do anything.

Hang in there.

Just five days and the launch will be over. Then the floor manager can step in, the restaurant can get on with running itself and I can have my husband back.

In the meantime there's a holiday to look forward to. After the investors had left, Nathan hugged and kissed me and promised two weeks in Mauritius – the honeymoon we never got around to. Nathan wouldn't suggest taking me away somewhere so expensive if he was having an affair.

I soothe myself with a checklist of reassurances that Nathan still loves me, that he hasn't tired of me even after ten years together. The holiday he's planning for us. *Tick.* The impressive bouquet of tulips, hydrangeas and white roses he surprised me with last week. *Tick.* Tickets to the plush cinema in town. *Tick, tick.* Thoughtful gestures, sometimes only small, but I know they mean a great deal.

Slowly I work through them, again and again, as if I were counting sheep. The repetition eventually calms me, and my eyelids begin to grow heavy.

I'm awoken by the noise of a zipper. I blink into the early-morning light pouring between the curtains. I blink again as my other senses slowly awaken; my gaze is drawn by the *clunk* as Nathan stands his suitcase on its end.

On hearing me stir, he looks over and smiles. He sits down beside me on the bed. The mattress dips as he leans in, giving me a peck on the cheek. He smells of toothpaste and his expensive aftershave.

'I was trying not to wake you.'

'Where are you going?' I croak.

His phone starts buzzing, he looks at it briefly, frowns, rejects the call and slips it inside his pocket.

'Did you sleep OK?' He runs a hand across my cheek, pushing the hair from my face.

'What time is it?'

His phone goes off again and this time he gets up, crossing to the far corner of the bedroom.

'Hi. Yeah, sure. Can I call you back in a minute?' he says quickly, his voice frayed. He hangs up, looks back at me, his smile strained.

'My flight's in three hours. I'm sorry, I should go.'

'Wait. Go where?'

'I have to travel to London.'

'London? I don't—'

'Something urgent has come up and I need to thrash out the details with a possible new investor.'

'But – it's New Year's Eve.'

'If I don't grab this opportunity now . . .' Seeing my expression, he tails off. 'Sorry, love. It's the last place I want to be going.'

'Can't it wait?' I feel myself bristling with frustration that his work always comes before me. He promised we'd be together to celebrate the New Year.

'Opportunities like this almost never happen. You know

how difficult it's been securing investment; I've got to grab this with both hands. We're having drinks with Brad Garcia; his family own a hedge fund worth fifty million and there'll be some important people there. He's flying out to New York on the second, so this is our only chance. Bex, after all the setbacks we've had, you know I can't lose this.'

And then the third person in our marriage slams into my thoughts.

'Is Katya going?'

He looks a little startled by my tone and gives me a puzzled frown.

'We're business partners so, yeah, I need her to sit in on this.'

'Right.'

'I'll be back the day after tomorrow.'

'Two days from now?' I sigh. 'You have no idea how to switch off.'

'Well, that's restaurants for you – it's an antisocial business, everyone knows that.'

'And I'm supposed to accept it? What if I need more?'

'Becca, come on; so much is riding on this.' He shakes his head in frustration. 'It's only until we open, and then things will calm down.'

I stare at him, unable to find the words. My chest is tightening, filling up with anxiety and dread. I know the reaction I'm having is over the top, but I can't stop it.

'I'm sorry. I know we planned something special.' He puts his palms together in a gesture of contrition. 'But I'll make up for it when I'm back.'

It feels like grief, the weight sitting on my chest that's making it impossible to breathe. The same sensation as when I lost the baby.

I should have told him about the miscarriage earlier. Why didn't I? But now's not the time, not when he's rushing out the door.

'I wouldn't be doing this unless it was absolutely necessary,' he says defensively.

Still, I have no words. I'm searching, scrabbling around my brain to find something that won't make me sound hysterical or irrational. Because right now all I want to do is scream the house down. Meanwhile, a dull ache is building, expanding between my temples.

Nathan checks his phone and his eyebrows knot. Hurriedly, he says, 'I've really got to go now, I'm sorry.'

He reaches for his suitcase, tugging it towards the landing, and then he stops, as if suddenly remembering that I'm still in the room. He smiles awkwardly and hurries to my side, planting a rushed kiss on my forehead before retracing his steps. He leaves this time, but he's forgotten something else. There's no *I love you* as the door closes, leaving me alone in the half-light.

THE FRIEND – BECCA

I stare into the Eye of Horus with mixed emotions.

In three days' time, the British Museum in London will celebrate the opening of 'Tutankhamun: Treasures of the Golden Pharaoh'. I scroll down the web page with envy and sadness, studying the Egyptian artefacts that they've managed to secure for the exhibition, overwhelmed with longing for the school trip that *I* should be taking the children on.

I'd spent an entire year teaching my class about my passion project – the pharaohs – and now my replacement will reap the rewards of my hard work. It doesn't seem fair, I think, picturing the children's faces lighting up as they walk between the wood-panelled rooms, staring into the display cabinets, the laughter ringing out on the coach ride home to Devon.

I take a breath, collecting my emotions, because it's really not that important. I was only a teaching assistant at the local school; there'll be other opportunities.

Another swoop of self-loathing for making Nathan feel guilty about leaving me. It's not his fault he needs to be back in London. The pressure he's been under to secure funding for Muse has been enormous, and all I'm doing is adding to it.

And *we* had to move, otherwise something terrible would have happened. Nathan was on the cusp of a nervous breakdown, working under his tyrant of a dad at the pub. He'd become a shadow of himself. Though some days it feels like that's what I've become.

A shadow.

Invisible.

'There'll be a great expat life out there. You'll make friends easily; everyone is in the same boat. It'll be a chance to start over.'

That's what everyone promised. But it's been none of those things. Nine months since selling our cottage in Devon, bundling our lives into the back of a van; moving from a quiet village to a bustling city. And now I feel more isolated than ever.

I'd hoped a baby might alter that – there'd be a little person to care for, someone who actually needs me. I catch myself before I burst into tears.

God, I feel so alone, but I can't talk to anyone about it. It's been difficult making friends in Amsterdam, and I wouldn't want to burden my best friend Soph and the girls back home; they'd only feel helpless they were miles away and couldn't give me a hug. And the last person I want to worry is Nathan – he's got enough on his plate.

So instead, I've been bottling it up, putting on a brave face while spending my days trapped inside a never-ending loop.

I wake up. I walk a hundred metres to the cafe on the corner with the pale blue awning. I exchange several words with the barista while I wait for my matcha latte.

Open laptop and resume job search.

I'm trying but it's been impossible to get an interview. The local schools want someone who can speak Dutch. There are a few expat colleges in the city but competition is fierce and I don't stand a chance with my lack of teaching qualifications. I've offered to help out in the restaurant but Nathan won't hear of it. He says it's not healthy for couples to work together. Recently, I've worried that's just an excuse and there's another reason he doesn't want me spending too much time there.

I squeeze my eyes tightly shut, trying not to think about Katya and what I did the other night.

Stop. Obsessing. About. Her.

The problem is, the less I do, the less I want to do. Minutes turn to hours and by 3 p.m. I'm typically collapsed on the sofa, scrolling through social media. Peering into the lives of others, wishing I had what they had. If only I could muster the energy, if only I could find my sparkle again.

I don't recognize myself any more. The other day, something really strange happened. I thought someone was following me. How crazy is that? I've even started carrying around a bottle of pepper spray. I think I might be losing my mind.

Numbly, I gaze through the cafe window. The sky is darkening, a patchwork of grey, and the air is thickening. Amsterdam seems colder and gloomier than the UK, and the thought of spring and summer feels impossible. I wake up every morning to rain, followed by darkness. And now snow is on the way.

The forecast is predicting a cold snap. They're saying the canals will freeze over, which hasn't happened in years. It's mid-afternoon, yet there's a sense that the world is creeping towards nightfall. That darkness is one breath away. A tram rumbles past. My matcha latte trembles in its cup.

I wasn't always this negative, this depressed. At first, I explored, I did the touristy things, like wandering the cavernous rooms of the museums and galleries, admiring the Vermeers and Van Goghs. But after exhausting every attraction, the newness of the city wore off and the seedier side of Amsterdam started to seep in.

The stag weekends. The sex shops. The prostitution. The smell of cannabis wherever I went. It became so suffocating I found myself building up imaginary walls to block it out, my world shrinking even further.

This cafe was meant to be an escape from the silence of the flat, but everywhere I turn I see painful reminders that I'll be spending New Year's Eve alone. The couple in the corner staring intensely into each other's eyes. The crowd of friends, talking over each other in Dutch, sharing a slice of warm apple and cinnamon pie.

I check my phone, searching for something to anchor me to home. There's a missed call from an unknown number. Nothing from Nathan. An uneasy feeling lodges in my stomach.

Think. Try to think about something else.

But within seconds I'm back where I started. Instead of focusing on what I need to do, I'm imagining Nathan's day. He'll have arrived at Heathrow by now, he'll be heading for the Underground. Suddenly it occurs to me – I have no idea where he's staying. An image of some plush hotel lands in my head. Is he sharing a room with Katya? No, Becca, that's absurd.

I check my phone again. Another missed call – number withheld. *That's weird*. I turn it off silent mode in case it's Nathan trying to get hold of me.

But instead of putting my mobile out of sight, I swipe to open Instagram, immediately checking on Katya's profile. She hasn't updated her page since last night's party. The first picture is still her and Nathan. Arm around his waist, gently leaning into him. Big cheery smile for the camera.

They look like a couple.

God, I hate her. I'll never be that pretty or talented. And I hate myself for hating her. For being so pathetic and bitter. I respond by rearranging my cup and half-eaten slice of cake into something aesthetically pleasing and post the photo on my Instagram with the hashtags #livingthedreamabroad and #dreamscancometrue, along with my location. Then I sink back into my chair.

There's a sudden bang behind us. The entire cafe turns. It's just kids in the street messing around with fireworks, but the shock of it stays with me, my heart thumping behind my ribcage as I scoop up my bag and head back out into the cold.

It feels like the temperature has dropped at least three degrees. My breath mists as I look up and down the quiet tree-lined avenue, following the long stretch of residential flats. Sixties, flat-roofed, ugly-looking things. A twenty-minute tram ride south of the centre, and it feels like I'm living in a different city entirely. *Things will be better when we move onto the canals.* Then I'll have the noise and the bustle to keep me company.

I should reach out to someone back in the UK, but I feel achingly tired, and the thought of connecting with home robs me of what's left of my energy. Tears spring to my eyes and I pick up the pace before I lose it, right here, on the pavement, in front of everyone.

And it's then, while I'm hurrying, that the feeling returns. A cold breeze on the back of my neck. The sensation I'm being watched. I glance over my shoulder several times to check, but nobody's there. It must be the hormones fluctuating. I tell myself I'm going mad, but I can't shake the uneasy feeling.

Laptop bag bumping against my hip, I pick up the pace and swing round the next corner, knocking into a woman pushing a buggy. The little girl drops her toy and starts crying.

Scooping the floppy rabbit off the ground, I place it back into her arms. The little girl's face immediately brightens. I have a sudden urge to stop and chat, to find out what it's like being a mum. To say something, anything, to break the deafening silence. The desperation must show in my face because the child's mother is eyeing me warily, edging away, and I feel a rush of shame.

It's the final straw. After days of bottling up my heart-ache, the tears arrive, and now they won't stop. I hurry home, burrowing my face inside my scarf, willing the ground to swallow me whole.

I stand in the entrance hall, listening to the stillness of the empty flat. The faint hum of the fridge. The hollow ticking of the clock. I dump my bag on the kitchen table, fighting the urge to collapse on the sofa.

For the next few minutes I pace around, resisting the urge to check my phone. I take a breath, then another, then head into the bathroom where I splash cold water on my face. But I can't wash away the sense of unease.

Crossing to the bedroom, I make the bed; it smells of us, of Nathan's aftershave. I open the windows, clearing the stale air. Then I head into the living room, where I wipe down the coffee table, plump the sofa cushions and throw away the vase of half-dead flowers. By 4 p.m. it's spotless.

Now what? *Don't stop, keep busy.*

I head for Nathan's study to try to make sense of the mess.

The box room is crammed with paperwork. Stacks of documents, towers of lever-arch files, and scraps of paper littering the floor. I open a cardboard box at my feet, it's filled with sketches, pencil drawings of the restaurant, documenting its infancy to opening. I can't help think about Nathan, how his face lit up with each new version of his dream.

My hand automatically reaches for my pocket.

Keep busy.

I force myself to look inside the next box. It's brimming

with official documents, endless forms we had to fill in to apply for residency in the Netherlands. But at the bottom is a photo. Our wedding day. Us, in love, kissing on the steps of the registry office. I wore a pink dress with white flowers and Nathan wore his cream linen suit. Smiling sadly, I lift it out of the box, placing the heavy frame on the bare shelf.

Keep busy.

I dive back into the mess, and this time I find something of mine. A box filled with books on Egypt. I begin unpacking, placing them on the shelves, until I come across *The Valley of the Kings*. The hardback creaks open like an ancient crypt, releasing a musty library odour. I slide down onto the floor and sit cross-legged, the heavy book across my knees, and begin reading. Within minutes I'm pulled into Ancient Egypt; it's 1150 BC and I'm walking through the labyrinth of passages inside Pharaoh Ramses IV's tomb. I can almost hear the echo of my footsteps, smell the dank air, feel the sand in my hair.

The past is soothing. The familiarity is as comforting as worn-in slippers; it takes the edge off my anxiety. As I lean back against the wall, exhaustion catches up with me. The words on the page blur, my eyes begin to close and soon I'm dreaming about sand dunes, hieroglyphics and ancient treasures.

My neck twinges. I lift my head; the room is pitch black. What time is it? I must have dozed off.

I check my phone: 5.36 p.m. Still nothing from Nathan. But I've missed three more calls from an unknown number.

Was I so soundly asleep I didn't hear it ring? Nathan would have left a message; this must be some pushy cold caller. I grit my teeth and get to my feet, making my way to the kitchen where I find Nathan's coffee cup and breakfast bowl in the sink. I fix myself a drink, take a breath, and as I stand marooned between the oven and the breakfast bar, my screen flashes. Anger flares, I swipe the iPhone from the counter.

'Whatever it is, I'm not interested!'

I'm about to hang up when I hear a faint: 'Twig?'

My breath catches.

'Twiggy?' the female voice says again in the poshest cut-glass English accent.

My brain scrambles. A distant memory, slowly being pulled to the surface. Cautiously, I bring the phone back to my ear and listen.

'Twig, is that you?'

I haven't heard that name in almost a decade.

'Tell me it is—'

It took me years to move on.

'Twig?'

To come to terms with what happened.

'Twiggy, I know it's you, darling.' I wait for her to continue but she sighs out theatrically. I think she's about to hang up.

'Georgie?' I croak.

'It is you! You still have the same number; I can't believe it.'

I inhale.

'I can't tell you how good it is to hear your voice.' A

27

pause. 'I'm sorry it's taken me so long to pick up the phone.'

My mind is reeling.

'You're being very quiet. I guess it's a bit of a shock.'

Silence.

'Yeah, you could say that,' I say eventually.

NOW

5 January

A small crowd has gathered by the canal while the sound of a siren wails in the distance.

A girl strapped into ice skates sobs into her mother's shoulder. The woman puts a hand to her daughter's head and strokes it, but her baby girl, her little princess, is inconsolable. Meanwhile, the snow continues to fall, twirling lazily, oblivious to the grisly scene hidden beneath the arches of the bridge.

'What was it? What did you see, meisje?' her mother whispers tenderly in her ear as she cradles her, rocking her gently back and forth. The girl blinks, she tries to talk but she has no voice. Her entire body is trembling with fear and cold as she slips further into shock.

The temperature is dropping. The ice is thickening. The snow is deepening fast, a dazzling blur of white across the canal, but the air is filled with death. Newcomers arrive, curious to find out what's happening, nudging one another out of the way to get a better look.

The flashing blue lights of a police car splinter the darkening sky. The siren crescendos, roaring inside the little girl's ears, then the car lurches to a stop beside the canal. The wailing is silenced and the air is suddenly still. Like a held breath.

THE TIKTOK DETECTIVE – JAMIE

Imagine solving the disappearance of the decade.

Imagine how famous I'll be. The press interviews. The breakfast show appearances. The book deal. Imagine how satisfying it'll feel, beating the coppers to it, showing the world I'm the next Sherlock Holmes, that I'm the greatest TikTok detective to walk this earth.

Imagine.

'Jamie?'

I blink from my daydream, returning to the overheated pub that's already crowded with locals for New Year's Eve. Aaron looks over from the bar. 'Guinness or Stella?'

'What you say?'

'Fucking hell, mate. Sometimes I think you're away with the fairies.'

'What's that?' I scowl.

'Ah, never mind.' Aaron returns to the barmaid and winks. 'He'll have a Guinness and make that another round of sambucas. Put it on the tab, will ya.'

It's hard to hear anything in this dive with the TV screens blasting. Some obnoxious windswept presenter reporting live from Big Ben. We've managed to find some space by the pool table. Aaron spills his beer over the green felt and sniggers.

'Cheers, boys!' He raises his shot glass.

The seven of us, mates since school, bump glasses, but my head's somewhere else. I look around, taking in the dreary room with its tired walls scuffed with marks, the floor that reeks of stale booze and vomit, the dartboard hanging at a drunken angle. I've been coming to the Hare and Tortoise with my mates since I was fifteen. Every Friday after work. Lock-ins on payday. This place has been my second home.

Not for much longer.

These fellas might be happy with their lot, but I've other plans. I want more from life and I know exactly how I'm gunna get it.

My name's Jamie Finn, I'm a twenty-five-year-old lad from south London. I live with my nan on a council estate in Lewisham and I work as a security guard. I make a decent living, keeping an eye out for shoplifters in department stores, manning the door at nightclubs as well as the odd hospital shift. You'd be surprised at what kicks off on a ward – there's always some lunatic wanting to start a fight. That's all fine, it pays the bills. But the thing is, I've always dreamt of more. Ever since I was a kid, I've wanted to join the police force, because that's what Dad did, and his dad before him.

I tried – honest to God, I did. I gave it my best shot, but when I flunked the entrance exams that set me off on a downward spiral. And then I got nicked for shoplifting and joyriding. Yeah, so, I've never been good with rejection.

Anyway, never mind that, I've found another way in.

Nowadays you don't need a badge to solve a crime. All you need is a smartphone and a camera that records. Oh, and a car, to get you to the crime scene quickly.

When I'm not doing my day job, you can find me over on TikTok at Crime_Tok_Detective where I offer insight, analysis and on-the-ground live reports. I cover everything from disappearances to murders to burglaries and spooky goings-on. The stuff you'd expect to see in a true crime documentary. Most days I feel like an MI5 agent, leading a double life. It's exhausting being me. LOL.

I'm not an armchair detective or a grief junkie or a ghoul or a TikTok idiot or whatever those journalist twats are calling us. I'm not anything like that. I'm just someone who can see through BS and is clued up when it comes to people lying. It's all in the eyes; you can tell everything just by the way someone looks – or won't look – at you. No copper's got the life experience that makes me qualified for this job.

I've got approximately twenty thousand followers. That's not to be sniffed at; but to make my channel grow, I need a proper mystery to solve, one that gets everyone's imagination going. I've been waiting for the right case, but it's difficult with all the competition; the world is filling up with amateur detectives trying to copy what I'm doing, and they're getting in the way. I have to stand out if I'm gunna be noticed.

The fellas laugh at me, they say I'm making a tit of

myself turning up at these crime scenes, videoing myself, but it'll be me having the last laugh soon, boys.

I look around the pub and at my drunk mates and my heart sinks. What am I doing here? I should be at home, poring over newsfeeds for potential stories. Checking the socials. Listening in to police radio. Going on the Dark Web.

The lads don't get it. Nobody does. Well, there is one person who understands, but I can't let myself think about her right now.

Ah, New Year's Eve has this effect, doesn't it? You start feeling down, reflecting on how shit your year has been. You swear the next will be better. It never is.

But this year *will* be better.

There'll be no more slaving away for long hours, putting up with arsehole bosses, being looked down on cos I'm security and not a real copper. Being told what to do.

Fuck that, this year will be *my* year.

'Jamie?'

I turn around.

'Want one?' Kaleb glances sideways then shows me what's in his hand.

'Nah, mate, I'm sorted.'

'What?'

'Yeah.' I show him my pint. 'I'm good with this.'

'You knocked your head or something? I'm offering you a pill.'

I take another slug of my beer.

'Suit yourself.'

Yeah, I will, I think, and return to mulling over the big

case I'm about to crack. Ah man, I want to be there now, feeling the rush, the thrill of solving a crime. The world hailing me as a hero. A new breed of detective. I see it all playing out before me. The build-up to midnight in the pub fades into white noise as I take stock of my bright future.

THE FRIEND – BECCA

From the window, I watch her collect her bags from the Uber, struck by how little Georgie has changed over the years. Her cat-eye sunglasses are pushed back into ombré hair that's falling in perfect waves around her shoulders. Looking effortlessly chic in a navy tailored blazer, skinny jeans, black leather ankle boots and her trademark fiery orange-red lipstick, she could be Sienna Miller's twin.

I've got butterflies in my stomach as I make my way downstairs. I'm nervous, excited and resentful, all at the same time. I take a deep breath and open the front door.

We both fall silent, staring at one another. Old friends, once as close as sisters, now lost for words.

'I can't believe it's really you,' Georgie says eventually.

How many times have I imagined this moment? And now it's finally happening, I'm speechless.

'Come on, you – how about giving your old friend a hug?' She steps forward, pulling me into her arms. I feel myself stiffening at first. Then I smell English Pear & Freesia, the same Jo Malone perfume she wore when we were teenagers, and I'm filled with a sudden longing for home. Any resentment I've been harbouring eases and I allow myself to relax in the embrace. I close my eyes for a second, the sensation almost bringing me to tears. I didn't realize how badly I needed a hug.

Georgie steps back, holding me at arm's length, her eyes running over me. I immediately feel underdressed in my tracksuit bottoms, slouch socks and Nathan's faded Guinness hoodie. Nervously, I run a hand through my new short do.

'It suits you.' Georgie smiles.

'She cut it too short.'

'It brings out your eyes.' Georgie brushes a loose strand from my cheek. Then she peers over my shoulder. 'You going to invite me in?'

'Sorry.' I push the door wide. 'You must be freezing.'

Georgie follows me up the three flights of stairs while my head drowns in questions.

'So did you work out I was living in Amsterdam from my Instagram?'

'I sent you a friend request,' she says. 'About a year ago. But I suppose you never saw it?'

I saw it. I didn't know what to do with it. So I pretended it never happened. And now she's turned up out of the blue, I have no choice but to face it.

'I'm surprised you haven't taken more photos of the city.' She moves on.

I go quiet.

'You must love living here?'

'How long do you plan on staying?' I change the subject.

'Just for one night. Bloody Eurostar was cancelled and

I refuse to pay through the nose for a flight. I'm so annoyed – I'm supposed to be at a rather fabulous dinner party in London tonight.'

'What are you doing in Amsterdam?'

'Passing through. Slowly making my way back home after a great-aunt's wedding anniversary in Lake Como. Exploring Europe, that kind of thing.'

A stab of jealousy. Still the same Georgie, still living the dream. Travelling the world, eating out every night in the most expensive restaurants, mixing with sophisticated people. Thanks to her family, she can afford to swan around Europe for the rest of her life. The reminder of how far our worlds have drifted apart, stinging.

'It's kind of you to let me stay,' she says as we reach the top floor. Georgie stops and looks around. 'This is nice.'

I can feel her assessing the apartment. She's probably thinking how poky it is. Georgie places her Chanel handbag down on the kitchen table and makes a slow turn.

'Well, this is cosy.' She looks around.

'It's a rental until we can buy closer to town,' I say apologetically.

'I like it.' She turns to me, her beautiful smile lighting up her face. Behaving as if nothing's happened between us.

'You sure you wouldn't be more comfortable in a hotel?'

'You have no idea how happy I am to be here.'

'Well . . .' I hesitate. 'If you're sure.'

'I'm positive.'

'Anyway, the flat's temporary,' I say, feeling the need to impress. 'All our savings are tied up in the restaurant.'

Georgie looks up sharply. 'Restaurant?'

'Nathan's opening a restaurant.'

'Nathan?'

'Yeah, we're still together.' I laugh nervously, realizing there's so much to catch up on. Twelve years' worth of news.

Georgie slowly makes her way around the living room, smiling at the things of mine she recognizes.

'Mummy mentioned you got married.' Her eyes skim my books, sculptures and carvings. She picks up the wedding photo from the shelf, studying it carefully. 'I didn't realize it was Nathan though.' A slight frown develops.

Georgie never approved. To her, Nathan was 'the older guy who worked behind the bar' at the Rat and Parrot in our village. Her plan was to see me married off to one of her rich friends with a title. Way back when we had our life mapped out together.

I feel a rush of heat to my throat but manage to keep my smile in place.

'You look happy,' she says, putting the photo back.

'Six years ago, now.'

'Has it really been that long since we've seen each other?'

'Longer.' I can't hide the edge in my tone.

Georgie turns and looks at me apologetically.

'I have missed you, you know. I'm so sorry, Twiggy, things got a little . . .' She pauses. 'I do think about what happened, the last time we spoke; it plays on my mind. I shouldn't have said those things . . .' She stops again.

'It was a long time ago.' I drop eye contact. 'We were just kids.'

'Still, I shouldn't have said what I did. I feel terrible and—'

'Cup of tea?' I cut her off mid-sentence and head for

the kitchen before I say something I might regret. 'I've got Tetley,' I call after her.

'No, thank you. Twiggy, there's something important I need to tell you . . .'

'Hang on a minute!' I put the kettle on and lean back heavily against the countertop, sighing away the past. It feels good to let go.

Rummaging through the cupboards, I return with a small plate of Jaffa Cakes and Walker's shortbread.

'I found a little expat shop that sells all my favourites . . .'

Georgie looks up and quickly wipes her eyes. I'm taken aback by the sadness in her face, because the Georgie I knew didn't do upset. I can count on one hand the number of times I've seen her cry.

She inhales sharply and smiles.

'You know what – it can wait. There're far more important things to talk about, I want to know everything that's going on with you. I need to hear all about your new life here.'

'I don't know what to tell you, really.' I take a seat, blowing on my tea. 'Are you still living in London?' I notice there's no wedding ring.

Georgie stares at the mug I'm nursing in my hands.

'I have a much better idea.' She moves towards her luggage. Reaching into her duty-free bag, she pulls out a bottle of Bollinger champagne. 'Where are your glasses?'

The alcohol helps take the edge off, softening the resentment I've been holding on to for all these years. Two glasses in and my barriers are coming down, the conversation is flowing freely and the knot in my neck is loosening. We've picked up where we left off. It's almost as if no time has passed at all.

Almost.

The worry over Nathan is also washing out to sea. I haven't checked my phone in over an hour, I'm feeling present, happy even. When did that last happen? I can't remember; in fact, I can't focus on much except Georgie. I find myself hanging on her every word, mesmerized by my old friend and mystified by how little she's changed.

Sure, there are a few more lines around her eyes and she's wearing her parting to one side these days. But the way she holds herself with poise – shoulders back, speaking slowly and with confidence – that's the Georgie I remember. I'd kill for that old-money elegance.

I don't realize I'm staring until Georgie nudges me.

'Hey. Where did you go?'

I blush. A little shake of the head, clearing the champagne haze. I'm not used to drinking, especially after all these months off alcohol trying for the baby, and then when I was pregnant. I bite back my grief.

What would Nathan think if he knew I was drinking? *Nathan isn't here. Nathan left you alone for New Year's.* I feel a small burst of rebellion. I drain my flute and Georgie immediately fills it up.

'That's my Twig.'

We clink glasses.

'Not so *Twiggy* any more. I must have put on at least two stone.'

'Are you serious? What's all this hate talk? Besides, you'll always be Twig to me.'

Georgie squeezes my hand and I feel a twinge of nostalgia, remembering the day I was given that name – the eve of my fifteenth birthday.

I should slow down the drinking. Pace myself before I become an emotional wreck. *Too late.*

My eyes mist up as I'm pulled back in time . . .

The smell of freshly cut grass. Apples ripening under the midsummer sun. The farmer had finally gotten around to chopping down the wall of weeds and long grass that separated our estate from Waverley Hall, the imposing gothic house where the Taylor-Johnsons lived. Mum warned me not to get too close, as if the overgrown orchard had been an invisible frontier to never cross. Them against us.

But I was a teenager, curious and nosy. I'd heard about the wild parties, and the entire village knew Mrs Taylor-Johnson liked to drink. Now, finally, I had a front-row seat, an uninterrupted view into their back garden and their privileged world.

As I crept closer, the sound of music filled the air and I instantly recognized her. Long blonde hair tied back in a high ponytail, her legs dangling from the old stone wall. Georgie was dressed in tight jodhpurs, a pastel pink polo-neck and knee-high brown leather boots. I remember thinking how hot she must be in all those layers.

'What are you doing here?' she called out in her cut-glass accent.

I froze. I remember standing stock-still as if someone had caught me stealing.

'I know you! I've seen you before, around the village.'

'Hi,' I squeaked, intimidated and a little star-struck.

'Is that where you live then?' She pointed through the tangle of apple-tree branches.

'Yeah,' I said quietly, my cheeks reddening with embarrassment.

'Hot, isn't it?'

I nod.

'Mummy's made some fresh lemonade. Do you want to use our pool?'

I glanced over my shoulder to see who was behind me, not quite believing that Georgie Taylor-Johnson could be inviting me into her home.

'Well, come on then,' she said with a smile. 'I've got a swimming costume you can borrow.'

She lowered her hand for me to grab onto and I remember the feeling of her skin, soft as a baby's, against mine. The touch felt electric. It took several attempts to pull me up; I was so scrawny, I didn't have any strength in my arms or legs, but when I eventually made it over the wall, we fell back onto the bright green velvety lawn in a fit of giggles.

Georgie turned her head towards me, eyes sparkling with mischief. 'I've never done that before: invite a stranger into my garden.'

But I didn't believe her, not for a second. I knew instantly that she was someone who enjoyed upsetting the apple cart.

My old best friend looks at me now, her eyes a little more lined, her gaze soft and slightly dewy. I can tell she too has been travelling back in time to that unforgettable summer.

'I never told you this, but I thought you had an eating disorder when we first met,' Georgie says. 'That's why I called you Twiglet.'

'You do realize the skinniness wasn't deliberate?'

I didn't have an appetite. Not after what I'd been through.

She smiles at me kindly. 'I know. Your family was even more screwed up than mine.'

We share a look and I feel butterflies in my stomach. It's like she still knows me better than Nathan does.

'And being so skinny meant you got pissed easily, which was highly amusing. Do you remember when you went through a bottle of Mummy's sherry?'

'Please don't remind me.'

'And then proceeded to throw up all over her beloved chaise longue? Oh God!' She sniggers. 'Mummy's face, when she discovered what you'd done.'

I feel myself cringing at the memory.

'They never got the stain out, you know.'

'I still die inside when I think about it.'

'It was hilarious, seeing Mummy so irate.'

'Your parents hated me.'

'She would have been more drunk than you that day, she just hid it better.'

'She never approved of us being friends. I was too common for her. Do you think she ever forgave me?'

'Who cares.' Georgie shrugs. 'She's got worse, since the crash.'

'Crash?'

'Drink-driving. Nobody died, fortunately, but they took away her licence. Now she's stuck at home and all she does is drink. I can't remember the last time she was sober.'

I go quiet.

'Looking back, even though she was the most neglectful and narcissistic mother in the entire world, I do feel sorry for her. It can't have been easy, putting up with Papa.'

'With his affairs?'

Georgie's smile fades. She tips back the rest of her drink. I hesitate. 'Are you still in contact?'

'God no. Haven't spoken to that arsehole for a long time.'

A pause.

'I'm sorry.'

I met him only once. An expensive tailored suit. Shoes so polished I could almost see my reflection. A gold signet ring on his pinkie and a mane of silver hair. Duncan Taylor-Johnson said a few words to me, something vaguely polite, and then replaced his sunglasses. I remember the look of heartbreak on Georgie's face when he cancelled their plans to spend the day together. I remember feeling overwhelmed with sadness for my friend.

At least my dad didn't pretend to be anything but a bastard. He wore it proudly, like a badge of honour. Unlike Georgie's mum, he didn't even have to be drunk to turn on us. I quickly jam the trauma of the past in its box, my eyes finding their way back to my old friend, who came to my rescue more times than I care to remember. My lifeline. The one person I could count on to save me.

Until she wasn't there to save me.

'Anyway.' Georgie inhales. 'Fuck him. Tonight is about us.'

'Fuck him!' we say in chorus, locking eyes and clinking our glasses in a toast. We burst into laughter, just like we used to, and then suddenly I feel overcome with sadness as the memory, the heartbreak of how our friendship ended, comes crashing back.

Tears find their way into my eyes and I remind myself that it was my mistake. I should never have invested so heavily in one person.

'Hey, what's all this?' Georgie looks at me with concern.

'Tipsy and emotional. Ignore me.'

'Is everything OK?'

'Everything's fine.' I swallow my grief.

'Come here, you.'

She gives me a cuddle. Her perfume is intoxicating. Combined with the champagne, it brings the feelings I've been bottling up, the trauma of the past few days, swimming to the surface. I want to let it out, I long to share my secrets, about the miscarriage, and about what my paranoia drove me to do the other night. God knows I need a shoulder to cry on. I haven't told anyone about what's happened, but I'm not ready to fully trust Georgie again. My heart is bruised enough as it is. And I'd be betraying Nathan. Oh goodness, he'd be furious if he knew she was here.

'Have you stayed in touch with any of the girls from the village?' she asks cheerily, but the thought of how my life has turned out sinks my mood lower.

'Yeah.' I swallow. 'I'm in touch with them all, I didn't leave Upcott in the end.'

'What?' She stares at me. 'I can't believe you didn't move! You hated that godawful place; you couldn't wait to leave.'

'Nathan was there, managing the pub for his dad. I wasn't going to leave him behind, so . . .' I shrug. 'It's just how things turned out.' I feel a twitch of bitterness. 'How about you? Are you still running around with that Chelsea crowd?' I can't keep the edge out of my tone.

Georgie looks at me apologetically. We fall silent for a moment.

'It wasn't them or you, you know, although I realize it must have felt that way when I left. Anyway, I'm careful about who I mix with now.' Her voice turns uncharacteristically solemn.

'Has something happened?'

Georgie stands up suddenly, crossing over to the window. She stares out onto the residential street, frowning. 'It's strange. I wouldn't have pictured you living in Amsterdam.'

'What makes you say that?'

'Drugs, clubbing. It's a bit of a party scene.' She laughs. 'Although not so much out here in the sticks. Don't you feel disconnected?'

'I guess.' I go quiet.

'Have you made friends?'

'I should make more of an effort to learn the language.'

'There must be some Brits you could go out with?'

'I've barely had a chance. Nathan's been so busy with the restaurant.'

'Nathan sounds like the centre of your world.'

47

I look up, taken aback by her sharpness.

She turns back to face me, smiling. 'We need to fix that.' Her pale blue eyes sparkle. 'Come on, get changed – we're going out.'

THE FRIEND – BECCA

Sliding open the cupboard, I reveal the only three evening dresses I own.

My heart sinks as I stare at the out-of-fashion sequins and unflattering hemlines. Out of the corner of my eye I notice Georgie undressing. She's still got her killer body. Effortlessly she changes into a revealing racy slip dress, the sort of thing that should only be worn to bed, but Georgie somehow pulls it off, even without a bra. She could wear a workman's boiler suit and still look sexy.

Making a snap decision, I pick out the antique pink off-the-shoulder dress I wore to my engagement party. I hope it still fits. My body isn't what it used to be. Lumps have started appearing, my hips have widened. I'm only thirty but it feels like I've aged dramatically this past year. And I hate my body even more since the miscarriage. It let me down – it failed me – and I can't find much to love about myself.

Georgie models her outfit in the mirror, turning from side to side, the expensive black silk hugging in all the right places and showing off her hourglass figure. Georgie looks stunning and I feel myself shrinking in comparison.

Even if I could afford designer dresses, I wouldn't look that good in them. Georgie bends down to her suitcase, pulling out her Valentino Rockstud heels, and that's when I notice the scorpion tattoo stretching across her shoulder blade, as black as an oil slick. I'm taken aback. The old Georgie would never have got a tattoo, and if she had, it would have been inconspicuous, perhaps a small butterfly on her ankle. This scorpion, it's not very Georgie, and somehow I feel strangely wrong-footed.

As she turns, I notice something else even more shocking. Bruises on her upper arm. She looks up, our eyes meet in the mirror and she flashes me a warning before diving back into the suitcase for a red pashmina shawl.

Should I say something? I'm not sure it's my place. Conflicted, I turn to face her, but she's now behind me, a red dress glittering like rubies between her hands.

'Try this one on.'

I look at her and laugh.

Armani. Maroon. Sequined. The sort of dress that grabs attention. I immediately shrink away from it.

'Go on.'

'I don't think so.'

She shakes the dress free, letting it unspool to the floor, the sequins dazzling.

'Try it on.' She forces it on me.

Warily, I take it from her, showing her my back as I peel off my hoodie and strip down to my underwear. Twelve years ago, I wouldn't have thought twice about getting undressed in front of Georgie, but I'm not *Twiggy* any more and it's impossible not to feel self-conscious next to her.

I thread my head through and zip it up, my lungs instantly tightening. Hesitantly, I turn around.

'Oh good God! You look incredible.' She stares at me.

'Really?' I turn to the mirror.

'I knew it'd be perfect on you.'

Readjusting my hair, I iron out the folds around my hips. It's a little tight, but it doesn't look dreadful.

'Do we really need to get this dressed up for a bar?'

'Here, wear this' – she hands me a matching red scarf to drape across my shoulders – 'and you'll need gold shoes.'

'Will silver do? I think I have a pair in here somewhere.' I root around the bottom of the closet while she tips her make-up onto the bed. By the time I'm back on my feet she's behind me, resting her head on my shoulder. Our eyes meet in the mirror. A moment's silence as she inspects me, and the butterflies take flight in my stomach.

'You'll look incredible in red lipstick.'

'No, no, absolutely not.' I hold up a hand at the MAC Ruby Woo she's picked out for me. 'Are you kidding? I can't pull that off.'

She turns me around, taking hold of my bare shoulders.

'Listen. It's important to stand out. You spend too much time hiding in the shadows.'

'But I hate attention.'

'Do it for me?' Her tone is suddenly serious, as if this moment carries more importance than it should.

'OK.' I nod obediently, turning back to face my reflection. 'Sure, why not.'

Closing my eyes, I let myself become her canvas. Georgie carefully outlines my lips and then fills them in, finishing off with a slick of clear gloss before turning her attention to her smoky eyeshadow palette. The sensation of the brushes across my skin awakens old memories, like the times we used to get glammed up and sneak downstairs for Georgie's mum's legendary parties. I suddenly realize how much I've missed this. And, I have to admit, somehow she's managed to make me look like an entirely different person.

I stare into the mirror, not recognizing my reflection. I haven't seen myself as sexy or pretty in a long time – and this new me, it's giving me courage. I feel ready. I open my mouth to share my secret, but the moment is stolen by Beyoncé.

Georgie plugs her portable speakers into her phone. Shaking her hips, she shimmies across the room to the bassline of 'Single Ladies'. She pours the last of the champagne into my glass and then I tell her to go ahead and open up the Pinot Noir from South Africa. A vintage Nathan had been saving for a special occasion.

Soon we're singing old club anthems at the top of our voices. Georgie's pitch-perfect voice drowning out mine. We dance around the bedroom like we're sixteen again. Twirling, I'm feeling light-headed and woozy. I miss a step and collapse on the floor in a heap of giggles.

Georgie flops down onto the bed beside me. Rolling onto her front, she rummages in her make-up bag and pulls out a small rectangular tin, her expression changing as she opens it up, mesmerized by its contents. She dabs the tip of her pinkie finger on her tongue, then into the tin. Then she brings a tiny mound of white powder to her nostril and inhales sharply.

She blinks quickly, a sharp shake of the head.

Georgie looks up, eyes wide and electrified. 'Want some?'

I feel my smile drop. I shake my head.

Georgie lifts her finger to her right nostril. Sniffing hard. 'Whooo-haaa.' She wipes her nose. 'This stuff is good.'

I stare at her, feeling uncomfortable. The cocaine has suddenly put distance between us.

Old Georgie was wild and unruly, but it was always alcohol, never drugs. This is new; it must be a hangover from her Chelsea years, and I don't like it. I have no idea what the street value of cocaine is but I'm aware it's a rich person's drug. And the way Georgie seems so *into* it, it's like it's replaced me somehow.

I paint on a smile and remind myself that most people have tried drugs. But I'm the square who's lived a sheltered life in a village. I won't say a word, or let on that I'm uneasy – the last thing I want is to remind Georgie of the person she traded me in for. *The boring one.* Not now she wants me back in her life. And if I'm going to enjoy tonight, I need to loosen up. It's New Year's Eve, for goodness' sake.

I might even have some fun.

THE FRIEND – BECCA

The crisp December air blows through the open window of the Uber as we zip past the Van Gogh Museum, bumping over tramlines. Skimming around the Rijksmuseum, leaving the grand neo-Gothic architecture in the rear-view mirror, we enter the network of canals and narrow streets – the beating heart of the city.

'Gosh, it's adorable.' Georgie stares out the window, fascinated by the houses that line the canals. Narrow and crooked, they lean into each other like an old married couple who know each other's secrets. The festive lights blink back at her. 'It's like a toytown.'

A sharp left, another tight corner and my stomach drops as we soar over the next bridge.

Locals whizz past on bikes, frantically ringing their bells at tourists blindly stepping into their path. The narrow pavements are crammed with out-of-towners spilling onto the streets. Large groups of twenty-somethings searching for a big night out. A city gearing up for midnight. The air is humming with energy waiting to be discharged. It's lifting off the cobbles, it's rising up from the canals, and I feel a prickle of excitement.

The bright lights of the city are pulling me out of my cocoon.

It's too late to get food anywhere but we find a rustic bar that's not too crowded. Georgie looks around at the dark wood-panelled walls and beer mats wallpapered across the ceiling. I'm sure she's not impressed; it's hardly Chelsea posh and we look overdressed in our sequins and heels. But we're attracting attention, which Georgie seems to like. She's already made eye contact with the bartender.

We find a seat by the window, a slim candle flickering lazily between us, and a waiter comes over with the drinks menu. He's tall and handsome with a mane of hair swept back off his forehead. Georgie summons him with her smile and asks, 'Can you take a photo of us?'

She hands him her phone and moves around the table, perching on the edge of my seat and looping her arm around my waist. Suddenly I'm back in the spring garden, filling up my lungs with her scent and my body with her warmth and I feel a whoosh of excitement at the thought – Georgie might post the photo of us on her social media. Show that posh crowd who her real bestie is. I lean into her and smile.

When the waiter returns the phone to Georgie, she turns the screen to face me. 'See? Gorgeous! Believe me now?'

Filtered by the soft candlelight, I suppose I do look vaguely OK. It's the first photo of myself I haven't hated and wanted to delete on the spot, and I feel myself inching from my cocoon a little further.

'I've sent it to you,' she says, then places her phone on the table. A WhatsApp message flashes on her screen, chased up by another, and something passes across her face.

'We'll have a bottle of champagne,' she tells the waiter, sliding her mobile back inside her handbag. 'My treat.'

'I'll get this.' I pull out my credit card.

She places her hand over mine.

'Darling, please, let me.'

'Don't be daft, you're my guest.'

But I flinch as I wave my card over the contactless reader because Nathan's trying to be careful with money and if he knew I'd spent over a hundred euros on Georgie, he'd go bananas. Then I remind myself it's almost 11 p.m. and my husband hasn't checked on me once.

'So tell me about you and Nathan,' Georgie says, as if reading my mind. 'Why aren't you spending New Year's together?'

'Oh,' I look at her awkwardly. 'There was some urgent business back in London.'

She frowns. 'On New Year's Eve?'

The waiter returns with a bottle in a bucket of ice. He fills our glasses and we toast again, although the mention of Nathan has soured my taste buds. I knock back a large gulp and Georgie gives me a look.

'There's a lot of pressure on him right now,' I say. 'He's back-to-back with meetings. Nathan didn't want to ask his dad for money so he's constantly networking, trying to secure extra funding. So much is riding on the restaurant being a success.'

She clears her throat. I sense a touch of wariness.

'You are happy, aren't you?'

'Yeah.' I take a breath. 'Course.'

'Twig?'

'I'm happy,' I insist. 'I need to get a job, that's all – find something else to focus on. And make some friends.'

She looks at me, her face etched with concern.

'What about your job in the UK?'

'Oh, it was nothing, I was only a teaching assistant.'

'That's not *nothing*.'

'Well, I don't know—'

'Which you gave up for Nathan, so *Nathan* could live out *his* dream.'

'I wouldn't put it quite like that.'

'But what about you? Where's my Twig in all this?'

'I'm here.' I smile thinly. 'I'll find something that gets me excited again.'

'It's me, you don't need to pretend.'

'I'm not pretending.' I hear a small catch in my voice, because all I've been doing these past nine months is pretend.

Georgie's staring at me; she knows me better than anyone, even after all these years apart. I can feel my resolve weakening. This mask I've been wearing, I can feel it slipping off and all at once I have this overwhelming need to talk to someone.

Not someone. My old best friend.

'We've been trying for a baby,' I blurt out.

57

She looks shocked.

'But it hasn't been going so well.'

'Oh, Twigs.'

Quietly I say: 'I lost it.'

I feel her hand on my arm. The touch, the physical contact, brings tears to my eyes. My cheeks heat up with embarrassment and I swipe them away before anyone can see.

'How far gone were you?'

'Six weeks.'

'Oh, my darling.'

'I didn't think it was possible to miss morning sickness and achy breasts.'

'How've you been coping?'

'I try to block it out. Pretend it never happened. Then I blame myself. God, I hate my stupid body for letting me down. Why can everyone else do it and I can't?'

She looks like she's about to cry too.

'I'd be frightened to try again. Is it weird to think that?'

'Nathan should be here supporting you.'

'It's the restaurant – it's taking up all his time. It's been stressful for him too. That's been his baby.'

'You've been going through this alone?'

'It's not his fault. He thinks I'm still pregnant.'

'What? You haven't told him about the miscarriage?'

I look away.

'Why not?'

I bite my lip. Teetering on the edge of breaking down.

'Twig?'

'I don't want to disappoint him again.' I take a breath. 'I feel like such a disappointment already.'

'It's too much to deal with alone. Look at you.' She reaches out to me and takes hold of my hand, gripping it tightly.

'I suppose what I feel is invisible. Nathan is so taken up with the launch – which is completely understandable; God, it's less than a week away – but I can't see where I fit in any more.' I let out a sigh. 'I suppose I'm resentful. Maybe even a little jealous.'

'That's OK. It's a normal feeling to have.'

'And it doesn't help that I don't have anything of my own. I hoped a baby would help with that.'

'A baby won't fix a marriage.'

'Every woman wants to feel loved, right?'

'If you don't solve a problem, life will give you more problems,' she says philosophically.

'I know it's my insecurity that's to blame. I'm projecting on to him. It's just . . . he works late most nights, so I'm sitting around, feeling lonely and—'

'Works late?' She looks at me pointedly. 'You don't think . . . there's someone else?'

'What makes you say that?'

She studies me closely. 'I'm picking up on something from you. Is there another woman?'

'No, no.' I shake my head. 'He wouldn't do that to me.'

She holds my gaze, her eyes searching mine. 'Who is she?'

'No one.' I reach for my drink. 'A figment of my imagination.'

'Twig?'

I don't want to make it real, to give it a name.

'Twiiiig?'

Or should I tell her about Katya? Get it out in the open. The thought of it makes me nauseous, but maybe facing it head-on will help. I'm hoping Georgie will reassure me I'm going mad.

'It's nothing. I'm paranoid.'

Her eyebrow lifts.

'Forget I said anything.'

She eyes me cautiously. 'It's OK to accept help once in a while, you can't always do it alone.'

I take another swig of champagne, reaching around in the dark for my Dutch courage. Then I force out the words.

'I followed Nathan's business partner home the other night.'

'You did what?' Both Georgie's eyebrows lift.

'I got it into my head they're having an affair. It was stupid. It's embarrassing.' My cheeks prickle with heat. 'I hung around outside Katya's flat waiting for Nathan to show up after he finished at the restaurant. Yeah, exactly, like some obsessive stalker. I was feeling so anxious, the only way I could calm down was to see for myself that nothing was going on.'

'So did he show up?'

I shake my head. 'Am I weird?

'You're not weird.' Georgie looks at me kindly.

'Anyone else in my shoes would do the same, wouldn't they?'

'Is she pretty?'

'She's everything I want to be.'

'Stop that!' Georgie says angrily. 'It hurts me to hear you talk yourself down. *You're* pretty. Nathan's bloody lucky to have you.'

'Let's chat about something else.'

'We need to unpack this and get to the bottom of why he's making you feel this way.'

I squeeze my eyes closed for a moment.

'Please.' My voice breaking up, I take a breath, pulling the bottle from the ice and topping us up. 'Tonight is about us.' I glance towards the bar; it's filling up quickly as the hour creeps closer to midnight.

'You can talk to me though. I'm sorry I haven't been there for you.' She reaches a hand across the table. 'But I'm here now and you can trust me. I'll always give you my honest opinion. Not that it's worth much.' She smiles. 'I mean, what would I know about marriage? I think I'm getting worse at relationships as I get older.'

I look up sharply, suddenly aware of what a selfish friend I've been. I've barely stopped to ask about her. I just assumed Georgie was happy being single, travelling the world, no strings attached. After all, Georgie has always run in the opposite direction from commitment. Now I think about it, she's barely told me anything about her love life. The Georgie I knew would have been boasting about the guy she's seeing, how good-looking he is, what wild sex they're having and what outlandish positions they've been trying out. I study her, wondering, despite her polished appearance, could she also be struggling?

'Are you seeing someone at the moment?' I ask tentatively.

'This might surprise you, but being me isn't all it's cracked up to be. It can get quite lonely.' Georgie goes quiet.

'Sorry, I didn't think to ask.'

'I don't know any more, Twig. Maybe some people aren't meant to be in relationships.' Her expression suddenly turns serious. 'A lot has happened since I last saw you. The thing is . . .'

Someone bumps into our table, sending the champagne bucket crashing and ice skidding across the floor.

'Sorry!' The guy in an oversized hoodie and low-slung jeans struggles to get back on his feet. His friend pulls him up by the arm, giving Georgie a goofy grin.

I look back at Georgie.

'What were you about to say?'

She stares back at me with a blank expression.

'So everything's OK with you?'

'Everything's fine, why?' Her smile is back in place. That unnerving note of jollity.

'So long as you're sure you're all right . . .'

More people arrive, filling up the small space, standing shoulder to shoulder, talking loudly over one another. It's becoming difficult to hear anything. It's getting harder to breathe.

'How long until midnight?'

'What did you say?' Georgie shouts above the noise.

'How long?' I tap my wrist, avoiding my phone. I don't want to be triggered again by Nathan's lack of contact.

She pulls her mobile from her handbag, her expression darkening as she reads the screen.

'Four minutes.' She frowns and gets up suddenly, disappearing towards the toilets, leaving me with a sense of unease. While she's gone, I think again of the bruises on her arm and how she's kept herself covered up tonight, despite how sweltering it is in the bar. I think, too, of how guarded she seems, as if there's something she can't bring herself to tell me. Maybe I'm not the only one keeping secrets.

When she returns, she's wiping her nose, she looks wired, as if she's knocked back a double shot of espresso, and suddenly I'm back on the outside, looking in on our friendship. Wondering where I fit in.

She drains the rest of her champagne. There's an urgency to the way she tips back her glass. Her eyes are frantic, darting around the room, unable to settle on anything. Something definitely feels off-kilter. I open my mouth to say something, to ask her why she's covered in bruises, and then the bar erupts into a chorus.

FIVE.

FOUR.

'Come on!' Georgie leaps to her feet and takes my hand, pulling me through the crowd.

THREE.

TWO.

The mass of bodies has swollen in every direction. I'm desperately searching for a pocket of air when a tug on my arm brings me stumbling out through the door.

ONE.

We spill out onto the street just in time.

'HAPPY NEW YEAR!' The city explodes into celebration.

It's a clear night, as if the clouds moved aside for us. The sky has caught fire. Sizzling and crackling, a thunderous rumble as rockets launch, exploding into a million glitter pieces. Bodies pressed up against one other, friends hugging, lovers kissing. The air is turbo-charged, it's electric. It's giving me goosebumps. The slow build-up tonight, released in an instant.

It's like a war zone, fireworks exploding from every direction. Groups of teenagers lighting them on the street. A wayward rocket shoots sideways along the canal and I let out a scream.

'This way!' Georgie pulls me along and we thread our way through the crowds, Georgie holding my hand tightly, leading us to a bridge over the canal.

Sparks fill the air, showering us in gold. Ribbons of colour trail across the sky, reflected in the dark canal water. It's like nothing I've seen before and the thick fog of anxiety I've been lost in finally begins to clear. It feels like I'm seeing Amsterdam for the very first time – the beauty, the splendour – through this wonderful new lens.

There's a reason Georgie came back into my life. She's here to show me how far I've strayed from my path. She's come to rescue me, just like she used to when things were bad at home. Everything she said tonight is doing loops around my head. How I should never have sacrificed my dreams for Nathan's. *I can't believe you're alone for New Year's Eve.*

I blink. Lost in the electric blues and greens, I try to focus, but the champagne has made me giddy and overly emotional.

I never wanted to need someone; I thought I could do this all on my own. I didn't realize how badly I needed a friend until Georgie showed up, and now I'm back in her circumference of light, I feel protected. Brave. Defiant. A fire has been lit inside me. Instead of checking my phone to see if Nathan has wished me Happy New Year, I slip it inside my clutch bag. Georgie notices and gives me a small nod of approval. Then she links my arm into hers, resting her head on my shoulder.

'You're my best friend – you know that, right?'

I give her a squeeze.

'Let nothing come between us again, 'K?'

'OK,' I echo.

'You make me feel safe,' she whispers, her mouth close to my ear. Almost too quietly to hear under the noise.

Safe. I frown, glancing sideways at her. Georgie's face is angled to the sky, her perfectly symmetrical features outlined by the light. There's a veil-like glow across her skin that blurs everything, except the strain. She looks as if she's fighting off tears.

Fireworks detonate around us. A thunderstorm of electric oranges and reds. Amsterdam is on fire.

'Isn't it glorious!' She turns to me, smiling. Her eyes are bright with light as she stares directly at me and any sign of sadness seems to have vanished. And once again, I'm left wondering – did I imagine it?

THE FRIEND – BECCA

'I'll order an Uber.'

'Let's not go home yet,' Georgie says with pleading eyes. 'You told me you never go out – so let's go out. How often do we see each other?'

I blink back the tiredness. I'm not used to staying up past 11 p.m., my body is aching, screaming at me. I want to collapse in my bed.

She reapplies her lipstick in her phone camera.

'Do you want to go to the restaurant? There'll be no one there, we can raid the bar.'

'I want you to forget all about Nathan for tonight. 'K?'

'We can open another bottle at home.'

She looks downcast. I don't want to upset her, but the last thing I can deal with is paying through the nose to get into some sweaty club crammed with people half my age. Plus, it's suddenly got bitterly cold; I can see the puff of air from my own breath.

She hesitates. 'Have you heard from Nathan?'

I wasn't going to look but the mention of his name triggers me. I check my phone and wish I hadn't.

Nothing. Not even a 'Happy New Year'. I could message or call him, but why the hell should I? He's the one who buggered off and left me alone; he ruined our plans. He doesn't even care what I'm doing. He just assumes I'm sitting at home watching TV. Either that, or he's busy with *Katya.*

Georgie looks at me apologetically – as if she's the one who's let me down. And that's the moment I realize: *Nathan can fuck off.*

'We both need some fun in our lives – what do you say, Twig?' She links arms with me.

I nod, although the fire in my belly is already starting to fizzle out. I've never been good at being mad. The few times I've lost my temper with Nathan I've ended up apologizing.

'Come on, you.' She leads me off the bridge. 'We need to party.'

'OK, but no clubbing. Just a quiet drink somewhere. Promise?'

She smiles. 'This way,' she pulls me away from the noise and towards a dark narrow alleyway that splices two canal houses in half.

'I'm not sure we'll find anything out this way—'

'Trust me,' she cuts me off. 'You and me – we're going to have the best fucking night of our lives!' A slur in her words. 'And when have I ever been wrong?' She gives me a sideways glance, a dangerous twinkle in her eye.

I recognize that look – the girl who likes to upset the apple cart.

* * *

It's a relief to escape the tourist-clogged streets.

Weaving through cobbled alleyways, we turn another corner, taking short cuts between canals. It feels like we've entered a labyrinth as we move further and further away from the overcrowded city centre and into the quieter residential streets. The sound of fireworks fades behind us.

Why haven't I explored around here sooner? I gaze across the canal at the sixteenth-century houses lining Amsterdam's most expensive postcode, the Herengracht, taking in the decorative facades and steeply pitched roofs with fascination and envy. The houses are far grander here. The windows are tall and wide, the light from within pours onto the street. It's an invitation to look inside. We stare into the opulence with astonishment.

'Now this is more like it!' Georgie's face lights up.

Slowing to a crawl, we peer into the lives of others, coming to a stop outside a five-storey house where the entire ground floor appears to be wallpapered in gilt-framed paintings dating back to the late fifteenth century. There are snowy scenes of children skating on the canals and windmills across the seasons. There's a grandfather clock pushed back into the corner while a crystal chandelier twinkles above. The soft light casts a snowflake pattern over the creamy walls.

'Gosh, aren't they terrified about being burgled?' Georgie stares in disbelief.

'The Dutch don't close their curtains. It's a thing out here, especially in these parts.' I put on a voice. 'The rich like to show off.'

Georgie looks at me but says nothing.

'Personally, I reckon anyone who flaunts their wealth is asking for trouble,' I say.

'I would move here in a heartbeat.' Georgie makes a slow turn, mesmerized.

'Shall we go back? There's nothing around here.' I hug my coat into me. A few snowflakes have started falling. It doesn't seem to be sticking to the ground but it feels like a storm is on the horizon.

'Just a few more minutes.' Georgie checks her phone, almost as if she's looking at directions, and then takes off again with fresh energy, her heels striking the cobbles. She walks purposefully along the water's edge, disappearing around the next corner while I'm still nursing my stitch.

My feet have swelled, my heels are rubbed raw. I slow, briefly considering whether to take off these stupid stilettos, and then I hear a high-pitched cry.

'Georgie?' I sprint after her.

I turn into the Keizersgracht to find Georgie standing stock-still at the edge of the canal, transfixed.

'What is it? Are you OK?'

Catching my breath, I look up, following her gaze across the water to the tall narrow building lit up like a Christmas tree. Light pours from every floor. The dark shapes of people are silhouetted in the window while the sound of trance music drifts towards us. Their reflections seem to stretch out across the water. Reaching for us.

'Hello!' Georgie looks sideways at me, smiling. 'I've found our party.'

'No.' I shake my head. 'We can't—'

But before I can argue my case, she's already five steps ahead. 'Come on, Twiggy, keep up!'

'It's a private party,' I call after her.

'So?'

'They won't let us in.'

'When's that ever stopped us?' She turns sharply onto the bridge. 'It'll be just like old times.'

I feel the pain of my blisters, the pressure building in my right heel. Wincing, I try to keep up with Georgie, but she was always far fitter and now she's found a new energy. Like a greyhound out of the trap, she's sprinting towards the prize, and there's nothing I can say or do to slow her down.

There are a few people outside, loosely grouped together, chatting, vaping. Unfazed by the cold, these beautiful twenty-somethings in their micro-outfits look like they belong on a *Vogue* shoot.

I feel my cheeks heating up with embarrassment as Georgie walks past, shoulders back, hipbones first, like a model on a runway, with barely a glance in their direction.

A set of stairs leads to an ivy green varnished door. There's no name plaque set against the buzzer, nothing to reveal who lives here. The thud of dance tunes, the laughter, pours through the open windows.

'Look, it's a private party,' I whisper. 'We can't be here – let's go, *please*.'

Georgie's eyes are glittering with mischief.

'Let me do the talking, 'K?' She looks back at me briefly. 'Wait!'

She presses the bronzed button.

The trill of the doorbell is barely audible above the music and I feel a wave of relief. *Nobody will hear us.*

I turn around, trying not to look at the beautiful people as I clop awkwardly down the steps. As I reach the pavement, I hear a rattle. The sound of a lock being pulled across. A creaking. And then, all at once, the chilled air is filled with the smell of expensive perfume and bougie candles and the pulsing *thud thud* of trance beats.

My heart sinks.

I turn back to Georgie, who's busy grooming herself, combing her fingers though her hair as a very attractive man holding a clipboard fills up the doorway.

Broad-shouldered and tall, hair slicked back off his face. Youthful; handsome, dressed in a crisp white shirt and dinner jacket. He looks and smells of wealth. Old Amsterdam money and I notice how Georgie's eyes immediately light up.

'Hi!' she says breathlessly.

His gaze slides between us, sizing us up, while Georgie playfully cocks her head to one side.

'It's cold out here.' She exaggerates a shiver. 'Are you going to let us in?' She flashes her megawatt smile.

A woman appears and drapes a tanned arm around his neck.

'Who are they?' she whispers to him in Dutch, eyeing us from over his shoulder. Her eyes glitter with iridescent gold make-up. Her lashes are thick with mascara. I feel her gaze running over us, and I'm immediately intimidated by her beauty.

'Come on, Georgie,' I say under my breath. 'Let's go.'

Georgie smiles at them with determination. 'Sorry we're late!'

Oh God.

The woman eyes Georgie with curiosity. She's stunning, with her winged eyeliner and a thick diamond choker wrapped around her long swan-like neck. With a mane of honey blonde hair, and no older than twenty-five, she gives Georgie a run for her money. She barely looks at me.

'Are you on the guest list?' Her accented English is perfect.

Without hesitation, Georgie says: 'I should be. I'd be horrified if I wasn't.'

The man defers to his clipboard. 'What's your name?'

'Georgina Taylor-Johnson.'

He scans the list, flicking through the pages and then shakes his head. 'I don't see you.'

'That can't be right.' She pulls out her mobile, pretending to search for the invite. 'Someone's obviously made a mistake.'

A pause, a moment where they both stare at Georgie with fascination.

'Uh, what a week! I've just survived a detox and debloat wellness retreat – it was a little off-grid, as these A-list hideaways often are. Perhaps that's why you didn't receive my RSVP. Hopefully the breakdown in communication isn't at your end.'

The woman whispers something into the man's ear. He leans into her and they both laugh. I feel my insides fold into little pieces.

'Georgie,' I hiss.

The woman takes another moment, eyes slowly running over me and then Georgie, sizing us up. Deliberating whether we're pretty enough to be invited in. Then, a small nod of approval in Georgie's direction.

'You're friends of Dieter Schmidt?' She looks at Georgie for confirmation.

'Dieter and I? Of course, darling,' Georgie agrees. 'We go way back.'

'And you know him from . . . ?'

'It's been a ridiculously long time since we've seen one another. So much to catch up on.'

It's as if they're speaking another language, one reserved for the rich and privileged. I feel like I've been shunted back on the outside. The memory of why Georgie and I fell out comes creeping to the surface.

'Where were you first introduced?'

'My goodness!' Georgie says with a theatrical sigh. 'We'll have turned to icicles if we stand out here much longer. Do you want to grab Dieter and check with him I'm not impersonating his old best friend?' A hollow laugh. A false note of irritation entering her voice.

The woman smiles timidly. 'That won't be necessary.'

'I can't wait to say hello. I'm just awfully sad we couldn't get here earlier,' Georgie says with a pout, the privately educated schoolgirl confidence shining through. Her lie so convincing, I almost believe it's true. I frown. Does she know Dieter?

I watch my old best friend with a mixture of embarrassment and envy. She's sexy and daring all at the same time. God, if only I could be that confident. I would never have the brass to blag my way into a private party.

The woman pulls the door wide, making room for us.

'Welcome to the afterparty,' she says in a mysteriously seductive voice.

'We're thrilled to be here.' Georgie steps inside, greeting them with an air kiss to both cheeks as if they are long-lost friends. Her high heels meeting the varnished parquet floor with a *clack clack*. She then slows, as if suddenly remembering me, flashing me a triumphant expression.

'Yay! Party time!' she mouths. Brows shooting up. Eyes twinkling.

I peer into the darkened hallway, searching the gloom for some sense of what we're getting into. Shadows stir, looming in the muted candlelight.

'Twigs, come on,' she calls out to me from the dark.

I hesitate, looking back into the cold night.

A face at the window.

Pale and lined, a bush of white hair. An old man is watching from an equally old and rickety houseboat moored outside. Backlit by the moon feeding in from the opposite end, his features appear strained. Disapproval? No, something else.

Several beats pass as we stare at each other. I feel a chill spread across my shoulder blades and then a noise, a shriek of excitement, pulls me back into the afterparty.

'Twiiiigs!'

I let out a shaky breath. And then I follow her.

THE TIKTOK DETECTIVE – JAMIE

I knew I shouldn't have gone out with the lads.

Where'd the night go? I stumble in the front door, hammered.

Kicking off my trainers, I make my way into the lounge where I find Nan, fast asleep in the armchair.

Fuck's sake, I told her it was dangerous to leave the electric heater on. I pull the plug from the wall and grab the quilted blanket, laying it across her; tucking her in. She looks so peaceful, bless her. I leave Nan sleeping while I fix myself a cheese toastie loaded with Worcester sauce and then head upstairs into the bat cave.

That's my bedroom, for all of you wondering. I keep it nice and dark with the curtains drawn at all times. Don't want no nosy neighbour getting a look in at what I'm working on. It's MI5 clearance only, remember. LOL.

But seriously. The stuff I'm putting together is top secret, especially as some of the websites where I search for crime stories ain't always kosher. The last thing I need is some curtain twitcher reporting me, or worse – stealing my scoop. You can't be too careful; especially now word's got out on the estate that I'm a bit of a big deal. I wouldn't be surprised if someone was watching me, following me, trying to copycat what I'm doing.

I needn't worry.

There's only one Crime_Tok_Detective.

And just wait until I solve my next case. They'll be rolling out the red carpet for me down the Hare and Tortoise.

Ha. It's funny, looking back, it's obvious I'd end up down this road. I've been obsessed with true crime ever since 2014 when the podcast *Serial* became a phenomenon. I was only fourteen at the time but I was instantly hooked. From then on, my life has been about researching wrong'uns. My shelves are filled with books on serial killers; when a new docuseries drops on Netflix, you can bet I'll be up all night binge-watching. Figuring out whodunnit is what gets me off – and nine out of ten times I'm right.

I got into CrimeTokking a few years ago, when everyone was starting to catch on that live feeds were the next podcast. But it was the case of missing teenager Elena Brookes, last summer, that changed everything.

Elena was on a girls' holiday in Ibiza when she disappeared on her way home from a night out clubbing. Nobody could work out what had happened to her. It was as if she'd vanished into thin air. The mystery surrounding her disappearance gripped the nation, and everyone was going wild chasing conspiracy theories. The hashtag #FINDELENA racked up over 300 million views on TikTok. It took CrimeTokking to a whole new level, and that's when I realized – what the fuck have I been doing with my life? That should be me, finding missing people. As soon as a story breaks, I need to be first at the scene, out and about with my iPhone, searching for clues, keeping the great British public informed with updates delivered in real time.

I take another bite out of my toastie while my eyes flick between the screens. I've got four monitors set up on my desk feeding me breaking news stories from around the world. Nan jokes that my bedroom hums so loudly it could take off.

I open a new browser and search for something to sink my teeth into.

Like I said, missing people are the best kind of news because there's mystery surrounding a disappearance and it's the unanswered questions that get the CrimeTok community buzzin' with conspiracy theories.

I'm talking Brits missing abroad, that kind of thing. When you think about it, all sorts can happen when you're in a foreign country, out of ya comfort zone, stuck in the middle of nowhere. You end up doing things you wouldn't normally do. You chat to people you wouldn't normally meet. You say things you should have kept a secret.

You make impulsive decisions that can end up costing your life.

THE FRIEND – BECCA

We've stumbled into another universe.

Or that's how it feels as another man, with slicked-back hair, thick-rimmed glasses and a midnight-blue velvet blazer, takes our coats. He slides them between the fur and cashmere jackets, handing us a circular gold token.

The smell of the place is the first thing to hit me. A heavy blend of tobacco and leather oud perfumes mixed in with bodies that's so powerful it makes me want to sneeze. I stand in the hallway, pinching the bridge of my nose, waiting for Georgie to finish chatting up the cloakroom guy, and think, *What am I doing here?*

'Come on, I need a drink!' Georgie eventually returns to me, locking her arm in mine. 'Let's mingle.' She pulls me along while I tug at my dress, feeling increasingly self-conscious, the pulse of music growing louder as she leads us towards the noise.

The downstairs is one long open-plan room with walls lined in gilt-framed mirrors. Chandeliers the size of small planets hang from the high ceiling. The gold, the varnished wood floor, the crystals, it reminds me a little of the Hall of Mirrors at the Palace of Versailles. This so-called *after-party* oozes money, and, my God, it's hot in here. It's an inferno with the number of bodies all crammed together.

Everywhere I look I see beautiful people – high society types dressed expensively, with some even wearing *Eyes Wide Shut*-esque Venetian masks. It's an arty crowd, mostly twenty- and thirty-somethings, talking over each other in a mix of European accents. My eyes are drawn to the group of girls in the centre, dancing suggestively. One of them finds a bottle of Dom Perignon and immediately pops the cork sending vapour lifting and froth fizzing onto the floor. They're a tangle of limbs as she pours champagne into the open mouth of her friend. They squeal and gather for selfies.

This is so not me.

I'm a homebody, I should be curled up with a camomile tea, finishing off my Netflix series. But Georgie, she's in her element, scanning the room for important people.

Georgie carves a path through the mass of bodies, lifting two champagne flutes from the woman serving a tray of drinks.

I immediately drink more than I should, desperate to take the edge off my nerves. I don't think I've ever felt such a thorn among roses.

'Let's check out upstairs.' Georgie jerks around in the other direction, I feel my hand grabbed again as she pulls me towards the narrow, almost vertical staircase that these old Dutch houses are famous for. It's a slalom finding a way up past friends that have stopped to chat and couples making out. The air feels electrified, buzzing with pheromones, and from their glazed expressions, everyone here seems to be on drugs.

A girl in a leather miniskirt, bare tanned legs and cowgirl boots is leaning back against a wall, her girlfriend whispering in her ear. She makes eye contact, immediately dismissing me, her gaze drawn to Georgie.

These are the circles Georgie's used to mixing in. She was raised on champagne and parties, it's all she's ever known. But it's been over a decade since I was at Waverley and even Mrs Taylor-Johnson's parties weren't this glamorous. I'm a duck out of water, stiff and awkward, uncertain how to behave and terrified of drawing attention to my ordinariness. I feel myself retreating back inside my cocoon, but then Georgie takes my hand, leading me up the next flight of stairs to where the music is even louder, the bass thudding right through my chest.

It's different again up here. A wild fusion of old and contemporary design with electric-blue lamps, luxurious velvet sofas placed next to futuristic-looking chairs, while large framed avant-garde paintings hang from the walls. I find myself imagining who must own this house. Who is Dieter Schmidt? An art collector? Clearly someone with an absurd amount of money.

Champagne bottles everywhere you look. A woman to my right bends over, snorting a line of cocaine off a polished wood side table. I fold my arms across my chest, feeling horrifically uncomfortable, but at the same time transfixed, unable to look away.

I've been granted access to a world I'd normally be excluded from and I'm getting goosebumps, a small thrill from knowing these are the sorts of people – with money and influence – that Nathan would love to have invest in his restaurant. God, he'd kill to be invited.

'Stop fidgeting.' Georgie pulls my arms apart. 'You look gorgeous. Please, you've got to stop hiding yourself.'

She swaps looks with a couple of guys standing around in a darkened corner, I feel a tug on my hand, a swoop in my stomach as she leads us towards them.

'Mind if we join you?' She holds out her empty champagne flute to the man with the bottle of Dom Perignon.

He maintains eye contact while filling up her glass.

Nathan is good-looking but these men, they're in another league entirely. Tall and chiselled, and in perfect shape. I'm instantly drawn to the rougher-looking one with the eyebrow ring and a tattoo poking out the neck of his black silky shirt, his jaw grazed with stubble, and I feel my cheeks flush, as though I'm on a first date, which is ridiculous, because I'm married.

'Hi, I'm Carter. And this is Lloyd.' He gestures to the man I can barely make eye contact with.

'You're American,' Georgie says.

'And you're British,' Carter smiles.

'Nice to meet you.' She kisses his cheek, their cheekbones clashing. He holds his skin against hers for a beat longer. Sparks already flying between them.

'Seems they're letting anyone in the door these days,' he jokes.

Georgie looks around. 'So what came before this?'

'You weren't at the gallery opening, then?'

She smiles. 'And where's our delightful host?'

He lowers his voice. 'The mysterious Dieter, you mean.'

'Oh please.' A toss of her head. 'How mysterious can he be?'

'No one gets to meet him. He's like a legend.'

'Well, someone must know him.' She plays along.

'She does.' Lloyd nods towards the painfully trendy woman who's entered the room. 'That's his wife.'

With a blunt-cut bob sweeping across her jawline, wearing a paper-thin designer dress and a grungy loose-knit cardigan arranged around her shoulders, she's someone you'd expect to see in the front row of a catwalk show.

A crowd quickly forms around her. She starts a conversation while immediately looking over their shoulders, eyes roaming for someone more interesting to chat to. I feel intimidated just looking at her.

'Not sure about that cardy,' Georgie says dismissively. Then she lightly touches Carter's chin, pulling his gaze back to her.

'I prefer what you're wearing.' He flirts back.

Georgie shrugs off her red shawl, revealing her dress. Carter can't take his eyes off her, while mine are drawn to her bruises. It's worse than I first thought. Did she have a fall? I wish I'd found my voice and asked her when we were alone.

'If you don't stop smiling at me like that, I'm going to have to kiss you,' he says to her.

'Do you want another drink?' Lloyd looks at me sympathetically.

I nod. 'Water would be great.'

'Water?'

'Please.'

I glance back at Georgie and Carter. The two are already entwined. His arm has snaked around her waist, her back is pressed against his chest as she shows him something on her phone. Georgie giggles flirtatiously at whatever he's whispering into her ear.

'Here you go.' Lloyd reappears with more champagne. 'That's all they had.' He grins.

I must slow down, I've had too much to drink, but then I drain half the glass in one go. The bubbles hit the back of my throat. He gives me a look and I laugh nervously. Now it's just the two of us, I feel self-conscious again, tugging at my dress. Smoothing over where I imagine it's bulging.

'Let's go somewhere we can chat.' He leads us from the noise towards a sofa by the window. Another avant-garde piece that probably cost as much as our entire flat.

Melting into the luxurious fabric, I'm grateful to take the pressure off my sore feet. The window looks out onto the canal, the moon is stalking the rooftops and the snow, it's getting heavier, a thick layer building on the street below.

'Hey, relax,' he says, as if he can read my thoughts about getting home.

Our eyes meet and I look away, dropping my gaze. When I look up, he's still staring at me and I feel a little bewildered. Men like Lloyd don't normally notice people like me, especially when the room is filled with beautiful women. I can't deny I'm enjoying it though, after months of being ignored – fading away in the shadow of the restaurant and *Katya*, it feels nice that someone is taking an interest. Whether it's genuine or not, I want to hold onto the moment for a little while longer, forget all about losing the baby. I tuck my wedding ring out of sight.

'So tell me, who is this Dieter?' I ask him.

He shrugs. 'I'm not sure. I'm Carter's plus-one. This afterparty is buzzing though, isn't it?'

'I haven't been to anything like this before.'

'Not a party girl then?'

'That's more my friend.'

I look over to Georgie. Her face is now inches from Carter. How is it possible to go from zero to a hundred in minutes?

'And are you having a good time?'

'What?' I say above the noise.

'I said, are you having a good time?'

I turn back and Lloyd has inched closer. He's so close, his leg is grazing mine.

'Yeah.' I swallow. 'I'm having a good time.'

He brushes the hair off my face, exactly how Nathan does. His touch feels electrified and I'm hit with a stab of guilt.

Becca, what are you doing?

It's OK, I reason, it's just harmless flirting, we're not kissing, we're barely touching. Just to be sure, I put some distance between us, if only a few centimetres, but Lloyd immediately closes the gap, casually hooking his arm behind me.

'The British accent is so sexy,' he says, controlling the momentum of how whatever this is between us is going.

My heart beats like it's on a date. I find the courage to look him in the eye and instantly wish I hadn't. Moss green, flecks of brown with thick dark lashes. This doesn't feel real, I'm going to laugh about this with Georgie in the Uber home.

'It's like a drug to us Americans. You sound so sophisticated. What do you do?'

'Oh, me, I'm a . . .' I stop. Suddenly worried how ordinary I'll sound if I tell him I work in education, or worse, that I'm currently unemployed. I think about Katya and why Nathan is so drawn to her. She's creative and exciting, and before I think it through, I blurt:

'I'm an Egyptologist.'

His eyebrow lifts. 'Oh. Tell me more.'

'Well . . .' I start blushing. 'What do you want know?'

'Are you the next Lara Croft?'

'Ha, not exactly.'

'I like the sound of you even more.' He grins. 'And when you're not rolling around in the dust, what is it you enjoy?'

'What do you mean?'

'How do you let off steam?' he asks casually, but I know it isn't casual.

'I don't know really,' I say quietly, regretting my fib.

The music switches to an R&B track and people get up and start dancing around us. The bass kicks in, the air is suddenly charged. I shift around in my seat awkwardly.

My heart rate picks up. I take another sip of my drink. Searching for something to say.

'I like reading, I guess.'

He laughs. 'That's cute.'

'So, erm, what do you do in your spare time?'

Cringe. Did I really just ask that? Talk about the worst pickup line ever. Although why am I even thinking about pickup lines? A nervous laugh. 'God, I shouldn't even be here.'

'Hey.' He places a hand on my leg. 'Don't run away. Not just yet.'

I stare at his hand as if it were on fire and I could go up in flames at any moment. I'm uncertain how to act. I'm not imagining it: lines *are* being crossed, which I'm partly responsible for, and I need to snap out of this fantasy right away, but my head is swimming. It feels like I've downed a triple shot of vodka, not a few glasses of champagne. Anxiously, I look to Georgie but she's kissing Carter. His hand has moved up her thigh. I turn back to Lloyd and smile awkwardly.

'I'm glad you made it to the party,' he says. Looking at me expectantly.

This is the moment I should tell him about Nathan. I should confess, tell him I'm searching for an ego hit because my husband's away on a business trip with another woman, and then I stop, because how desperate does that sound? I've spun a narrative to excuse my behaviour. Nathan would be so furious – no, disappointed, if he could see me now. I feel a rush of shame.

I bring my hand to my neck to loosen an imaginary collar. My blood feels like it's reaching boiling point.

'It's really hot in here, don't you think?'

'Yes, you most definitely are hot.' He smirks.

What's wrong with you, Becca? But the voice in my head sounds strange, echoey.

'You know, these afterparties are legendary.'

'Are they?'

'Especially for what comes later,' he says with a lazy smile.

My stomach contracts.

'Why, what comes later?'

'I've heard it gets real loose.'

'Loose?' I search around me, feeling woozier.

'But only if you want to lean into it.'

'I'm not really sure I understand.' I catch the eye of the guy serving drinks. Middle Eastern looking, with floppy dark hair hanging in front of his eyes. A tattoo of an eagle wrapped around his bicep. He flashes me a concerned look which forces me to do something, and suddenly I rise up onto my feet. Although it's more of a stumble, because the floor feels like it's tilting, and . . . I frown. Weirdly, all the pain has gone. In fact, I can't even feel my feet any more.

My dress is damp with sweat and the room feels like it's shrinking. I try to get Georgie's attention but she hasn't come up for air.

'Georgie,' I say, raising my voice.

She's stroking Carter, drawing suggestively across his back with her finger while she kisses him. There's a sense of desperation about the way she's behaving, and that's not how I remember her.

'Georgie,' I say more loudly.

She drags her eyes away from him and looks at me, frowning.

'Can we go. I'm not feeling great.'

'But we just got here.'

'Please.'

'But I'm having fun.'

I grimace. All I want is fresh air. I need air.

She untangles herself from Carter, a small roll of her eyes as she stands up and comes over.

'What's wrong, Twig?' Her eyes soften.

'I'm tired and I feel sick.'

'Why don't you eat something,' she continues gently, gesturing to the small plates of sushi and caviar floating around the room.

Perhaps some food in my stomach will help. Although the thought of raw fish mixed with a belly of alcohol makes my stomach gurgle.

'I thought you guys were getting along.' She looks back at Lloyd. 'He's hot, no?'

I laugh in astonishment. 'I'm married.'

'I know that, silly. But listen, it's just a bit of fun.'

'I can't do this.'

'Isn't it nice to have a flirt?'

'I'm not flirting.' But I feel a twinge of guilt as the words leave me.

'Look, it's OK to enjoy yourself.' Georgie fixes me with her eyes. 'I'm worried about you. From what you've told me tonight, everything you've been through, you could really do with having some fun.'

I glance back. Lloyd catches my eye and smiles, revealing his perfectly straight white teeth. I realize how much I want to kiss him.

'I'm old enough to be his mum.' I banish the thought.

'You're only thirty!'

'I feel old.'

'You need to get your power back. You've forgotten who you are. What makes *you* happy.'

'That's not what I said earlier,' I say firmly.

'You're starting to believe your own lies.'

'I love Nathan. With all my heart, and' – I glance back at Lloyd – 'I *am* old enough to be his mum.'

'Where is the Twiggy I knew?' A head-tilt of sympathy. 'The one who drank all of Mummy's sherry, the girl with big dreams who couldn't wait to escape that hellhole of a village. Where is she?'

'I can't do this now.'

'And anyway' – she smiles mischievously – 'young guys love experienced women.'

I shut my eyes and exhale.

'Please. Can we leave?'

Georgie looks back at Carter and gives him a cutesy wave. She lowers her voice to a whisper. 'I really like him. I want to see where this can go.'

Can go? But she's only just met him.

'Let's stay. For another half hour, 'K?'

I check the time on my phone: 3.30 a.m. *Still* nothing from Nathan.

I'd be having an anxiety attack if it weren't for the fact I feel like I'm about to throw up. I swallow, my throat is dry and the room feels like it's suddenly five degrees warmer. I glance again at Lloyd but his face is in soft focus. Come to think of it, everything's a little blurred. A haze of electric blues and vape smoke.

'Pretty please.'

I feel foggy and confused.

Georgie gives me a squeeze and then leaves my side for Carter's. Within seconds she's entwined. He locks his arm around her waist, pulling her firmly against him, and my heart sinks. I'll never prise them apart now.

I don't want to ruin her night, but something doesn't feel right. Carter seems overly possessive, and I don't like how he keeps looking over at me.

He fires me another look. Jesus, does he want me gone? I suppose I could leave them to it.

No, wait, even though I've given Georgie the spare key, she'll never find her way back to mine with all the alcohol and drugs she's taken. And what if this Carter forces himself on her? I feel responsible for her. I should hang around and keep an eye on her. But I'm feeling a little weak, so I lower myself into a nearby armchair and shut my eyes briefly.

THE FRIEND – BECCA

When I open my eyes, it feels like I've been asleep for hours.

The thud of the bass shudders right the way through me and something strange seems to be happening to my vision. I give my head a little shake, searching for somewhere I can wait for Georgie, but when I glance across the crowded room, I'm struck by how everything has changed.

The room's filled out, there's barely enough space to move. The music is different. Lloyd has disappeared – and so has Carter.

Scanning the crowd, I search for Georgie.

I couldn't have shut my eyes for longer than a minute, could I? I frown, feeling confused. I check my phone: 4.15 a.m. What the . . . ? How the hell did that happen? The handful of times I've got drunk, it never felt like this. It takes far more effort than it should to stand up; it's as if I'm having an out of body experience, my limbs are heavy, my skin won't stop tingling, and why are my hands sore and achy? I'm thrown off balance as I make my way to the darkened corner where I last saw Georgie.

There's a new couple on the sofa, making out.

'Did you see my friend? She was just here?'

The guy looks up and frowns.

'Long blonde hair? Black dress?'

I realize that could be half the people in this room and he responds accordingly, pulling a face. He shrugs and turns his head away. The girl he's with shoots me an apologetic look. I search again but I can't see either of them. I can't see Lloyd either. The room blurs in and out of focus, I give my head another shake but I still feel jittery.

She's probably gone to the toilet, that'll be it.

Forcing my way through the makeshift dance floor, I head towards the landing where there's a queue snaking right the way down the stairs.

But no Georgie.

I squeeze past to tuts and sideways glances. I smile sheepishly, promising I'm not jumping the queue, and knock on the bathroom door.

'Georgie?'

The sound of a toilet flushing.

The squeak of taps.

A brief surge of water.

The door swings open and the woman who welcomed us into the afterparty staggers out, willowy and fragile, dabbing her nose. She bumps into me and I catch her before she trips.

'Hey, have you seen my friend?'

She sniffs loudly, wiping her nose several times.

'The one I arrived here with?'

A blank look.

'You invited us in?'

'Oh yeah.' She runs her fingers through her blonde hair and staggers past.

Jesus, is everyone here off their head on drugs?

'Georgie?' I call after her urgently. The next person in line barges me out of the way, closing the toilet door before I can check if Georgie's inside. I knock on the door. 'Hey. Is my friend in there? Georgie?'

I turn around to angry faces peering back at me. 'Get in line!' Then someone shouts 'Crazy lady!'

Crazy? I know I'm not cut from the same cloth as them, but that's harsh.

'Is there another toilet?' I search around.

They eye me warily, as if I'm a bomb about to detonate. I push past, making my way upstairs. As I inch closer to the top floor, the stairwell shrinks, the ceiling lowers. I can almost reach up and touch it.

A couple kissing on the landing breaks apart, giggling. But as soon as they see me, their laughter falls away. They give me a wide berth, quickly making their way down the stairs.

Is there something on my face? Why is everyone looking at me strangely? I wipe at my mouth in case my red lipstick's smudged and then continue along the landing but my head feels syrupy, while my legs are full of lead. It takes a few seconds to realize – I'm the only one up here.

All at once, the party feels a light year away. The music is muted, reduced to a dull thump. The walls are dreary, stripped bare, there's a cold draught coming up between the floorboards and the air smells earthy and damp. None of the rooms are open, so I try the doors, but they're locked. I reach out a hand to steady myself and that's when I notice it. Branching off from the corridor.

A final set of stairs.

The stairwell is so narrow there's barely room for one person and at the top is a much smaller door with a light creeping underneath. An attic? I climb towards the light and catch a whiff of something else. A tang of perfume lingers on the stairs. The ghost of someone who's just been here.

'Georgie?'

'No one's allowed up here.'

I startle, turning quickly to find a woman with short hair, gelled flat to her scalp, dressed severely in a trouser suit, standing a few feet behind me. Where did she come from? She's eyeing me suspiciously, a tightness in the corners of her mouth.

'I'm looking for my friend,' I tell her.

'You won't find her up here. Party's that way.' She points to where I've come from.

I glance back to the secret room, catching a flicker of movement in the crack of light beneath the door. A shadow shifting around.

'Maybe she came up here looking for me.' I make a start on the stairs.

The woman crosses her arms.

'She's not up there.'

'She's had a lot to drink, she probably got lost.'

Her eyes pinch. One prolonged stare. Waiting for me. My cheeks flush under the spotlight of her glare. Sod her, I'll try again in a minute when she's gone, I think, and turn, but the movement throws me off-kilter. I reach for the wall to steady myself.

'Careful.' She moves aside.

I feel her watching me the whole way down.

Back on the ground floor, I return to the room of mirrors and chandeliers, forcing myself deeper into the crowd to look for Georgie. I'm feeling wobbly, like my legs are different lengths. What was in that champagne? I give my head another shake and push through the throng of people. The party has doubled in size and the room's as hot as an oven. The large front windows are misty, my temperature is rising and I can feel sweat pooling between my shoulder blades. I make a beeline for the drinks bucket filled with ice.

Grabbing a handful of ice, I feel a brief shock as I hold the cubes to my temple. I run them across my wrists but it does nothing to cool me down. My chest is tightening, I lose my footing and someone shoves me out of the way. The man in the velvet blazer gives me the once-over, a look to say I'm *that person*, the annoying drunk at the party.

Suddenly the party feels hostile. Everywhere I turn, I'm seeing pinched faces, groups swarming together, glancing my way as they speak in low, threatening whispers. The masks have taken on a sinister shape. The noses appear as sharpened beaks, the eyes filed down into demonic orbs. I shiver even though I'm the opposite of cold. Jesus, am I hallucinating?

'Are you OK?' A voice from behind.

It's the tattooed waiter, regarding me with a deep frown.

'Miss, are you all right?' he says insistently, full of concern. 'Do you need some help?'

'Have you seen Georgie?' I can hear the hysteria in my voice.

'Georgie?'

'Never mind.'

I hate myself for being rude, but all I can think about is Georgie. I lurch past him into more bodies. Searching. Eyes raking the room, until my gaze lands on a woman with ombré hair wearing a silky lace dress.

Oh thank God.

'Georgie!' I reach for her, my hand lands on her shoulder and she turns around.

The woman, who couldn't look less like Georgie, glares at me.

'Sorry!'

She edges away, eyeing me warily.

I can't stop apologizing, but my voice has shrunk to something small and brittle and I feel my knees weaken. Abandoning my search, I turn towards the exit, desperate for some air. I need air or I think I'm going to pass out. I let my feet carry me forward, my head rattling around like a lollipop on a stick. I make it out onto the steps in time, drinking in the cold night. So cold it makes my lungs stutter.

It's still snowing. The moon slides out from behind a cloud, turning the streets silver. I search up and down the length of the canal. It's deserted, bar the few partygoers braving the cold to smoke.

'Georgie?' My voice is now barely a whisper.

I stagger down the steps, my heels sinking into the snow.

'I think she's drunk,' a woman close by says to her partner.

I feel more confused than ever. Where should I look now? Nowhere without my coat, that's what, but my brain isn't thinking logically, so instead I follow footprints in the snow, although they could be anyone's. Georgie wouldn't have gone without her coat in this weather, would she? This feels all wrong. Georgie wouldn't have left without me, she wouldn't have abandoned me. Only a few hours ago she was calling me her best friend.

I carry on, the cold stinging my face. This is crazy. I'll freeze to death out here, I should go back, search the party again. I turn around, wobble and slip, landing on my back with a *thunk*. Pain spikes through me, but within seconds, the stabbing sensation in my side vanishes. I lie in shock, not completely understanding what just happened. Then I laugh it off, the stress of tonight catching up with me. But now I'm down, I can't seem to get up. My legs refuse to work, and my head feels like cotton wool, fluffy and full of air. Weirdly, I can't feel the cold any more.

Reaching around in the snow, I manage to find my clutch bag. I fish out my phone, the screen lighting up the dark. There's one continuous stream of messages from Nathan.

Happy New Year. I love you baby. I hope you're having fun tonight. X

Then:

Sorry I didn't message at midnight. Battery died.
Back at my hotel now. x

Where are you?

Three missed calls.

Are you OK? Why aren't you picking up.

Five missed calls.

I won't go to sleep unless I know you're OK.

PICK UP. Is everything OK with the baby?

He's been trying to get hold of me for hours. The messages are only coming through now. There must have been no signal inside the house. My heart sinks. Oh God, oh God, how could I have been so bloody stupid to let my insecurities get the better of me. I've behaved terribly, and now, *this*. Why did I get so drunk? I find Georgie's last WhatsApp message and ring her phone. It goes straight to voicemail.

'Where are you? I'm outside the party. Call me. Please!'

But the words come out garbled. Which is no surprise because my head feels like it's being held underwater. I can't concentrate. *Focus, Becca.*

My phone buzzes in my hand. I look at the screen. Nathan! I go to answer it but my arm gets stuck. Why can't I move? I stare at the screen helplessly, watching it ring off. The phone slides between my fingers, sinking into the snow.

What's happening to me?

Up is now down and the Christmas lights, the small fairy lights looped around the arch of the bridge – they twinkle and swirl, the honey yellow, dripping into the dark canal water.

And suddenly there's a shadow looming, a man standing over me.

Then everything turns to black.

NOW

5 January

A young police officer in a windproof jacket heaves a sigh as he gets out of the car, snow swirling into his eyes and sticking to his hair as he cuts a path through the crowd. He approaches the girl on the side of the canal who's sobbing so hard her face is bright pink and her nose is dribbling. He offers her a tissue before flashing his ID at the mother.

'Are you the woman who called the police?'

She nods, craning her head up to look at the tall figure.

'You reported finding something suspicious in the canal?'

'I warned my daughter, I told her, don't skate under the bridge, it's dangerous, I could see a hole in the ice and I was terrified she would fall in.'

The officer crouches, one knee ploughing the snow, meeting the little girl at eye level.

'Hello, I'm Pieter, what's your name?'

She curls herself away from him.

'Lotte,' her mother answers for her. 'Whatever she found must have really frightened her, I've never seen her like this.'

'Hi Lotte, do you want to tell me what's made you so upset?' the officer asks.

The girl buries her face into her mum's shoulder.

'Don't be scared. I need to ask you a few questions and then you can go home, OK?'

She nods.

'Did you see someone fall through the ice?'

She shakes her head.

'Did you find something?'

A nod.

'Do you want to tell me what you found? It's OK, you can tell me.'

Slowly, the girl lifts her gaze, her eyes are swollen and glistening with fresh tears.

'See, I'm not that scary.' The officer smiles.

She stares back at the man with wide arctic-blue eyes. Her face is pale and haunted.

'What did you find under the bridge?'

'I saw a face,' she whispers.

'A face?' He frowns.

Her bottom lip trembles.

'Oh heck, it's OK,' the mother comforts her daughter, rubbing her back. 'Don't be frightened.'

'*Who* did you see?' he says urgently. It comes out sharper than the officer intends but, not having a family of his own yet, not understanding what it's like to be a father, he sometimes forgets to measure his tone.

'It's all right, don't be frightened.' Her mother strokes her head, warning the officer with her eyes. 'Tell this man what you saw and then we'll go home.'

'A face,' she repeats. 'There was only a face.'

THE FRIEND – BECCA

An ugly noise, a bleeping sound, drifts into my consciousness and then out again. Steady and rhythmical, followed by a humming, the buzz of machines. The murmur of voices and now the soft squeak of feet approaching quickly, then disappearing. Slowly, I peel open my eyes, blinking into the brightly lit small space.

The cubicle is warm and airless. There's a curtain on a rail wrapped around a bed which I'm lying on. I'm wearing Georgie's dress, my tights are laddered, my shoes are missing and there's a dull ache behind my ears, spreading down to the base of my skull. I reach around to feel the back of my head, wincing as I make contact with a hard lump.

An unpleasant coppery taste is in my mouth. Blood? From where I bit my tongue? I feel queasy, the contents of my stomach sloshing around and burning my insides. I try moving, the pain in my head intensifies, but a fragment from last night is dislodged. A handsome man with dark peaty eyes, the way he was gazing at me, almost as if he was peering right into my soul.

A sudden whipping noise jerks me back into the cubicle. The curtain, on what looks like a cheap shower rail, is pulled back and a man dressed head to toe in pale blue scrubs appears at the foot of my bed.

Young, confident, a tawny mop of hair threaded with copper; he's very good-looking, although his shadowed eyes betray the strain of exhaustion. Behind him, nurses dash back and forwards. A woman with her chin tilted to the ceiling holds a white gauze over one eye. A teenager with a bandaged hand is pushed past in a wheelchair. Someone cries out in pain. The man who's obviously a doctor pulls the curtain across, putting some distance between us and the pandemonium.

'English?' he says in a soft Dutch accent.

I nod, but even that hurts.

'I'm Doctor Hendriks.' He sits down heavily, clicks the end of his torch and shines the light into my eye. I blink quickly.

'Look left.'

Obediently, I follow his finger until I feel a sharp scratch. It's as if something is tearing at my eyeball. My eyes fill with tears, I try blinking but the light is too bright all of a sudden.

'How many fingers am I holding up?'

'Three.'

'What's your name?'

'Becca.'

He looks at me.

'Rebecca Peters.'

'And what's today's date?'

'Today?' I repeat as if it must be a joke. Then a white-hot jab of pain shoots between my temples.

'Do you know what year it is?'

I open my mouth to speak and shut it again.

'What do you last remember?'

I look at him blankly.

The doctor pushes himself away, the wheels of his chair spin across the floor. He slides the torch back into his top pocket, a fresh look of concern entering his features.

'How did I get here?' I squint, searching around me for clues.

'Someone found you unconscious and brought you into Spoedeisende hulp.'

'I'm in A&E?'

'You've had a nasty bang to your head. Do you remember falling?'

I look down at my hands. My knuckles are swollen, there's dirt or something dark crusted under my fingernails and my hands ache. A throbbing pain, as if someone's drilling right down to the bone. How did I get these injuries? A hazy memory of an argument drifts towards me and then leaves as quickly as it arrived.

'Do you remember where you were last night?'

'Yeah, of course, I was at . . .' I wince as I try to drag up the memory. 'There was a house party . . .'

'Are you on holiday? Which hotel are you staying in?'

'I live in the south, in De Pijp.'

'Do you know how you came to be at this party?'

More fragments float behind my eyes – the handsome man with an American accent – and I pause, because there was someone else, with floppy dark hair, towering over me in the snow. Was I that drunk?

I feel nauseous and my head is pounding. This is worse than any hangover I've experienced.

'Who can I contact for you?'

Nathan. I look up sharply. Oh God, he was trying to get hold of me, I missed his calls; he must be losing his mind with worry.

'The man who brought you here, is he a friend?'

I sit up, looking around urgently. 'I have to go.'

The doctor touches my shoulder, gently pressing me down onto the bed.

'Do you have anyone who can collect you?'

'What time is it?'

'A family member?' He glances at his watch. 'It's 9.45 a.m.'

What? 'How long have I been here?'

'Several hours.'

I don't understand. I was so drunk I passed out?

'Rebecca, is there a friend or a family member who can take you home?'

'My husband, he's um . . .' I blink quickly. The memory of him kissing me before leaving for his flight lands in my thoughts. 'He's away with work, and my friend, she's . . .' I stop, my stomach sinks further. *Georgie.* The thud of the music, the heat of the party. My senses are suddenly electrified as I'm dragged back inside the canal house. The panic of not being able to find Georgie rising in my chest. Where did she go?

I push myself upright.

'I have to get home,' I tell the doctor insistently. I need

to know Georgie got back safely. Thank God, I gave her a key to the flat.

'Before you leave, I need to explain a few things. We've run some tests.' He turns to his notes. 'The good news is the CT scan shows no fractures.'

'So I can go?'

'There's minor concussion, it's important to rest.'

'I feel fine.' I swing my legs to the ground but the sudden movement makes me dizzy.

The doctor's eyes flicker up to meet mine and I smile weakly, trying to disguise my nausea. 'We're waiting on a few more results.' He grabs his pen, returning to his notes. 'Are you allergic to anything?'

'Not that I know of.'

'Are you taking any medication?'

I think about the drawer filled with supplements.

'Just some prenatal vitamins,' I confess, and then immediately regret it.

'Are you pregnant?'

A fluttering sensation fills my chest.

'Rebecca?' he asks, a new urgency in his voice.

There's a clawing at my insides as I'm forced to relive the miscarriage.

'I'm not pregnant,' I say eventually.

'That's a relief.' He smiles. 'A fall like that would have put the baby at risk.'

I look away. I'm holding on by a thread.

He takes my contact details; he checks his watch.

'It shouldn't be much longer until we get the results. Try to rest in the meantime.'

The doctor hands me a glass of water before disappearing behind the curtain. The cold liquid hitting my stomach makes me feel queasier. I sink back, noticing my stilettos parked by the bed and my clutch bag on the chair. *Oh, thank God.*

But closing my eyes only makes me feel worse. I think I'm going to be sick. I turn and heave, but nothing comes out. What the hell was I drinking?

Another memory shakes loose, a waiter with a tray of champagne flutes. Then I remember the look he gave me and, now I come to think of it, everyone was staring at me strangely. As if I was deranged. I didn't do anything crazy at the party, did I?

I shut my eyes tightly again. I'm not thinking clearly. A frazzled-looking nurse pulls the curtain back, attaching a clipboard to the end of my bed.

'Shouldn't be much longer now.' She smiles kindly.

Panic is rising in my chest as the confusion of last night takes hold. Why did I get so drunk? I should have known it would hit me hard, having been off alcohol for months. I hope Georgie's OK. She'll be all right – I try to scrub the worry away – she could always handle her drink better than me. Still, I need to get home. The image of my friend swims behind my eyes as I slide off the bed and begin collecting my things from the chair.

'Wait! The doctor told you to rest.' The nurse holds up a hand but I brush past, wrenching back the curtain. My ears are ringing. The pain between my temples is increasing.

Weaving through the rabbit warren of corridors and

medical bays, skimming past a waiting room heaving with people nursing New Year's Eve injuries, I eventually find the exit. I leave through the sliding doors, blinded by the dazzling morning light.

The chilly air bites at my cheeks, but I can breathe again.

I can't stand hospitals; they remind me of those dark years growing up. Mutely sitting by Mum's bedside, clutching her hand tightly as Dad covered up what he'd done – lying to the A&E doctor that her fractured ankle was another clumsy fall down the stairs. She always found it in her heart to forgive him and take him back. And then it would happen again. And again. Those were the dark years, before Georgie rescued me and adopted me into her world.

A new image arrives. A flashback to us giggling; listening to cheesy tunes, trying on clothes and doing our make-up as we got ready to go out. Last night – it started off so well.

I let myself into the flat. It's deathly quiet. For some reason the heating hasn't come on and it feels even colder and more unwelcoming than when I left it.

'Georgie?'

Silence.

I walk quickly between the rooms; everything is exactly how we left it. Two champagne flutes stained with red lipstick, two empty bottles, Georgie's make-up tipped out on the bed, her clothes flung across the floor. Her suitcase flipped open. Her phone charger still plugged into the wall.

'Georgie?' I push the bathroom door wide open. Make-up is scattered around the basin. The sink is coated in iridescent sparkle. I run the tap, flushing away the finely milled powder and look up to meet my ghostly reflection in the mirror. Skin bleached white. Bloodshot eyes and thin spidery veins woven across my nose and cheeks. It's as if I've been sandblasted by an arctic wind. How long was I out cold for?

A new image arrives. A warm breath on my cheek, hot across my collarbone. Two dark eyes staring directly into mine.

A face hovering over me when I was outside the party in the snow.

The heat of a body pressed up against me.

What? Stop, that's not right, Nathan has blue eyes. I push the thought far away. What's happening to me?

'Georgie?' I call out.

I look over the flat again, I even check inside the bath in case she passed out there. The realization *she never made it home* slowly dawns on me.

Plugging my phone in to charge, I ring Georgie again. The fifth time in seven minutes and it goes straight to voicemail. I'm so frustrated, I want to throw my phone across the room. Instead, I leave another message pleading for her to get in touch. I can't bring myself to read the dozens of new messages from Nathan. He must be losing his mind, but I need a moment to think, to pull the pieces of myself back together.

What the hell am I going to tell him? That I got so

drunk I ended up in A&E? He doesn't even know I lost the baby. I close my eyes for a moment. I feel nauseous from just playing out how that conversation will go.

All at once I'm hit with the memory of chatting to some impossibly good-looking American and then I recall how I hid my wedding ring. I played along with being single. I was attracted to a man who wasn't my husband. My eyes fly open and my cheeks burn with shame.

I'm an awful person. Dad kept his gambling secret from Mum. Georgie's parents kept secrets from each other. I vowed I'd never become like them. And here I am, doing the same. *Keeping secrets.* Tears spring in the corners of my eyes. How could I be so bloody stupid?

The pain is escalating, drilling at the base of my skull, and I drop down on the chair by the window, gazing numbly onto the street, watching snow flurries drift past the window, listening to the hum of the fridge, the ticking of the clock.

The silence is deafening.

Georgie will be fine, I try to reassure myself. We're not teenagers any more, she can look after herself and she's an experienced traveller. She went on to a club. She'll be having wild sex in some hotel room. Her phone's run out of battery. But she'll be in touch soon. Her things are here, she won't want to leave without them.

I close my eyes, pushing hot tears onto my cheeks. The sensation brings another flashback. Vitriol, rising in my voice. Me, yelling? I swallow. That doesn't sound like me at all. No, that didn't happen. Now I'm really confusing things.

I get up, although my movements are slow and heavy like I'm walking underwater. Each step sends a small shockwave through my system. A *thud thud*, and once again I'm dragged back into the dimly lit rooms, the trance music rattling through the speakers as I fight my way through the sweaty mass of people. I force myself to remember the moments leading up to when I last saw my friend.

I only shut my eyes for a second, she was there, right there on the sofa with Carter, yes Carter, I remember his name now, and then, then she was gone.

There was no argument.

I glance down at my hands, studying the purple marks appearing around my knuckles. It must have happened when I bumped my head, although that doesn't really explain the bruising. I head for the bathroom, suddenly desperate to wash the night off me. I strip off, leaving Georgie's designer dress in a heap on the floor, and step into the heat of the shower. I turn the temperature even higher, to almost scalding, and begin scrubbing. I've never felt so dirty in my life.

By the time I get out, my fingers have wrinkled into prunes and my skin is flushed red. I throw on my jogging bottoms, instantly feeling more comfortable in my loose clothes. I pour a glass of water, press two paracetamol pills from the blister pack, wash them down with the water. Already I'm feeling calmer. I'm silent for a few moments, thinking. One final deep breath, then I pick up my phone and call Nathan.

* * *

'Jesus Christ, I've been going out of my mind.' I can hear the fear in his voice. 'Are you OK? Where've you been?'

'I'm so sorry.'

'Didn't you see my calls?'

Panic.

'I left my phone at home,' I lie.

'So where were you?'

'A friend called on me to watch the fireworks, it was all last minute.'

'Have you any idea how worried I've been?' His voice is breaking. I've never heard him this upset. My heart contracts, and at the same time it's giving me a small thrill – hearing how much he cares.

'Everything's OK, I'm fine—'

'I thought you'd been in an accident; I was about to ring the hospitals.'

'Please, you don't need to worry.'

He exhales. 'OK,' he says, taking a deep, calming breath. 'You're safe, that's all that matters.'

'I'm so sorry I worried you.'

'So where did you end up last night?' His voice softens. 'Were the fireworks any good?'

I panic again. The truth sticking in my throat.

'Just in the city centre.' *What am I saying?* 'But I was home not long after midnight.' I can't bring myself to tell him the truth. Not over the phone.

'You shouldn't go out without your phone, not at night – anything could happen. Why didn't you message me when you woke up?'

Just tell him the truth, Becca.

'I had a lie-in, I was exhausted.'

'Is everything OK?' he says quickly. 'Is the baby OK?'

Tell him about the baby.

'Everything's great.'

He blows out another heavy breath of relief. 'Were you out with the girls from the expat group?'

'Yeah,' I swallow. 'Just a few of us.'

Oh God, now I've started lying, I can't stop. But I know how he'll react if he finds out it was Georgie. 'Anyway, how was your night?' I change the subject quickly. 'How did the meeting go?'

'Ah, I don't know. I think it went OK,' he says absently. 'But it's so hard to tell with these things.'

He sounds despondent and I feel even worse for adding to his stress.

'Is Brad going to invest in the restaurant?'

'That's what I'm hoping for, but I need to get him to commit to something on paper. It might take a bit more work.' He turns his face away from the phone, his voice fading. I can hear a noise in the background. A woman's voice? *No, Becca, don't start this again, what's wrong with you? You're the one who's lying.*

'Hey, babe, I have to go, I've got another meeting before Brad leaves for New York, but I'll call you tonight. Please pick up this time. Love you.'

He hangs up and I feel sick with guilt. I wish I'd told him the truth; a problem shared is a problem halved, and I could do with his advice right now. Nathan's always so great in a crisis.

Returning to the silence, I try to take my mind off

things by clearing away the glasses, recycling the bottles. Everything is taking three times longer than it should. I stop to catch my breath, down two more glasses of water and open the fridge. I know I should eat something, but the sight of leftovers is enough to turn my stomach.

She'll be fine.

From what I remember, Georgie didn't seem drunk last night. Then I think about all the cocaine she was taking, how she kept checking her phone, how distracted she seemed. And she left the party without me. Did I say something to upset her? No. I dismiss the idea. I'm confusing things again. We were having fun, she told me as much.

She'll show up soon, I tell myself, trying to soothe my anxiety.

My head is pounding, a roaring between my temples, I don't think I've ever felt this sick in my life. I cross to the bedroom and lie down. But I can't relax, it's impossible. An uneasy feeling has lodged in my stomach, a worm tunnelling through my insides.

THE FRIEND – BECCA

I get a twitch of guilt from looking through her things, it feels private, but I have to do something.

I'm not sure what I'm expecting to find in her suitcase, but anything feels better than staring at the ceiling. I pull out a lipstick, mascara, some loose tampons and a blister pack of antihistamines. Her wallet isn't here but her passport is. As I rummage through Georgie's clothes, feeling the expensive fabrics against my skin, I get a whiff of her perfume. It's as if she's in the room with me, and my mind walks me back in time.

Summer 2015, and we were making the most of the heatwave, stretched out in our bikinis by her pool. Georgie was wearing her trademark oversized Gucci sunglasses, sipping on a cocktail while I tried to read my book.

I was struggling to take in the words, I was having to re-read big chunks of text because my heart was beating so fast. In less than two weeks' time, Georgie and I would be living together.

Georgie's father had bought her a two-bedroom flat in Cheyne Walk as a present for finishing her A-levels. She planned to have a year out before university, living the high life in London, and I would stay in her spare room while I figured out what I wanted to do next with my life.

It would be my first time away from Devon. I'd been to the Lake District on a camping trip, but that didn't really count because it rained for five days straight and Mum was crying the entire time because Dad had spent our holiday money on the horses and her arm didn't work properly after he told her never to bring it up again.

This would be different.

Georgie and Becca's big adventure.

I was nervous, I was excited and I was relieved because I'd been starting to listen to what everyone had been telling me for years. That I was Georgie's *pet*, her 'local friend' who she killed time with but wouldn't be seen dead with outside the village.

Now I would prove them all wrong.

So you can imagine the embarrassment when Georgie went back on her word.

My heart skips a beat just thinking about that awful moment she broke the news there'd been a change of plan, a friend from her posh private school – Fiona – would be having my room instead. She didn't even offer me much in the way of an apology, other than they 'had more in common'. I could hear her mum's voice coming through in her. I could picture the conversation they must have had. How she'd persuaded Georgie that I would hold her back. That I wouldn't be accepted into her Chelsea world.

A little piece of me died that day. I'd been living in

Georgie's orbit, feeding off her sunlight, and all at once, everything went dark. Like a lunar eclipse. A blackout.

I had been replaced – just as everyone predicted I would be – by a much cooler, glamorous crowd. The Chelsea rich kids also living off their parents' trust funds. And twig-thin council estate Becca ceased to exist.

While she partied with her new beautiful friends, I buried our plan to travel the world. I didn't bother with university and focused on getting a job nearby so I could afford to leave home. I had to get as far away from that toxic house as possible.

Instagram had not long become a thing and I would check Georgie's profile, obsessing over her photos until the envy became unbearable and I removed myself from social media altogether.

I stopped going out, I wanted to shrink out of sight. I was convinced there must be something wrong with me, why else would she abandon me like that? Eventually, time was a healer and I did move on, I made new friends in the village, girls with a similar upbringing to me, and I hung out with them down the pub and my friendship with Nathan blossomed into a relationship. Nathan became my life raft. He stepped into Georgie's shoes; he rescued me from the storm. Which sounds a little pathetic, I know, but after an upbringing like mine, all I wanted was to feel safe.

Every now and then, I'd catch myself daydreaming about what it would have been like if we'd gone on to live together, just like Georgie promised. And then I'd hack down the idea, before it made roots, reminding myself that it would never have worked out. How could it? We were from different worlds.

Tears find their way into my eyes as I run my hands through her things.

She came back to find me and now I've lost her again.

I know the hangover's to blame, it's why I'm overly emotional. I'm also aware I'm overreacting about Georgie, that she's probably fine. But something's triggering me, twisting deep inside me. I'm not really feeling myself. I get up and walk to the bathroom to splash water on my face and a flash of pink catches my eye.

Half hidden in the folds of the duvet, a Juicy Couture cosmetic bag.

I lay flat on my stomach across the bed and carefully unzip the soft velvet pouch, expecting it to be full of expensive face creams. But what's inside couldn't be further from any beauty treatment.

I stare at the needles and syringes in silent horror.

THE FRIEND - BECCA

Georgie, diabetic? I study the small vials of insulin, part relieved to discover my friend isn't a heroin addict, part devastated there's yet another side to Georgie I didn't know about. But mostly, I'm terrified for her well-being. I've a feeling of dread in the pit of my stomach. How long can a diabetic go without insulin?

I type the question into Google and it tells me a window of hours to several days – depending on whether she's type 1 or type 2 diabetic – before her blood sugar level plummets and she falls unconscious. I think about all the alcohol she drank, the cocaine, her erratic behaviour suddenly seeming even more reckless. Does she have a death wish?

No, come on, Becca, Georgie wouldn't have been so stupid to go out without taking an emergency supply with her. Would she?

I try calling her again. I check my email; I send her another message on Facebook and Instagram. Then I pick up the phone and ring around the hospitals.

* * *

In daylight, they all look the same.

I'm in the right neighbourhood – where all the rich people live – but which one of these grand homes did we end up in?

I peer inside the ground-floor windows, desperately hunting for a clue, something to trigger a memory. I can picture the chandeliers, the giant glittering orbs suspended from the ceiling, but I've already walked by several homes that could fit that description. A middle-aged man reading a paper in his front room looks up, our eyes meet and I hurry on before he thinks I'm casing the joint.

It's like searching for a needle in a haystack, it's hopeless and yet I feel desperate I'm not doing more. I should be knocking on doors, calling out Georgie's name, stopping people in the street, because this is my fault. Georgie was my guest; I was supposed to be looking after her. If I hadn't been so obsessed with my problems, if I hadn't drunk so much champagne . . .

I take a deep breath of the chilly air.

I'm trying to stay positive. Georgie hasn't been admitted to any of the local hospitals, which is a good sign, at least, although it doesn't throw any light on where she might be. This hangover isn't helping; everything appears bleak and hopeless, like I'm wading through treacle. My thoughts keep relentlessly returning to the medication I found. A sand timer is running down in my head. Images of Georgie passed out cold somewhere, or worse, keep shooting into my thoughts, rapid as gunfire. *Pah pah pah*.

And there's something else. Niggling. A memory about last night, just out of reach. I don't know how, or what I did, but it feels like – I don't know, like I might be involved somehow.

No. That's crazy. What would I have to do with this?

I inhale sharply, it doesn't even bear thinking about.

I stop. I take another breath. *Stay focused*. This is bad but it could be worse. If I can find where the house party was then I can ask the owners if they remember seeing Georgie or the guy she left with. What if Georgie went back to collect her coat, or maybe she left something else behind? Someone must know something.

Should I contact the police? Or will they think I'm overreacting? The idea of knocking on doors and stopping strangers in the street now seems hysterical. It hasn't even been twenty-four hours yet. What would Nathan do? He always knows what to do in a crisis and I feel a sudden longing for my husband. I'd give anything for one of his cuddles right now.

It's just gone midday and the winter sun is breaking through. It's so bright it feels like it's searing my retinas. My temple throbs; I wish I had my sunglasses and I desperately need water. Jesus, this hangover is like nothing I've ever experienced. I squint into the sunshine, eyes roving back and forth along the canal searching for clues, but all I find are the charred remains of last night's fireworks, half buried by the snow. It feels like a graveyard it's so eerily quiet with the ghost of New Year's Eve haunting the streets.

I make another slow turn. A horrible chewing sensation in my gut.

Where the hell are you, Georgie?

I walk for nearly twenty minutes until finally I see something I recognize. An old rickety houseboat converted from a 1960s cargo ship. Battered and faded by the changing seasons, it stands out like a sore thumb among the smarter-looking models. Then, an image of a pale face at the window flickers into my mind. Someone was watching us? But before I have time to pull apart the memory, I'm distracted by two workmen in high-vis jackets directing traffic, while a removal lorry reverses into position.

That's odd. Who moves house on New Year's Day?

The loading doors swing open, clanging against the sides of the lorry. A man dressed in overalls and a beanie hat jumps out of the cab and disappears inside the house directly opposite. Seconds later, two more emerge, pulling out a painting I recognize.

Then a velvet sofa is carried out, the sofa *I* was on last night, and my mind spins me back twelve hours. A hazy memory of chatting to the handsome American, his arm slung around me.

This is it – number 34 – this is where the party was, only—

Confused, I approach one of the removal men.

'What's happening here?'

He ignores me and disappears inside. I peer into the hallway where there's another man in dungarees balancing on a stepladder trying to reach a chandelier. The sour smell of alcohol, sweat and stale cigarettes drifts towards me, turning my stomach over, and I cover my mouth to stop myself retching.

Seconds later, the man I spoke to reappears hugging a

cardboard box, chin tucked over the lip. He scowls and brushes me out the way.

'Is someone moving out?' I follow him.

'What does it look like,' he says brusquely in a thick Dutch accent. Heaving the heavy load into the back of the lorry, he dusts off his hands and walks past me. I hesitate, then chase after him.

'Has the house been sold?'

He shrugs.

I swerve out the way as three removal men clamber down the stairs groaning under the strain of a solid marble table.

Maybe they've seen or heard something?

'I was here last night,' I say to one of them.

The stocky bald man wearing an Ajax football hoodie shunts air through his nose. 'So you're to blame for making our life hell today.' He exchanges looks with his friend as if they're sharing a private joke.

'Do you know how I can contact the owner?'

'We get paid to remove things.'

'I left something behind last night.'

He shrugs.

'Something very valuable.'

He walks off.

'It's important I get it back. Please, who can I contact?'

'Look, miss.' He turns in my direction. 'We don't know anything. The job goes through an agency, you'll have to contact them.'

Thwarted, I take a step back, trying not to give in to the mounting panic I'm feeling as I watch furniture being carried out. The evidence of last night's afterparty is being erased, piece by piece.

Georgie's not missing, she just hasn't been in touch yet, I remind myself. I'm reading too much into this. No doubt there's a perfectly reasonable explanation for the sudden clear-out.

I turn in the other direction, my gaze sinking into the canal, as if the answers might be hiding somewhere in the dark water.

My phone vibrates in my pocket. I fish it out so quickly, I almost drop it.

Caller withheld.

'Georgie?'

'Mrs Peters? It's Doctor Hendriks.'

It takes a few seconds to register the name. It feels like days not hours have passed since I woke up in hospital. I've been so worried about Georgie, I've almost forgotten how the night ended for me.

'You left before I could discharge you.'

I look back at the removal van, my head drowning in questions about why someone might be gutting an entire house hours after Georgie went missing.

'Is there something I can help you with?' I say impatiently, and then immediately feel bad for snapping.

'I'm afraid I have some bad news.'

'What's happened?'

'Mrs Peters, we found something concerning in your blood results.'

'Wh-what do you mean, *concerning*?'

'Are you familiar with the drug Rohypnol?'

THE FRIEND – BECCA

'I was drugged.' I feel like I'm having to repeat myself. 'My drink was spiked and my friend is missing.'

The young desk sergeant looks at me with concern and I feel like screaming.

'But you can't remember his name or any details of this man?' he asks.

The words are landing, but nothing's going in because all I can hear is *Rohypnol Rohypnol* ringing in my ears.

A sedative.

A dirty street drug.

A date-rape drug.

Our night out seemed so fun and spontaneous at the time but now the stupidity of the situation is dawning on me. The one thing you never *ever* do on a night out is leave your drink unattended.

A memory of him smiling as he handed me the glass of champagne bulldozes into my thoughts. The sensation of the bubbles stinging my nose as I drank it quickly. He must have slipped something into my drink then.

My stomach squirms, I cover my mouth and swallow

hard. Since I've found out my drink was spiked, I've been feeling increasingly nauseous. The thought that someone was planning to—

I stop, unable to let my mind go there.

There's a quiet knock at the door and a woman enters the interview room.

'I'm Inspector Van den Berg,' she says as she approaches.

An inspector, oh thank God, someone will take me seriously now. I feel a huge wave of relief because the first officer I spoke to had barely shown interest, let alone any sense of urgency.

We shake hands, and she takes a seat opposite. Pale and drawn, she's not wearing any make-up and she has a short functional haircut, not too dissimilar to mine. Somewhere in her fifties, maybe. Casting her eyes across my missing person's report, she sighs out, drinks from her plastic cup and pulls a face.

'Urgh. This coffee tastes like shit.'

I smile awkwardly, a little taken aback by her abruptness. I keep forgetting how direct the Dutch can be.

'I've been on duty since last night,' she says unapologetically.

Her accent is strong but her English is perfect, which I've also come to expect from anyone who's Dutch. As she reads the notes made by the desk sergeant, I suddenly feel drained at the thought of having to go through what happened again.

'Your drink was spiked at a party.' She looks up. 'How are you feeling now?' Her eyes are full of concern.

'I've been better.'

'Were you assaulted? Because we can arrange for a forensic medical examination.'

'That won't be necessary.' I frown, because I would know. Surely I would know if someone had forced themselves on me?

'Mrs Peters?'

I'd definitively know. I calm myself. I'd feel it afterwards, I'd be sore. Oh God, just the thought of someone poking around inside me after the miscarriage fills me with dread.

'Mrs Peters, are you OK?'

And then there's the shower I took when I got home. My skin, bright pink from where I scrubbed it raw. Any evidence I might have had on me – now washed down the plughole.

But what about Georgie? What if she's been assaulted?

'It's my friend you should be worrying about.' I catch the sob in my throat.

'Georgina,' she confirms. 'Who you think might also have been drugged?'

'If I was, she definitely would have been.'

The inspector nods thoughtfully. 'We'll get to that. If we can rewind for a moment.'

'OK, sorry, I know I'm not making much sense, I just . . .' I stop, take a breath. 'I should have reported her missing sooner. I knew something was wrong, Georgie wouldn't just disappear without telling me.'

'And what's your relationship with' – she looks down at her notes – 'Georgie Taylor-Johnson?'

'We're old friends, we grew up together.'

'You live in Amsterdam and she'd come to visit?'

'We were spending New Year's Eve together.'

'Do you have an address for her?'

I look at the inspector for a moment, thinking hard.

She frowns, noting my pause.

'She travels a lot,' I say quickly, 'she was on her way home from visiting a relative in Italy.'

'But you see each other often?'

'Actually,' I falter. 'It's been a while. This was more of a reunion.'

She notes that down too.

'Do you have any contact details for her next of kin?'

I draw another blank. I have no idea where her mother moved to after she left the village. And as for her dad – the inspector's guess is as good as mine.

'I know their names, if that helps.'

She looks at me closely.

'What about a photograph? Do you have anything recent?'

'Yes, I have that.' I pull out my phone, thumbing through the pictures. I show her the one we took in the bar. Heads bowed together, smiling. It's a little blurred, it's grainy, but there's no mistaking Georgie's beauty. Her buttery hair spilling over her bare shoulders, her plump red lips, her megawatt smile for the handsome waiter behind the camera. It takes me a second longer to notice I'm also in the photo.

'She's an attractive woman.' The inspector studies the image.

'I know.' A note of pride. Then I realize how strange that might sound. 'It's hard to compete with a friend who looks like that.'

'Compete?' She lifts an eyebrow. 'Are you in competition with your friend?'

'That came out wrong,' I say awkwardly. Why am I so nervous? 'What I meant was, I'm aware of how pretty she is. And how someone might want to take advantage of that.'

She notes that down, nodding contemplatively.

'Blonde, blue eyes, around 165cm?'

'I think so.'

She zooms in on the photo. 'And what was she wearing?'

'A black dress and a red shawl and designer shoes with studs and her handbag was Chanel.'

'So she has money?' The inspector says it casually but her observation triggers me to panic.

'Do you think someone might have mugged her?'

'Any distinguishing marks or features?' the inspector continues.

I picture the bruises on her arm, the patterning, it was as if someone had grabbed her roughly. Should I tell the inspector about that?

'She had a tattoo of a scorpion on her shoulder,' I reply.

'Where was this taken?' She sends the photo to her own mobile then hands my phone back.

'A bar in the centre . . . let me think, what was it called?'

She notes the time from the photo.

'High Spirits! That's it.'

'And were you taking drugs?'

'Me?' I laugh. 'God, no.'

'And does your friend use drugs?'

'What?' I frown.

'Party drugs? Was she taking anything last night?' The inspector keeps her tone and expression neutral.

'Oh, erm,' I flounder. I don't want to say anything that could get Georgie into trouble or for the inspector to write Georgie off as a party girl and dismiss the seriousness of the situation. 'No, not that I know of.'

She holds my gaze for a moment longer and I feel the heat rise in my face with the lie.

'Do you think she could have gone with the man you saw her with, to buy drugs?'

'I said she wasn't doing drugs.'

'Uh huh.' The inspector nods.

But now she's suggested it, I can't help but wonder – did Georgie leave to buy cocaine? Even if she did, that doesn't explain why she didn't come home. Unless . . . I breathe in sharply. Unless the drug deal went wrong and something happened to her.

'Everything OK?' The inspector watches me closely.

'Yeah.' I give my head a little shake.

'And the house party you went to was on which canal?'

'The Keizersgracht.'

She raises an eyebrow, noting it down.

'What number?'

'Thirty-four.'

'Whose party was it?'

'I don't know.'

'You have no idea?'

'Someone very rich – an art collector, I think.' I press two fingers between my brows, trying to force myself to remember his name.

'It's easy for me to find out who lives there.'

'Georgie talked her way in. That's the sort of thing she does.'

'You weren't on a guest list?'

'We were walking around the area and came across it.'

'Lucky timing.' She looks up. Grabs my eyes with hers and smiles.

'I guess,' I say doubtfully. I hadn't given it much thought until now, but I suppose it was a strange coincidence. 'I don't feel so lucky now,' I add quietly.

'Then what happened?'

'We started chatting to some American guys and then I felt dizzy and sick. And that's when I lost Georgie. The rest is all a blur until I woke up in A&E and then the doctor told me I'd been drugged.'

'Did Georgina seem distressed at all?'

'Well, erm, not especially—'

'The man she was with . . .' Her eyes drop to my report. 'Carter, was he forcing himself on her?'

I look up, trying to search my memory. 'I don't know, I don't think so.'

'And you can't be certain her drink was spiked?'

'But mine was. Isn't that enough for you to do something?'

'Do you have the medical report from the hospital with you?'

'Report? No – the doctor rang me.'

'I can get that from the hospital with your permission.' She makes another note. 'And you think it was the American you were chatting with who spiked your drink?'

'Lloyd,' I blurt out, suddenly remembering his name.

'Did Lloyd spike your drink?'

'It had to be. Who else?' I feel another thrust of frustration.

'But he left the party without you?'

'Yes, but—'

The inspector moves her gaze to my wedding ring.

'You're married?'

'That's right,' I say defensively. 'My husband, Nathan, he's away on business. He's back tomorrow.'

'But your husband knows about what happened?'

I shift in the chair, suddenly uncomfortable. Where is this leading? It's starting to feel like I'm the one being interrogated.

I feel my eyes pinching. 'I don't see what this has to do with my drink being spiked.'

'But you were out, chatting to some men at a party.' She puts the pen down. 'Is this something you do often?'

'What do you mean?'

'Chat to men at parties.' She holds my gaze. 'As a married woman?'

I meet her eyes. 'No! Why are you even asking me this? I don't know what you're trying to get at.'

She studies me closely and asks: 'Is everything all right at home?'

I hesitate. The strain of the past nine months inflates like a balloon in my chest. I think about the miscarriage, questioning myself. Why have I kept it from Nathan? And just as I regain control over my breathing, the memory of what I did the other night – spying on Katya – tiptoes into my thoughts.

'Mrs Peters?'

Sweat pricks at the back of my neck.

'Has Georgina gone home with men in the past?'

Jesus, she's making us out to be a couple of sluts. Is she taking this seriously?

On noticing the strain in my face, the inspector says more carefully: 'Mrs Peters, this is the Netherlands. We're open-minded. If you like engaging in extramarital affairs, that wouldn't be an issue. I'm just trying to understand the situation.'

I shake my head with frustration. 'The *situation* is my drink was spiked and my friend is missing.'

She nods thoughtfully. 'I'm going to be totally honest: it feels like you and your friend might have been looking for something else on your night out.'

'That's not what I said.' I lean forward. 'I'm not into that kind of thing, I don't share my husband.' Then something spears my insides as Katya's face swims into view.

I let out a breath, noticing how quickly my temper has flared.

'Most cases of spiking don't get as far as sexual assault or theft,' she continues in a voice that sounds like she's reading from a transcript. 'I can assure you we take it seriously, and I'll file the missing person report, but at the moment, the information we have to go on is circumstantial. We can't say for certain that the man you met spiked your drink, or if Georgina was also targeted. And without a full name or a detailed description of the men, it's going to be difficult to investigate this further. Do you see my problem?'

'What about CCTV?' I say desperately. 'Can you check cameras in the area?'

'In a quiet residential street?' She frowns at me. 'This isn't London.'

'Or Ring doorbells? You must have them here. Georgie could have knocked on someone's door, trying to get help.'

The inspector pulls a face. 'OK. We'll look into it.'

'Something's wrong, Georgie would be in contact by now.' My voice frays.

She leans back in her chair and folds her arms. 'This is Amsterdam. People get lost here all the time. The most likely explanation is she's out partying, she's doing drugs, or she's gone home with this guy she met at the house party. I'm sure she'll turn up soon.'

'Listen,' I lean in. 'She's diabetic. Her medication is at my house. What if she's passed out somewhere?'

'Did you check the hospitals?'

'That was one of the first things I did,' I say angrily.

'We can check again. Most diabetics know to carry insulin.'

'I'm not overreacting.' My lower lip wobbles.

'Nobody is saying you are.'

Why won't anyone listen to me? After months and months of feeling ignored in my marriage, here I am again, trying to be heard.

'She wouldn't have left the party without telling me. That's not Georgie . . .' I choke on my words.

Her eyes soften. 'You care a great deal about your friend, don't you?'

I nod. Swallowing a sob.

Reaching into her pocket, the inspector pulls out a pack of tissues and passes them across the desk. She waits for me to wipe my eyes and blow my nose.

'You must be exhausted,' she continues gently.

'I haven't been sleeping,' I confess.

A sympathetic tilt of the head.

'I'm sorry.' I keep wiping my eyes. 'It's not like me to be so emotional. I'm normally the one comforting others.' Jesus, why do I feel so untethered?

'You don't need to apologize.'

Could it be a reaction to the Rohypnol? I've read about comedowns; I've heard stories of people acting completely out of character when on drugs. It's like I don't know myself at all right now.

'Some water?' She keeps her eyes fixed on me.

'I'm fine,' I say, but I feel hot under the scrutiny of her gaze and instinctively bring my hand to my mouth and start chewing at the skin around my nails.

Her eyes pinch.

'Those bruises look painful.'

Pulling my hand away, I study them as if it's the first time I've seen them. The skin has changed colour again, the bruise has ripened into a deep mauve. Fragments of a memory return. An argument. *Bitch!* The word echoes. Then my thoughts scatter, the memory falling away again.

She takes a closer look at me. 'How did you get those?'

'I think I fell. The doctor said I have concussion.'

A beat passes. She doesn't take her eyes off mine.

'Were you in a fight?'

'A fight?'

She nods.

'Me?' I laugh. 'God, what is this?'

'Is that impossible?'

What's happening? I twist my hands together anxiously. I came in here feeling confused and I'm leaving more frustrated than ever. I glance down, noticing my hands are trembling. I've never been that person who flies off the handle; it often takes me several days to realize I'm angry and then I brood, festering on it until it goes away, but this is different. I feel different. My throat is tightening, an angry heat is spreading into my chest and up my neck.

I get up suddenly before I say or do something I might regret.

The inspector raises an eyebrow in surprise.

'*Yes*, that is impossible,' I bluster, glaring at her.

Why is she writing that down?

THE TIKTOK DETECTIVE – JAMIE

Georgie Taylor-Johnson has been missing for twenty-four hours.

A photo and a description of what she was last seen wearing and an e-fit of the bloke she was last seen with has been circulated by the Dutch police.

Buried on their regional website among half a dozen similar reports of women who've gone missing over Christmas and New Year's. Blink and you'd miss it. The sort of report that would go unnoticed if it weren't for my super sleuth skills.

It's her best mate's post on Facebook that really caught my attention though.

Hi everyone, I'm really worried about Georgie, we went to an afterparty last night and I haven't seen her since and she's not answering her phone, and I'm not sure she has her medication on her, so if anyone's been in contact with her, please can you let me know, it's urgent.

My eyes flick between the four monitors I've got set up in the bat cave. Enlarging the photo Rebecca Peters posted nine hours ago, I stare into Georgie's eyes and a strange sensation comes over me. She's a stunner all right, in a posh way – polished with long blonde hair, sparkling blue eyes, pillow lips . . . My gaze lingers there a while longer.

She's perfect.

Perfect clickbait.

And everything surrounding the disappearance will fuel the conspiracy theories, because there's too many un-answered questions and mysterious circumstances. And the fact she's vanished without her meds is a worry. Ramps up the urgency.

I shut my eyes and imagine what they'll say when I find her. The headlines. The press interviews. Soon I'll be more famous than Sherlock Holmes.

'Jamie, you up there?'

Shit, that's Nan. How am I gunna break the news to her?

Quickly, I print out the info I have on the case so far. Between the missing person's report, Becca's social media post (on her Instagram, Facebook and Georgie's Facebook page and on X) and my Google sleuth searches, we know Georgie was visiting her old mate Becca Peters in Amsterdam, and Becca's husband, Nathan, is opening a restaurant called Muse, serving premium nosh. Georgie had been travelling round Europe and showed up at Becca's gaff around 5 p.m. on New Year's Eve, they went out for drinks at a bar called High Spirits, CCTV shows the girls walking away from the city centre at 12.35 a.m., heading towards the posh part where they blagged their way into a gallery-opening afterparty.

The house at 34 Keizersgracht is owned by some multi-millionaire Dutch art dealer called Dieter Schmidt, whose gallery burnt to the ground a year ago. Insurance fraud rumours have been swirling ever since, but so far his nose is clean as a whistle. Becca and Georgie chatted to a couple of American lads in their twenties and Becca thinks her drink was spiked.

Becca doesn't know what time she left the party.

Georgie never got to Becca's house.

Georgie is a diabetic. Her medication was found in Becca's house along with her passport.

Georgie has an Instagram account where she posts pictures and videos of her travels and Michelin-star meals; she's been everywhere from Japan to Australia to the Maldives, although there's been barely any activity on her page for the past year.

Becca and Georgie grew up together in Upcott – a village in Devon. Becca relocated to Amsterdam with her hubby, Nathan Peters, nine months ago. Nathan used to manage the Rat and Parrot in Upcott. Becca used to be a teaching assistant and, by the looks of her Instagram, is currently unemployed. The restaurant allegedly cost over a million and the opening has been delayed several times.

Little bit to go on there, it's something at least. I need to do more digging and move quickly before anyone else catches on to the story.

'Jamie, love. Breakfast's ready!'

I look down at my suitcase and inhale sharply. Everything is riding on this.

'Jamie! Come on, love, your sausages are getting cold.'

That's Nan again. Bless her heart, where would I be without her? She's one of the reasons I'm doing this. When I'm famous, I'll be earning enough to rescue her from this dump and into a warm home with central heating that doesn't have damp or draughts or black mould. She raised me, looked after me when no one else did, and now it's my turn. That, as well as showing the ghost of my dad that I was robbed.

I'll show 'em. Show those pigs that rejecting me from the police force was the biggest mistake they ever made. I'm going to prove to the world I am a somebody.

I'm Crime_Tok_Detective.

I glance out of the window to the estate. It's still dark outside, these winter months are the worst, they drag on for ever. Amsterdam will feel like another universe compared to this shithole.

Better pack another woolly jumper, I caught the weather forecast on the news and it mentioned snow and ice. The coldest winter in fifteen years.

I zip up my suitcase, lift it off the bed and lug it down the stairs. Nan is waiting in the hallway. She stares at me and then my luggage. A look of nervousness in her eyes.

'I said your breakfast's ready. I made you a fry-up. You can't leave now.'

'Sorry, Nanna.'

'Where you going, love?'

'Away for a few days.'

'Away?' She looks wounded. 'Why didn't you say?'

'Didn't want to worry you. Now eat your food before it gets cold.'

'Who will take me to bingo on Wednesday?'

'Frank will drive you.'

'I don't like Frank.'

'I've got to go now, Nanna. I've got an early flight to catch. Love ya.'

'But how long will you be gone for?'

I open the front door.

'Don't you bring that dreadful girl home with you this time. She's not right for you.'

An icy blast reaches inside and Nan readjusts her shawl across her shoulders. Her hands still blue and mauve from the fall.

'I don't like it when you go.'

I steel myself. *Don't go soft now. She'll be OK.* I take a breath and lean towards my beloved nanna, planting a kiss on her forehead. She's the only person who's ever shown me kindness. The rest of the world – can fuck off. My hand trembles, I find it difficult to control my bitterness. I didn't get a good start in life, but that's all going to change. I grip the handle of my wheelie case with determination.

I'm going to make Nanna proud. Next time I see her, I'll have been crowned a hero.

THE FRIEND – BECCA

'Why didn't you tell me it was Georgie you went out with?'

'Because I knew you'd react like this,' I say through the door.

'Becca, please, can you come out here?'

I'm hiding in the bathroom, looking at myself. Disgusted by my reflection. Appalled with how I've behaved and with all the lies I've told. I can't bring myself to face Nathan.

'I'm trying to understand,' he continues. 'But you did say you never wanted to see her again.'

'I know I did. But that was a long time ago.'

A heavy sigh. 'Can't believe you'd let her back in your life after the way she treated you.'

I squeeze my eyes shut. 'I'm sorry, please don't be angry,' I say quietly.

'Becca, please come out and talk to me.'

'I feel terrible.'

'I'm not angry with you. Why would you think that?'

I take a shuddering breath.

'Unlock the door.'

And another. I stare at the lock, my chest fluttering

with anxiety. I don't think I've ever felt so out of control. I want things to go back to normal, to how they were before we moved here. But this is ridiculous, I can't stay in the bathroom hiding. Gingerly, I slide the lock across.

I'm expecting disappointment. Anger even. But my husband's face is full of sadness. A dewy sheen in his eyes.

'You should have told me about the baby.' His voice is thick and raspy.

'I didn't know how.' Mine also cracks.

'Are you OK?' He reaches for my hand, threading his fingers through mine while looking me straight in the eye.

'Bex, talk to me.'

'I feel confused.'

'Why didn't you tell me? How could you keep this from me?'

'You've got so much on, I didn't want to stress you.' My voice breaks up.

'What's got into you?' He gives me a long penetrating stare. 'You come first. Always. You must have been going through hell.' He kisses my hand. 'Come here, you.'

Nathan pulls me in for one of his bear hugs, his body heat warming me up like a cosy electric blanket. I'm instantly reminded of why I married him. The attraction I fleetingly felt for the man at the party pales into insignificance. I would never risk what I have with Nathan, not for anyone. These past months have tricked me into believing we were broken, but we're not, we're stronger than ever.

'Promise you'll never keep secrets from me again.'

I settle my cheek into his shoulder. 'Promise.'

'God, you don't know how much it hurts that you felt you couldn't be honest,' he says, his voice cracking in my ear. 'You haven't seemed yourself for weeks. I'm really worried about you.'

'I think I'm losing my mind.' But my response is muffled against him. He doesn't even hear.

'We'll get through this. When everything calms down, we'll try again. Lots of couples go through problems.'

'I know,' I say quietly.

'We'll have the tests; we'll do whatever it takes to make us a family.' He squeezes me tightly.

'OK, but I need time.'

'Of course, take as much time as you need.'

'I can't think about anything until I know Georgie's safe.'

I feel his body tightening. It's as if Nathan has a physical reaction whenever I mention her name.

'Someone's got to know something. I can't just sit around here waiting, it's driving me crazy.'

He slowly releases me, plants a soft kiss on my forehead and then crosses the bedroom to the window.

'Jesus,' he hisses. Peering down on the street. 'He's still there.'

'Who?'

'Some weirdo.' He narrows his eyes. 'He was outside when I got in this morning and he's been skulking around ever since.'

'You think it's something to do with the neighbours?'

We've had problems with the couple in the flat below. Loud parties, drug dealers coming and going. Nathan's had to call the police a couple of times.

144

'You didn't tell anyone from that party where we lived?'

'Of course not. Why would I?'

'What if he's a journalist?'

'What does he look like?'

'Scruffy. Like a journalist.' Nathan's frown deepens. 'Hey, stay indoors today, he doesn't look right. I don't want you crossing paths with him.'

'He can't be a reporter, the police aren't taking Georgie's disappearance seriously.'

'That's if she's even missing,' he says under his breath.

'Why would you say that?'

'Because it's *Georgie*.'

'Yeah, but she's been gone nearly two days . . .'

He releases an exasperated laugh.

'She'll be shacked up with a guy somewhere.' Nathan's eyes pinch. 'Probably hasn't even come up for air.'

I know where this is coming from. He's being protective. He knows how much she hurt me. To him, Georgie was the spoilt posh girl in the house on the hill who looked down on him whenever she came into the pub. If I'm honest, she could be really dismissive of him. I could see why he hated serving her.

'You think I overacted by telling the police?'

'Jesus, no! You did the right thing reporting it – your drink was spiked, for fuck's sake.'

'I'm really worried about her.'

'And I'm worried about *you*.' His jaw clenches. 'You were *drugged*. *She* let that happen.'

All at once, my chest feels like it's about to explode.

'Me losing the baby isn't her fault!'

I let out a small gasp. Where did that come from?

We're both quiet for a little while but whatever's eating Nathan quickly returns.

'She's back in your life for five minutes and you end up in A&E. All of it's her fault.'

'I'm fine, you don't need to worry.'

'So fucking typical of Georgie to drag you to a party where something like this could happen.'

'She didn't drag me.'

'And you were drinking more than you would have. I bet she had something to do with that?'

'It's not Georgie's fault.' My voice shrinks.

He huffs, frustrated. 'I also know what Georgie's like, she would have made it impossible to say no.'

'I guess she—'

'See, I knew it. She didn't care before, and she doesn't care now.'

'Nathan, stop this!'

'She sold you a dream, but that's all it was.'

'It was *twelve years ago*.'

'Yeah, well.' He runs his hands over his face 'I haven't forgotten.'

I know he's just being protective, and a small part of me is enjoying seeing him care this much, but at the same time, I can't deal with it, not while Georgie's missing. Georgie's changed, I know she has, even though she looked and dressed the same, she seemed different. Vulnerable. Almost as if she was the one who needed protecting. I wish I could make him see that.

I look at Nathan closely. Maybe now's not the time.

'You look shattered. Do you need to go to the restaurant right away?'

'God, if only I had time to chill out. We're opening in three days.' He continues to stare at the street. 'I just hope she turns up soon, I don't want this to blow up on us right before the launch.'

'Nathan!'

'That's not the kind of press we need.'

'I hate that this is happening.'

He looks back and gives me an awkward smile.

'Oh God, I'm sorry.' His eyes soften. 'I know she's your friend, I just . . .' His voice cracks.

He's trying his best but the strain is showing.

'Look, you don't need to explain.'

He walks back over to me with a pained expression. He takes hold of my hand again and kisses it.

'I'm sorry, you know how I feel about anything to do with her. You mean everything to me. Finding out you were drugged, it's terrifying. The thought of someone hurting you, wanting to . . .' His voice cracks again. 'God, Bex, I can't lose you.'

We both fall silent. I rub my thumb over his. He just smiles at me and I know it's working.

Beneath Nathan's stoic exterior is someone very fragile. He's lived in the shadow of his domineering dad for years, he's taken so much crap from him, it's incredible he's still standing. The restaurant is his chance to break free, prove that he can go it alone. I know how much is riding on this being a success. And now I'm adding to his stress.

I have to do something to fix this.

An e-fit of the man I saw Georgie with at the party has been circulated as a person of interest, along with a missing person's report, but the police are making no effort to find him and it's not a great sketch. I could barely remember what Carter looked like apart from his dark hair and chiselled jaw and perfect set of straight white teeth, which could describe a million and one good-looking men in the world. I feel I've failed Georgie somehow. The weight of responsibility is crushing. And if I sit around any longer, I might explode. I wait for Nathan to head off to the restaurant and then pull on my hoodie and grab my coat.

I'm about to leave via the main entrance and then pause. What if Nathan's right and there is a weirdo outside? I take the fire escape instead, which spits me out into the communal gardens.

It's edging in the direction of another snowstorm again, but for now, it's just light flurries. Glancing over my shoulder to make sure no one's following, I quickly unlock my bike, wheeling towards the gate. Twenty minutes and I'll be in the centre. But as I'm about to head off, a hooded figure appears out of nowhere and grabs my handlebars.

Lurching forwards, I almost topple over the front tyre. When I look up, there's a man in a dark tracksuit and an army green parka jacket pointing a phone in my face.

'Crime_Tok_Detective, solving crime in real time.' He

removes his fur-trimmed hood and grins. 'Smile for the camera, sweetheart.'

'Hey.' I push the phone away but the man thrusts it right under my nose.

'What the— What do you think you're doing?'

'Tell us what you know about Georgie's disappearance?'

I jam my foot down on the pedal but he grips my handlebar tightly, using his free hand to film me.

Mousy hair, long overdue a cut, swept across his forehead. A scraggy beard and sallow skin. Wearing a woolly red scarf, frayed at the edges, he's kind of attractive if you like your men aggressive and dishevelled. And he's tall, well over six foot, with broad shoulders, and suddenly I feel intimidated.

'Whose idea was it to go to the afterparty?' He leans in and I get a whiff of beer.

Urgently, I search around for help, but the fire exit has taken me to the quiet backstreets. I hear a dog barking. The distant sound of a car engine starting, then fading, as it heads in the opposite direction.

I'm all alone.

'Are you a journalist?' My eyes drop to his phone. 'Are you filming me?'

'Did you and Georgie fall out?'

The air is punched from my chest. How does he know that?

'If you were such good mates, how come you ain't in any of her photos?'

'We didn't fall out!' I grit my teeth.

'You're lying about being best friends though, aren't ya?'

'Stop putting words in my mouth.' I try getting away again, but he wedges his body between me and the road and I'm no match for his strength.

'Why'd ya leave the party without her?'

'Get out of my way.'

'What sort of mate are ya?'

I pull my hoodie down lower, trying to cover my eyes.

'Were you jealous of Georgie?'

'What did you say?' I turn and glare. 'No! How could you say something like that?'

He angles the camera even closer.

'Cos she's smokin' hot.' A hollow laugh. 'Have you always felt like the ugly friend?'

I can feel the anonymous stares of those watching the feed, holding their breath and waiting for my reaction. My heart drums in my ears. Panic, building and building, and then, from out of nowhere, my arm shoots out. I shove him so hard I send him stumbling backwards onto the kerb.

He falls to the ground and I push off quickly, before he can get back on his feet, but not before I hear him say to everyone watching:

'Girl's got a temper. She's out of control.'

THE TIKTOK DETECTIVE – JAMIE

I'm off to a flying start, catching Becca off guard like that – well done me. And my followers seem to love the straight-talking brutal approach. I might not be the best-looking bloke around but I'm up front. And that's what people want. They're already cooking up conspiracy theories, the community is growing and chatting among themselves.

I refresh my TikTok profile. Whoa! Five thousand new followers. I look in on the GoFundMe crowdfunding page I've set up asking for donations to help with the search. It worked for Elena Brookes' family: her mum and dad raised a whopping £60,000 from the public to help find their daughter, to pay for private investigators and suchlike; and bloody Nora, it's working for me too. Already £3,200 in the pot. What the— I blink at the amount, not quite believing it. High-five me. QUIDS IN!

My high is followed by a sudden swoop of butterflies as I think about the next video. Now there's cash on the table, it feels like the pressure has risen tenfold. Maybe a swift pint before I start filming? To take the edge off, you know. Ease the nerves. I glance along the canal, squinting at the neon signs and flashing banners.

Just this minute I checked into Hotel 69 in De Wallen – that's the red-light district, if you're wondering. I'm above a knocking shop, which explains why it was dirt cheap, LOL, but I'm OK with that. It feels buzzy around here, like I'm in the heart of the city. Plenty of tourists passing through, having a gawp, and the perfect starting point for my investigation.

But first, how about that pint?

Crossing over the nearest bridge I head into the narrow side streets, passing by windows with prozzies and shops selling weed. I check out the prices for Casa Rossi – bit steep for a live sex show, I'll see if I can find something cheaper later on. My eyes are pulled next door to Boutique Kinky, where the shop window is full of giant dildos and patent leather gimp masks.

WTAF.

I carry on until I come across a bar I like the look of – the British Bulldog. Feels like home from home and I grab a seat at the window, which happens to be a great place to people-watch. I order a pint of Heineken, course, what else? And pull out my phone, logging back into my TikTok account.

Swiping away dozens of new notifications, I clear my throat because suddenly it's jammed up with phlegm. I glance down at my hands – they're shaking. Come on, lad, pull yourself together, you're not gunna make it as the next Sherlock Holmes if you're a quivering wreck, are ya?

But I can't help thinking about the competition, the

experienced journalists and rival TikTok sleuths hot on my heels. I'm hit with another wave of panic. I need to up my game.

I take a slug of beer. Ahh, that's nice. Cool and refreshing, and it does the trick. Carpe diem – seize the day, my friends, seize the day. I take another deep draw, then reverse the camera and press record.

Hiya folks, how we all doing? Welcome back to Crime_Tok_Detective, your go-to true crime channel, right here on TikTok, for insight, expert analysis and on-the-ground live reports. You know what to do: like and follow.

For all of you that don't know me yet, name's Jamie Finn, I'm a south Londoner, born and bred, and I'm the person the coppers love to hate. Why? Because I stick my nose where it's not wanted. I ask the questions they should be asking. I do the digging nobody is prepared to do. Jamie Finn goes the extra mile and I've travelled all the way to Amsterdam to bring our girl Georgie Taylor-Johnson home.

I'm reporting live from the famous red-light district. Take a look at this (swings camera around). If you wanna find a pretty lass who's gone missing in Amsterdam then look no further than where everyone is shady as fuck. Here you'll find it all – sex trafficking, drug dealing, diamond smuggling, money laundering – I heard even the tulip industry is dirty, a front for people trafficking. Yeah, you name it, it goes on around here.

Police working the case seem as thick as pig shit.

There's barely any enthusiasm to find our girl. They've no explanation about what's happened to her. They're writing her off as just another party girl. There's a new police statement from Inspector Van den Berg who says they're treating it as a missing person enquiry, and although they're concerned about Georgie's disappearance, there's nothing yet to suggest the involvement of a third party. Blah-blah-blah.

So, CrimeTokkers, it's up to us to start asking questions.

Here are five puzzling unanswered questions about Georgie's disappearance to sink ya teeth into. Who was the mystery guy in the e-fit Georgie was seen chatting to? Who spiked Becca's drink? Why has no one come forward to say they remember seeing the girls at the party? Why are there no photos of Becca on Georgie's Instagram? Girls not besties after all?

And here are five possible explanations for her disappearance.

1. Georgie's been kidnapped by an eastern European gang.
2. Mystery bloke has harmed her.
3. Someone else at the party has harmed her.
4. Becca has harmed her.
5. Something shady was going down at the party which Georgie found out about.

Or maybe she's just had enough and fucked off somewhere? What do you guys think?

Hang on, I'm already getting feedback from you

lovely folk. Katie from Warwick thinks the police should be dredging the canals. Ben from Dover says 'abducted and sold to an Albanian gang'. John says abducted and sex trafficked, Jen in Bracknell says Becca and her husband sold her to a gang to pay for his restaurant. Fuck me, Jen, that's dark. Paul in London says the police should be arresting the art dealer. You guys are sick, but keep 'em coming and tell me what you want me to investigate next.

You know where to come for the most up-to-date news on Georgie's disappearance. And if you haven't followed me already, follow me now so not to miss out on the latest coverage. Until next time, CrimeTokkers. And remember, spread the word – #FINDGEORGIE. Let's bring our girl home, yeah.

I sign off with hashtags to reach more followers: #CrimeTok #armchairdetective #crimeanalyst #CanYouHelp.

Whoa, fuck me, my hands, they're shaking. I'm buzzin'! What a rush, hey. Never felt anything like it, even when I was shoplifting. This is something else, I tell you.

I've started so many things in my life and not finished them. I've messed up opportunities, but I don't want to be that person any more. I was born to do this. I've got something to say and people are sitting up and taking notice. The lads back home won't be laughing at me now.

Knocking back the half-pint I have left, I grin, thinking about who I'll target next.

THE FRIEND – BECCA

Georgie feeds back into my thoughts as I pedal faster, rising from the saddle, my coat filling with air as I whizz along the canals, putting as much distance as possible between me and that scary man who ambushed me.

Who is he? A sweat has broken out on my face and neck. Who? And why? He said something about TikTok. He can't be a reporter, he looked like he'd crawled out from under a rock. Although he was asking the sort of questions you'd expect from an unscrupulous journalist. Firing shots in the dark to get a rise out of me. Filming my reaction, like I'm some entertainment show – that's sick!

And yet I can't shake off what he said – *were you jealous of Georgie?*

I'm still trembling with shock and adrenaline when I reach the Museumplein. I still can't believe I pushed someone to the ground. With shaky hands, I lock my bike against a railing, pause, take a breath and then turn into the wind. I've worked up a sweat yet I'm feeling colder and colder. I pull my coat tightly around me and, hunching into the biting gale, I make my way towards the gleaming white building up ahead.

Shaped like a giant yacht sail in the middle of the green, it stands out among the historic buildings and museums. It's an eyesore and magnificent all at the same time. Visitors are funnelled through a dome-shaped tunnel. My heart starts to beat a little faster as the glass doors slide apart, revealing an atrium with light pouring in from above.

My footsteps echo. Every sound is magnified inside the stark white hall. I immediately start fidgeting because people like me don't fit in places like this. The last thing I want to do is draw attention to myself.

This was a terrible idea. In fact, I'm not entirely sure why I'm here, or what I hope to achieve. After remembering the name of the art dealer, it didn't take much searching to find Dieter Schmidt's gallery. I make a slow turn, gazing at the elegant architecture, taking in the modern art and sculptures, lit up from below by hundreds of tiny spotlights. This must have been where everyone came to celebrate before the afterparty.

In the far corner, there's a quiet murmuring. Half a dozen people, loosely grouped together, speaking softly and nodding; admiring a painting that resembles something a toddler might do. A few messy streaks of paint across a wide white canvas. I spot a waiter circulating with a tray loaded with champagne glasses, and then I notice the tattoo wrapped around his bicep.

Is it him?

I duck out of sight behind a sculpture worth a whopping 176,000 euros, spying from across the room. He's about ten feet away but even from a distance I can tell he's tall with broad shoulders. Sleeves rolled up to his biceps, the inked feathers disappearing beneath the fabric of his crisp white shirt. Was it him serving drinks at the afterparty? The sight of his tattoo shakes loose another memory. I stare at him a moment longer before a voice from behind startles me.

'Can I help you?'

Dressed in a trouser suit and slingback heels, her pink hair gelled flat against her scalp and sculpted into precise ringlets around her ears, the woman holding a portfolio of information on the artwork gives me a knowing look.

Have I met her before?

She eyes me warily and another hazy image flickers to life, only for it to slip down my sinkhole of a memory.

'They're magnificent, aren't they? Can I give you any additional information?'

She's British. Her voice is posh and measured, and familiar.

I respond with a guarded reply: 'I'm fine, just having a look around.'

She continues to look me up and down, frowning at how I'm dressed. 'Let me know if you need anything.' I can feel her following me around the room with her eyes and I fold my arms tightly across my chest as if that will somehow protect me from her glare. Slowly, I make my way through the gallery, weaving between the sculptures and installations, trying to appear inconspicuous, when really I must stand out like a sore thumb in my battered high-top Converse, faded jeans and bobbly clothes.

Glancing over my shoulder, I try getting a better look at the waiter. It is him, isn't it? It's as though he feels my stare and immediately looks straight up at me. Our eyes lock and something flashes across his face.

Anger, or maybe fear? But he knows who I am.

Another memory stirs.

His cheek against mine, his face so close I can feel his breath on my skin. A rush of heat sprints up my neck. *Stop*, that can't be right. I look back at the waiter and I feel another prickle of heat. No, no, I'm getting muddled again.

I hear rapid footsteps – clacking heels crossing the atrium in my direction.

'We're closing the gallery for a private viewing in five minutes. I'm afraid I'm going to have to ask you to leave.'

'Oh, but I've just got here.'

She stands taller, her eyes pinching.

'The gallery will reopen tomorrow at 10 a.m. Sorry for the inconvenience.' The tone is conversational but the way she's looking at me is less than friendly and her cold stare suddenly prises a memory open.

The smell of rising damp, a narrow staircase leading up to the top floor. There was an attic in the house and *she* was there, warning me off.

'This way.' A curtness to her tone as she ushers me towards the exit in exactly the same manner as she did on New Year's Eve.

The light beneath the door. The dull thud of feet on floorboards. The shadowy figures moving around in the attic.

Oh Jesus, it's all coming back now.

What or who was she hiding up there?

Tucking my chin into my coat, I try to keep warm while I loiter around outside, desperate to grab the waiter when he clocks off.

The next ten minutes drag; it feels like hours not minutes have passed by the time a black Mercedes pulls up and a sharply dressed man in his forties, wearing a navy suit and crisp white shirt, gets out. He puffs out his chest as he buttons up his blazer. He's tall and good-looking in an arrogant way. Have I seen him before? A man who could be a nightclub bouncer follows closely on his heels and they disappear inside the gallery.

It's 4.45 p.m. and the light is fading. The temperature is steadily dropping, I can barely feel my fingers and blowing into my hands isn't helping. It's far too cold to wait around outside, so I head to a tourist cafe. I grab a seat at the window, order a double espresso and open a fresh Google search on my phone.

Thumbing through the Dutch *Hello* magazine photos and high society pictures of Dieter Schmidt and his glamorous wife, it doesn't take long to work out that the guy I saw entering the gallery as I was leaving is regarded as a pillar of the community. A multimillionaire art dealer and philanthropist who's behind the funding of a new art education programme soon to be rolled out in schools across the country. So was that his bodyguard he had with him?

I still can't quite believe we managed to blag our way

into his home. It feels surreal – all of it does, starting with Georgie showing up on my doorstep after a decade of not hearing from her.

I continue searching, reading up about how Dieter's previous gallery was burnt to the ground by vandals. He quite literally built his new one from the ashes of his last. Then I fall down a YouTube rabbit hole watching a conspiracy group tear strips out of the gallery owner, accusing him of fraud, highlighting how shady his lawyer is.

Another Google search reveals some very disturbing reports about a witness to the fire who was gunned down at close range outside his home. The shooter fled in a getaway car waiting nearby. I feel my eyes widen and my heart rate pick up as I read about links between Dieter's lawyer, the Dutch mafia and organized crime.

What did we get ourselves into?

The mystery of who was in the attic at the afterparty and why I was stopped from looking for Georgie is now doing laps around my head. I need to speak to the waiter immediately. I stare restlessly across the green at the gallery, lit up like a lighthouse in a storm. Which is kind of ironic because I think it might be the least safe place in Amsterdam. *Where is he?*

Forty-five minutes of silence pass by. I've almost given up hope when there's a flash of movement. The fire exit swings open, the door smacking into the wall, and a man in an oversized leather aviator jacket, clutching a helmet under one arm, looks around anxiously and then walks briskly across the visitor car park.

It's him.

I leave my coffee and sprint for the door, but I'm running across the green so quickly, I forget to look left. A woman on a bike swerves around me and screeches to a halt. She rings her bell, swearing loudly. I look up, and the waiter is staring.

The second our eyes meet, he rushes to put on his helmet and slings a leg over his motorbike. The engine roars to life.

I'll never make it in time.

'Wait!' I raise a hand and wave.

He squeezes the accelerator and, before I've thought it through, I've thrown myself into his path. He skids to a standstill, flicks up his visor, his dark eyes creased with irritation.

'Are you crazy?'

'I just want to talk.'

He revs, the back wheel skids from side to side, exhaust fumes pluming into the chilly air. But I keep my feet planted even though my heart is racing.

'I need some help,' I plead. 'I'm trying to find my friend.'

He glares at me.

'I know you were at the party on New Year's Eve, I just want to find out what happ—'

'Move out of the way.'

The engine roars, his wheels spin, but I remain rooted to the spot. I have no idea where this burst of courage is coming from. I've not done anything brave in my entire life.

'Five minutes,' I yell above the noise. '*Please!*'

He frowns, as if considering my plea. I think he's about to help me and then he slides down his visor.

'PLEASE.' My voice cracks.

'OK, OK.' A quick glance over his shoulder. 'But not here.'

'Where then?'

'Paradox Coffeeshop.'

He jerks towards me, I jump back and he takes off at speed, wheels spinning, the smell of burnt rubber riding the air. As the ringing in my ears fades, I glance down at my hands. They're trembling.

THE FRIEND – BECCA

He's rolling a joint when I arrive at the coffee shop.

The location couldn't be further from the sophistication of where we've just been. A narrow, dark, cave-like room with steamed-up windows, crude metal tables and bar stools. The air is thick with smoke, and the smell of marijuana immediately makes me light-headed.

He's chosen a table right next to a flashing fruit machine and I feel the room tightening around me as I make my way towards him, squeezing through groups of people. I hesitate and slow as I approach. Maybe this isn't such a good idea? I don't know the first thing about him. What would Nathan think if he knew I was here?

He looks up, our eyes meet across the room and now he's seen me it feels too late to turn back. Plus, he's the only link I have to the afterparty. My only hope of finding Georgie.

Cautiously, I approach the table and take a seat, clutching my handbag tightly into my chest as if it were some imaginary armour.

'You found it OK then?' He looks at me through long dark lashes, the dim amber lighting making him appear even more attractive. Wow, this guy is beautiful.

I feel suddenly shy and all the questions I'd planned to ask slip from my grasp. I swallow nervously. I try gathering myself.

'Why did you come to the gallery?' he says angrily in a heavy accent. But his English is perfect.

'You remember me from New Year's Eve, don't you?'

He says nothing.

'I was at that afterparty with my friend, Georgie, and she's missing.'

He looks away.

'I know you were there that night. I saw you. Why did you run away from me just now?'

He returns to his spliff, frowning with concentration as he carefully rolls it between his fingers.

'I think you might know something that can help me find her.'

'Why would I know something?' He shrugs.

'Did you see the men we were with that night?'

'I was busy working.'

'What about Georgie? Did you see her leave the party?'

He shakes his head, still avoiding my gaze.

'Look, I need your help.' My voice catches. 'My drink was spiked!'

He looks up sharply, grabbing me with his eyes.

'I need this job, OK? I can't afford to lose it.'

The intensity of his stare brings on a sudden flashback. His face against mine. His warm breath on my collarbone.

The sensation so powerful, it knocks the breath right out of me.

This is crazy, why do I keep imagining us together? I look back at him and something stirs inside me.

Oh God, did something happen between us?

I search my memory, trying to think how, when, *how?* And all at once I'm hit with an even more terrifying thought.

Did he spike my drink?

His hot breath on my skin.

Oh God, please no. My heart skips a beat as I frantically try to stitch the pieces of New Year's Eve back together. He was the one serving the champagne. He was giving me looks that night and then . . . My stomach drops. There's the unaccounted-for time.

I stare at him, blinking uncomprehendingly. I can't speak, I can't move. The doctor's voice: *Rohypnol, Rohypnol*, going around and around in my head.

'Everything OK?' he says, but his voice seems a very long way away as I walk through those last moments before I lost consciousness. Stumbling around in the cold. The rhythmic pounding of the music fading as I suddenly found myself alone in a dark street and then—

I look at him warily, panic climbing in my chest.

'It was you!'

'Me what?'

'You spiked my drink.'

'Excuse me?' He recoils.

'It was you, I know it was.' I hear the fear entering my voice. Oh God, what did he do to me while I was passed out? I glance down at my hands, at the bruises – was I trying to fight him off? I haven't told anyone where I am. How could I be so stupid, coming here to meet him alone.

'You think *I* drugged you?'

I look around, searching for the quickest way out. People are starting to take notice.

'What else did you do to me? Tell me!' Although I'm not entirely sure I want to know.

'You're crazy.'

'You slipped a pill into my champagne . . .'

'Are you kidding?' He gives me his best injured eyes. 'I would never—'

I leap to my feet.

'Hey, hang on.' His hand lands on mine. It feels as heavy as a brick, pinning me down, and the room seems to shrink, the walls creeping inwards. What did he do to me that night? I was so certain I'd know if I'd been raped; but what if I was wrong, what if I was too out of it to know? Adrenaline pumps into my veins. I snatch my hand free and make for the exit.

'Wait!' He jumps up after me and the cafe falls silent. People turn on their stools to stare at us. Pale, stoned faces peer at me through a haze of cannabis smoke.

'Stop!' he shouts, then he lowers his voice. 'Please, sit back down.'

'I'm calling the police.'

'I could never do something like that . . .' He stares into my eyes, silently begging me to believe him. 'Look, it was me who found you in the street.'

I blink.

'I took you to the hospital.'

'What?'

A shard of memory catches the light. His face against mine as he hauled me up off the ground.

'I had to carry you the whole way there – no taxi would take us, they thought you were too drunk.'

More images flash behind my eyes, rearranging themselves into order. His breath on my neck as he wrapped his arm around me, trying to keep me on my feet. I can feel the cold burst of snow on my face, his body heat feeding into mine. Then he took off his coat to keep me warm.

I look back at him apologetically.

'I couldn't just leave you there, could I?'

My emotions swing like a pendulum. Fear. Relief. I'm flooded with gratitude. 'Thank you,' I say quietly. If he hadn't found me, I might not be alive today. 'Why didn't you say something earlier?'

'I told you: I don't want to get involved.'

'But you *are* involved. And you can help me find Georgie.'

'Maybe the guy you were with put something in your drink? But I didn't see anything.'

'He left the party, so why would he go to the trouble?'

'He changed his mind?'

'It doesn't make sense.'

'I don't know then.' He sits back down and tells me to do the same with his eyes. 'Sorry if I frightened you.' His tone no longer has that hard edge to it; there's a softness there. He returns to his joint, placing it in his mouth and lighting up. He takes a long drag and then offers it to me.

I stare at it cautiously, as if it might be poisonous, and then something comes over me. That same rush of defiance I had when Georgie turned up on my doorstep.

'Fuck it,' I mumble, taking it out of his hand, our fingers brushing. I inhale and immediately start coughing. He gives me a bemused smile and I blush.

I shake my head, trying to stop the smoke from tickling my lungs.

'I've never tried weed before,' I wheeze.

His eyebrow goes up. 'First time?' A dimple pits his cheek. He holds it out for me to go again and I wave him off.

'I like the smell, I always have. Mum used to have a cheeky joint whenever Dad was out – it was her way of relaxing.'

'I've been smoking since I can remember. Helps me chill out.'

Our eyes meet across the table and I let out a ghost of a laugh. I'm not sure why I'm giggling, especially under the circumstances, but the strain of today is lifting. I have so many questions, but for now, it feels good to let go with a stranger.

He brings the joint back to his mouth, taking another drag.

'I'm Becca, by the way.'

'Hi Becca.' He blows out smoke from the corner of his mouth.

'What's your name?'

A brief pause.

'Rami.'

'Do you live around here?'

'Across town on a houseboat.'

'That would be my dream.'

'I share with this old guy, Hans. He's a widower. I pay him a bit of rent, but it's cheap. I think he likes the company more than he needs the money.'

'Where's it moored?'

Another brief pause.

'Where you were on New Year's. Outside Schmidt's place.'

'You live *there*?'

'It's how I got the job,' he says. 'They were at a loose end for a party and needed an extra pair of hands. I was working on the deck that day, doing a bit of sanding, and Freya – that's the woman you met at the gallery, she works for Schmidt – asked me if I would step in. She paid for me to have a haircut, bought me some smart clothes . . . It became a regular thing after that.'

'Waitering?'

He shoots me a look of innocence. 'Yeah, waitering.'

For a moment I wonder if he's hinting at something seedier. An escort? He's beautiful enough to be one and I can imagine all those rich married women and social-ites fawning over him. I've never seen eyes as dark as his.

The sensation of him cradling me in his arms jumps out from nowhere. His face mere centimetres from mine, the warmth of his breath slicing through the cold air. My skin tingles. That weed was strong. I try to focus on what he's telling me.

'It's good money, cash in hand. Only downside is dealing with rich wankers.' He takes another long drag on his joint. 'But you put up with a lot when you're desperate, you know.'

He lifts his hand back to his mouth and this time I notice the marks. A crossover of scars on his knuckles, each telling a story and I wonder what his is. How did he come to live with a widower on a canalboat in Amsterdam? Now he seems relaxed, I push again for answers.

'You do remember seeing me that night, don't you?' I ask gently.

He sits back, thinking about what I've just said.

'What about my friend?' I press.

'Not your friend, but yeah, I did see you.' He looks away shyly.

'OK.' I feel myself reddening. 'So you noticed me. What about the guy I was chatting to?'

'I got a look at him. Sleazy type.'

I lean forward eagerly.

'Did you recognize him? Has he been at parties before?'

'I see a lot of faces.'

'Did you see where he went? Was he with Georgie?'

A small hesitation. 'You were on the sofa together, but that was the last I saw of him.'

'Did you get a good look at him?'

His eyes dart between me and the window. He shakes his head.

'Well, what do you remember?' I say angrily.

'Hey, easy.' His eyes flash. 'I understand your frustration – if I'd lost my friend, I'd be asking the same questions – but it was busy that night, I was looking after the guests, keeping Dieter happy. He's very precise about the way he likes things. He notices when you slip up, you know?'

I study him closely. The guarded manner in which he's folded his arms over his chest. He's not letting anyone in. What's he holding back, dammit? I want to scream at him to tell me, but I know that's not going to work so I try softening my approach.

'This Dieter sounds controlling. I know people like him, who rule by fear.'

He shifts uncomfortably in his seat.

'Is that why you didn't want to be seen with me at the gallery?'

He looks away.

'I'm not going to say anything.'

Rami leans in, his expression suddenly darkening.

'Listen,' he hisses, 'you need to stop asking questions.'

'What are you so afraid of?'

'I'm trying to help you.'

'You can't say something like that and then ask me to drop it.' I frown, bewildered.

'These people operate in a different world, OK? The sort of business they do, it's not always above board. Your friend is attracting unwanted attention. She shouldn't have been at that party and they're not happy about it.'

'Is that why your boss cleaned out his house the day after the party?'

He looks behind, suddenly nervous.

'He was trying to hide something. Wasn't he?'

Lowering his voice, Rami says: 'Stop asking questions.'

I think again about the attic, the way Freya warned me off.

'Was something going down that night?'

Another glance out the window at the street.

Did Georgie see something she shouldn't have? Or did they drug me to split us up? A million possibilities are racing through my head, not one of them the least bit tangible. I couldn't know less about the art world and the sort of things Rami's referring to, my ignorance putting even greater distance between me and Georgie. All this time I've been focusing on the guys we met, but what if I've been looking in the wrong place?

I feel a thrust of urgency. How can I get Rami to open up to me?

'If they were doing something illegal, you have to tell the police!'

'Please, just leave me alone.'

'What about my friend, don't you care what happens to her?'

'I told you to drop it,' he says fiercely.

'I can't.' My voice is edging on hysterical. 'She's my friend!'

'Friend?' He pulls a face.

'Yes, *friend*.'

He shrugs. 'If you say so.'

What does he mean by that? My jaw tightens. I feel the frustration swelling in my chest. Building and building and spreading. What is he not telling me?

He stubs out his joint and gets up suddenly.

'Wait, hang on a minute.' I hear the desperation in my voice.

'There'll be an explanation for what's happened. Your friend's probably met some guy. She's gone off travelling.'

'That's what everyone keeps telling me.'

He gives me an apologetic look.

'How do I get hold of you?'

Rami warns me off with his eyes.

'But what if I need to get a message to you?'

He grabs his leather jacket and helmet from the stool. 'I hope she turns up soon. Really, I do. And I understand what it feels like to lose someone.' A note of sadness enters his voice. 'This city, it has a way of swallowing you.'

He leaves quickly but his words stay behind, chilling me to the core. I gather my things, suddenly desperate to leave this dark hole of a place, and that's when I feel it. The same sensation as before. A cold breeze across my neck, as if someone's watching me. I turn sharply and our eyes meet.

There is someone watching me. And filming me.

THE TIKTOK DETECTIVE – JAMIE

Crime_Tok_Detective LIVE
11.23 p.m., 2 January 2025

Hi folks, it's barely been a minute since my last video, but I'm back, and for those of you who are new here, welcome to Crime_Tok_Detective, your go-to true crime channel, here on TikTok, for insight, expert analysis and on-the-ground live reports.

My phone has been blowing up since I posted the video of Becca meeting some mystery man in a seedy weed shop. Shame I couldn't get close enough to record what was being said, but it seemed intense, right? What was that all about? Who is he? Someone from the party? Let's check what you guys are saying.

Benji in Warwick reckons she's bangin' him, no doubt about it, but Nadine in Bristol thinks he's involved in Georgie's disappearance. I've got Rebecca in Hull saying 'affair'. Brian says 100 per cent affair – wow, there's a lot of you thinking sweet innocent Becca is up to no good behind her hubby's back but, hang on, what's this, some of you are saying there's a conspiracy going on, that Becca and this fella have kidnapped Georgie. OK then, I guess I've got my work cut out for me. I need to find out who he is, what does he do for a living? What's his relationship with Becca and where was he on the night Georgie went missing. If anyone has any intel, you know where to send it. As always, smash the like button and share your theories . . .

But first – you guys are gunna wet your pants when you find out where I am. I shit you not, I am officially the best detective in town. A ton of you told me to go to the actual house, so by popular demand I've returned to the scene of the disappearance – and I've managed to find a way in.

Bear with me, folks, I'm on a live feed here, I'm going to move you over to my head cam so I can use my hands to get into this art dealer's gaff.

(rustling)

You still with me? OK, good, I'm going in.

(whispers)

I gotta keep my voice down now so nobody hears me, apart from you guys, of course. I've found an access point though the neighbour's back yard. Looks like they're out for the evening so I'm using their garden bench to give me a leg up onto the wall *(groan)* . . . and *(thunk)* I'm over. Oooff, that almost killed me. LOL. But, wow, look at this place, it's five fucking storeys!

(pans camera from the ground floor to the attic)

Let's quickly recap on what we know so far for all you CrimeTokkers out there. The girls ended up here on New Year's Eve after they crashed Dieter Schmidt's afterparty. We also know the art dealer cleared out the place the very next day. If that ain't suspect, I don't know what is. OK. So let's poke our noses around and see if we can find a clue or piece of evidence that might shed light on what the fuck went down here that night.

(picks lock on back door)

Misspent youth, don't judge me, lol.

(wipes brow, continues to pick lock)

That took way longer than it should have, but I'm in! *(gasp)* How the other half live, eh? This room, it's gotta be at least five times the size of my lounge back home. Would you just look at those high ceilings? *(pans camera around)* You can imagine what it would have been like on New Year's Eve with all that fancy art on the walls and those posh snooty types partying, swigging champagne, snorting cocaine – Colombia's finest, of course – off the polished side tables and, oh man, I've suddenly got the chills. Guys, my skin is tingling! No word of a lie. I'm feeling overwhelmed with emotion right now because *(takes audible breath)* this is the last place Georgie was seen alive.

(pans camera around the dark unfurnished room)

Nobody saw her leave. No one knows IF she left. What if she's still here? I'm getting chills just thinking about it. What are you guys saying on the feed?

Holy shit! 75,000 of you are tuning in tonight, and I'm getting loads of requests and questions. Whoa – slow down, people, I can't read that fast.

Darren in Bracknell says he's thinking about Georgie and praying for her safe return. Nice one, Dazza! What's your theories on that, people? It's a good thing she's got us in her corner instead. And bless you all for all the donations to help keep the search alive. I know if Georgie could speak, she'd be saying a big thank you from the bottom of her heart . . .

Hannah in Brighton says: Call out Georgie's name.

Georgie?

(silence)

Georgie, can ya hear me?

(silence)

Jesus Christ, I'm getting goosebumps. This place is creepy AF.

I'm gunna take a look around. Hang on tight, folks, we're going upstairs.

(climbs stairs to first floor)

Guys, you still with me? The reception's going, it's suddenly dropped to one bar, Christ, this place is like the Bermuda triangle.

(enters room)

It's dark in here, there's a bit of light from the street coming through the windows but it's pretty spooky and terrifying, and I don't want to put my torch on in case I attract attention.

(siren wailing in the distance)

Although sounds like the pigs are already onto me. Fuck's sake!

OK, CrimeTokkers, we don't have long. *(looks through window down onto the street, checking for police)* I've arrived on the floor where the last confirmed sighting of Georgie was. This is it, guys, this is where her mate, Becca Peters, saw her chatting to some mystery guy on the settee.

(pans to corner of the room cloaked in darkness)

I'm getting the chills again, just being in the same room as she was two nights ago. Have the police even searched this gaff? Why haven't they got any leads yet? I know I said it before, but it's fucking suspect that the owner of this property, that Dutch geezer, Schmidt, gutted the place the day after the party. Why would you do that?

(sirens drawing closer)

I'm not gunna abandon Georgie! Let's keep searching, team, never mind about the Old Bill, what's the worst they can do?

I'm taking you up to the top floor, here we go, hold on tight!

(breathless)

So not much to see on this floor, there's a few smaller rooms and some empty cardboard boxes – this bloke really did leave in a hurry. Hang on. I've found something . . .

Check this out . . . there's another staircase.

(siren outside)

Guys – think there's an attic . . .

(runs upstairs)

My heart's in my mouth! Something about this don't feel right . . .

(pushes door open)

(gasp)

Jesus! *(pans camera around tiny space)*

All my hairs are standing on end! No exaggeration. Are you getting this? *(zooms in)* Can you see these marks on the wall? Looks like there was a struggle up here. And what's that on the floorboards? *(moves across room)* There's something carved into the wood. Gunna get a close-up.

Fuuuuck. Guys, are you getting this?

(zooms in)

Oh my God, someone's written *HELP ME*.

(sound of boots on stairs)

Shit, I think the coppers are 'ere.

NOW

5 January

A crowd has swelled, pressing up against the blue-and-white tape cordoning off the area. On seeing the police car arrive, they immediately pull out their phones and begin filming the inspector as she makes her way towards the crime scene.

'Get them out of here!' She barks orders at an officer in Dutch.

Scowling, she ducks beneath the tape, being careful not to slip on the ice. *Detective Van den Berg falling flat on her face* going viral on social media would not please her superiors. She frowns again, because how could that even enter her head when she should be focusing on the much more serious and pressing matter.

The body in the canal.

But that's what crime fighting has been reduced to. The world is putting their trust in armchair detectives over trained professionals with years of experience behind them. It's absurd but it's becoming the way of the world. And it's making Detective Van den Berg's job almost impossible. The public are searching for reasons to crucify her team and she's becoming increasingly disillusioned by the process. Unless something can be done to control these keyboard warriors, the future of law enforcement is looking grim.

Will there be a world where she has to work alongside these predators? She'll have retired by then. Only ten days and she'll never have to think again about another podcaster or TikTok detective. She breathes a heavy sigh of relief.

Her father will be disappointed by her early retirement. He travels into her thoughts as she crosses the bridge, passing the old-fashioned chocolatier with the red awning he used to take her to for a treat on his day off. You couldn't pick out a more picturesque spot for such an ugly grotesque thing to have happened. But that's Amsterdam all over – picture-postcard on the surface. A dark underbelly lurking beneath.

Memories of happier times fall away as she approaches the water's edge. The noisy whir of the police boat swells, rising in pitch and volume. Divers in thick black wetsuits plunge beneath the ice, preparing the body to be winched out, while others rake the canal bed for evidence of how someone might have ended up there.

It could be anyone. A homeless person. A tourist who fell in after one too many. She's trying not to jump to conclusions, but her years on the job are forewarning her – this is no clumsy accident.

She shivers; despite her thermal layers and her wind-proof jacket, the cold has found a way in, spreading around her ribs. She blows into her hands then folds her arms tightly and waits. She might be here for some time. An uneasy feeling is growing inside her. Could this be the woman they've been searching for?

THE FRIEND – BECCA

It looks like a building site.

It's cold. Dark. There are dust sheets over the furniture, wood shavings and a finely milled carpet of sawdust across the floor.

'Nathan?'

We're three days from opening, what's he doing leaving the restaurant looking like this? No wonder Nathan's stressed. I'm getting heart palpitations just thinking how he's going to turn this around in time.

'Nathan?' I call out again, stepping over boxes. Wood chips crunch beneath my trainers while a chill penetrates to my bones.

When he didn't come home, I assumed he'd be here. I check my watch again, it's 11.46 p.m. Where else would he be?

I know he's busy and I'm starting to understand why he was so stressed this morning, but I need to speak to him urgently. I can't be alone in the flat with all of Georgie's things for a second longer, not after what Rami told me. My mind's been in a tailspin, going over the fresh memories from New Year's Eve, trying to work out why Rami's so frightened. Has Georgie got tangled up in something nasty? Should I tell the police? Should I report that creepy guy who's following me? Nathan will know what to do. Nathan always knows.

Where is Nathan?

I flick the lights but they don't come on.

Turning slowly, I inhale the dust and the stillness. It's not helping that the furniture's shrouded in shadows; it feels like someone might jump out from under the sheets at any moment.

Out of the darkness, I hear a noise.

'Nathan?' I say hesitantly.

A shiver feeds its way along my spine.

'Hello? Anyone here?'

The restaurant is suddenly eerily still, like someone has turned down the volume. With the moonlight feeding through the windows, I carefully pick my way towards the back of the room, an uneasy feeling swelling inside my chest.

As I draw closer, I hear a noise.

The soft murmur of voices.

My gaze shoots across the dining area to the door on the far side. It's coming from the stockroom out the back. I hold myself very still, barely breathing.

What if it's burglars? Or that weirdo? Did he follow me here?

Picking up a bottle of Gordon's gin from behind the bar, I raise my arm, my heart drumming.

Creeping towards the noise, with the moon on my

back, I reach out my other hand for the door handle and hesitate.

What if they're armed?

Don't be ridiculous. I've been watching too many true crime shows on Netflix. Still, I tighten my grip around the glass bottle as I turn the handle and tentatively step inside the darkened corridor. Shelves crammed with pots and pans, tins and spice jars run the length of the wall, and at the end of the tunnel is a light. And the blurred outline of two people, hunched over. The sound of urgent whispers drifts towards me.

It feels like I'm intruding on a private moment.

Nathan's bowed over, his head in his hands, while Katya crouches beside him, kneading his arm.

I feel suddenly small and insignificant. Embarrassed to be there – which is ridiculous, because Nathan's my husband. I remain quiet for a moment, watching Katya comfort him, torn between jealousy and concern. Why is he so upset?

I clear my throat and they both startle. But instead of appearing embarrassed or ashamed, Nathan turns his head away from me. Katya gives Nathan's arm a squeeze and then gives me a look – something unfriendly – before brushing past me and disappearing along the corridor and into the bar next door.

'Nathan?'

No answer.

'What are you still doing here? It's nearly midnight. And' – I glance back to the dining area – 'why are all the lights off?'

He turns and looks at me. His eyes immediately drop to the bottle of gin I'm holding. I can't read his expression and it's making me uneasy.

'Nathan?'

'Where were you tonight?'

'Me?' I frown. 'At home, waiting for you. Why?'

He rises up from the stool and comes towards me, his phone gripped tightly in his hand. His face is strained.

'Isn't that a normal question you'd ask your wife?' An unnerving note of coldness.

'It's not something you normally ask me.' I rub my forehead, feeling a little put upon. 'And where've you been all evening?'

'Here. Exactly where I said I'd be.'

'Um, OK.'

'So – I've been truthful with you.' He gives me another look.

There's a cough from the other room. I look across in time to catch Katya stepping away from the door. She pretends to busy herself behind the bar, rearranging bottles.

I return to Nathan, who seems engrossed by whatever is on his phone. His brow furrows as he studies his screen. A brittle silence opens up between us, which I immediately feel I have to fix.

'Look, I went to check out the gallery of the guy whose house party we ended up at. In fact, there's something really important I need to ask you—'

His shoulders lift.

'I thought you were staying at home, resting?'

'I couldn't sit there doing nothing!' I defend myself.

'Georgie's out there somewhere, and I think she might have got mixed up in something serious. The art dealer, it seems like he's connected to organized crime—'

'What?' Nathan pulls a face.

'People are saying he burnt down his own gallery to claim the insurance.'

Nathan lets out a sigh.

'That's fraud. This is serious, Nathan. The police aren't doing anything to find Georgie and now there's this weirdo stalking me and—'

'So you didn't meet up with some guy in a coffee shop earlier, then?'

A sharp intake of breath.

'What?'

He shows me his phone.

'What is that?' I squint at the screen.

'Yeah, so this has been trending on TikTok . . .'

Is Georgie's best friend having an affair?

My breath catches – 1.2 million views. What the hell?

'That's him, that's the weirdo who's been following me!'

But Nathan is barely listening.

'And who is *this* guy?' Nathan jumps the video forward to me and Rami. We're leaning into each other, sharing a spliff. Laughing. There's no getting away from it – we look like a couple.

'Friend of yours?'

I open my mouth to defend myself but the words get caught.

'Looks pretty cosy.'

I hear the pain in his voice and I look up sharply. 'God, you don't think—' I try to catch his eyes. 'You *do* think that?'

But he shakes his head like he's still not ready to hear what I have to say.

'You actually believe I'm having an affair?' I try again to get through to him.

A clank from the dining area.

I lower my voice to a whisper. 'Is *she* listening in?'

'Katya was the one who alerted me to this.'

Of course she did.

'She said it's been trending everywhere. And I agree, it looks really suss. The way you're looking at each other.' His voice splinters, as if he's fighting back emotion. He clears his throat but he can't hide the hurt in his eyes and I feel more guilty than ever.

'He was a waiter at the party. I thought he might know something.'

'He's a good-looking guy.'

'Nothing happened.'

'You look like you're flirting. Are you attracted to him?'

'It was made to look that way.'

'The camera doesn't lie!'

'Nathan. I love you.' I glance back towards Katya. I sense her watching, listening in, and my skin prickles. I turn back to my husband and whisper, 'Look, this is just some creepy guy making up stories for views.'

'But have you seen the comments? What they're saying about you? About us? They think you might be involved somehow. Katya said a couple of journalists showed up at the restaurant earlier, asking questions.' He rakes a hand through his hair. 'This is the last thing we need before opening.'

'I'm sorry, I was only trying to find Georgie.'

'Georgie.' He exhales her name.

'Nobody seems to give a shit about her except me.'

'Christ, it's like you're obsessed with her.'

'Obsessed?'

'It's happening again, isn't it?'

'What is?'

'You know what I mean.' He throws me a look.

I fall silent. The memory of how I fell apart is suddenly vivid in my mind and I'm whisked back in time to my parents' house. I'm curled up in a ball, sobbing on my bedroom floor. When Georgie dropped me, I felt almost suicidal, terrified I'd never be able to escape my abusive family. I was living in constant fear, knowing it was just a matter of time before Dad turned his fists on me too. Then came the relentless checking of Georgie's social media. Spying on her parents' house, hoping she might be home for the weekend. Desperate to catch a glimpse of my former best friend. Praying that she might change her mind and want me back in her life. Nathan's right, I was obsessed.

But that was twelve years ago.

I've moved on.

It's *not* happening again.

I'm just overwhelmed. I've been through a lot: losing the baby, then roofied, and then my friend disappearing . . .

I frown, because when you lay it out like that, and

include the past nine months – which have sucked away all of my confidence, strength and identity – it's seeming perfectly reasonable that I might be acting a little out of character. But then that doesn't explain the other thing, the *thing* that keeps eating away at me, like a piece of the puzzle is missing and, somehow, I'm involved.

'You haven't been yourself,' Nathan continues. 'It feels like you've been hiding a lot from me recently. You didn't even tell me about losing the baby, for fuck's sake.' His voice is breaking up.

'I'm sorry.' I shake my head, bewildered, because Becca-of-a-year-ago would never have behaved like this.

'You didn't tell me about your night out. About Georgie. Maybe something did happen between you and those blokes you met at the afterparty? Why else lie about being there?'

'What? No! Why would you say that?'

'And now this waiter . . .'

'Nathan . . .' I take a tentative step towards him.

'All those people who've seen the video must be laughing behind my back.'

'Nobody's laughing at you.'

'I don't know what to think.' His shoulders sag.

I take his hands in mine. 'I would never ever do anything to break your trust. I know you know that.'

He looks up, his eyes misty. 'Do I?'

'What have I ever done to make you doubt me? I've been nothing but loyal and supportive.'

'When you're with Georgie, it's like you change. You become a different person—' He stops and glances around, as if his mind has suddenly been pulled in another direction.

He stands up straighter and nods thoughtfully. 'Look, let's talk about this at home.'

'I don't want to leave you like this.'

'I have to finish up here, I'm way behind.'

'You sure I can't help?'

'Look, I need some space to clear my head.'

'I love you.' I catch his hand and squeeze it tight. 'I'm sorry for stressing you out.'

'It's fine,' he says brusquely. He plants a kiss on my forehead and I feel a faint wash of relief, the tension easing a fraction.

'Don't wait up for me, OK.'

I hesitate, I can sense he's still angry, which instantly triggers me to cling on tightly. Should I stay and try to fix things? I think about going home alone. A room full of her things; the ghost of Georgie haunting our flat, and the thought makes me colder than I am already. But I should probably give Nathan some space.

With a heavy heart, I let myself out via the fire exit, taking the bottle of gin with me.

The city is strangely still and quiet. The cobbled streets are dusted in a thin layer of snow and glittering under the moonlight. I pull out my phone, in two minds about whether I should order an Uber or delay going home, when I hear a quiet *Becca*.

A softly spoken voice behind me.

I turn to find Katya rubbing at her arms as a cold wind whips up.

'You shouldn't take it personally.' She gives a sympathetic tilt of the head. 'He's really stressed out at the moment.'

'Yeah, I know.' I cross my arms. 'I can see that.'

'So,' she smiles innocently, dragging a piece of hair behind her ear. 'We should try to do everything we can to ease the pressure.'

Katya says *we*, but I can tell she means ME. She's shifting the entire blame my way while acting like she knows what my husband needs better than I do.

'I need to head off. Is there anything else?'

She looks injured.

'Becca . . .' Her eyes flick to meet mine, her face softening. 'I didn't mean to offend you. I'm just . . . there's a lot going on and there's so much at stake. Nathan's not telling me everything. He's got his barriers up and I'm concerned . . .'

I feel my hackles go up as she continues to imply how close they are. How he's been confiding in her rather than me. Her innocent concerned act doesn't fool me. I bet she's enjoying driving a wedge between us.

'What are you saying?'

'We're behind schedule.' She flicks her eyes back inside. 'Way behind. And this guy who's been following you and posting TikTok videos, it's not good for business. We can't risk any negative press before the launch . . .'

'You think I'm enjoying being stalked and harassed?'

'I'm also risking everything.' Her eyes flash. 'I've invested my entire savings into Muse, I need this to work. This *has* to work, and . . .' She hesitates. 'I wasn't going to bring this up, but . . .' She pauses again, lowering her voice. 'I wanted to check. Are you OK?'

'Yeah, why wouldn't I be?'

'It's just . . . Look, I saw you.'

'Saw me?'

She observes me silently.

'Saw me where?' I go on, although I know what's coming. I can feel the heat starting to spread.

'Outside my flat the other night.'

Reaching and tightening around my throat.

'You don't need to be embarrassed; I understand.'

But I am embarrassed. My cheeks are burning with humiliation as I'm reminded of how I followed Katya home. How I spied on her flat from across the street, waiting to see if Nathan would show up.

'It's OK, I won't tell Nathan . . .'

There. The silent threat.

'I like to think you'd be able to come to me if there was a problem between us,' she says gently.

I stare at a patch of snow, unable to meet her eyes.

'There's nothing going on, if that's what's worrying you.'

'That's not it,' I mutter, but I can tell she doesn't believe me. I don't believe me. I was stalking her, for heaven's sake. If she decides to tell Nathan, it will make things even worse between us. I can feel the power balance tipping, and it's making me even more anxious.

'If you're feeling overwhelmed, there are people who you can talk to. Counsellors, that sort of thing,' she continues in her saccharin sweet voice.

'Right.'

'We're friends, aren't we?'

'Yeah.' I swallow. 'Course.'

She places her hand on my arm, giving it a light squeeze. 'Come speak to me next time.'

I smile thinly. I can't tell if she pities me. Or if she's enjoying the power trip. I'm so confused.

Then she turns and walks off in the direction of my husband, leaving me alone in the darkness. I feel whiplashed, uncertain. Nathan's right, it is happening again. The unravelling. God, I'm so tired I feel drunk, my thoughts are slow and clouded. I'm not sure I know who I am any more.

I look down at my hands, at the bruises.

Or what I'm capable of.

TWO DAYS EARLIER

THE TIKTOK DETECTIVE – JAMIE

I collect my phone from the copper sat behind the re-inforced glass screen, checking it over for scratches. Fuckers. Who do they think they are, arresting me and keeping me in overnight? And now I've done my back in on that excuse for a bed. I'm gunna file a complaint!

They make me sign some forms before handing back my coat and a sealed plastic bag with my wallet, hotel key card and my belt.

'This way.' The pig who arrested me frogmarches me towards the exit. You don't need to force me, mate, can't get out of this hellhole quick enough.

'One more thing, Mr Finn.'

What now? I roll my eyes and drag my feet as I turn around. For the love of God, not her again. It's that inspector woman who's been grilling me for the past two hours about why I was nosing around in Schmidt's gaff. Doesn't she have something better to do – like find out what's happened to Georgie?

'You've got off lightly with a warning. You're lucky Mr Schmidt hasn't pressed charges.' She peers at me. 'But

195

if we catch you back there again, or anywhere near his other properties, you'll be arrested, immediately charged and detained. Do you understand?'

I cross my arms. 'Like I said, just trying to help find Georgie.'

'That's our job. Leave it to the professionals.'

'Yeah, but are you doing your job?'

'Stop interfering, Mr Finn.'

'Don't say I didn't warn ya. I've told you what I found in that attic. You should be sending a forensics team up there.'

'For all I know, you vandalized the property as well as breaking and entering. Decades of police investigations under our belt, but as soon as someone buys a microphone off Amazon suddenly they're Sherlock Holmes.'

'Don't get me mixed up with those podcasters.' I wink at her. 'I ain't nothing like 'em.'

'We have a no-tolerance policy in the Netherlands.' Her eyes flash. 'Anyone interfering or profiting from our investigations *will* be punished.'

I see you, Inspector Van Der Whatnot. I see the way you're looking down yer nose at me. Anger lights up like a bonfire in my chest. She's thinking, how would someone like me solve a crime. It's written across her face; she's decided I'm scum and that what I do isn't important.

She gives me another demeaning look. I reckon she feels intimidated by a real man like me. I've been nicked before; her threats don't scare me. I bite my tongue to stop myself giving her a piece of my mind.

The pig pushes me towards the exit. The doors slide apart, and I'm blinded by the early morning light.

A sharp prod in my back.

'Hey! Easy.' I swing around and stumble as this GI Joe wannabe shoves me into the high street. 'I could do you for that!'

'Have a good day.' A smile plays on his lips.

And I could wipe that smirk off your face in no time.

Nah, I bite down on my anger, he ain't worth it. Let him go back to his pig pen, better save my energy for the important stuff.

It's cold AF out here, should I head to Muse and get the latest on Becca and her hubby? My followers are gagging for intel on those two since I caught her playing away from home. But then there's that other thing I need to do. I turn on my phone, my heart jump-starting. 'Come on, come on,' I mutter, waiting for it to boot up. Why does it always take so effing long, stupid thing.

The screen lights up, few seconds later – WTAF.

My jaw falls slack as I thumb through the hundreds of notifications. I kept the camera rolling as they arrested me and it looks like . . . I swallow. *Jesus*, I've been catapulted to hero status.

UR MY HERO.
Keep up the good work foot soldier.
Only you can save Georgie.
Fuck the pigs!

I give my head a little shake, I'm feeling dizzy with shock. I had a feeling this case would catch on, but not like this. My heart is clattering, it feels like it's gunna jump out of my chest. There's a message from one of the lads back home.

Seen this? Mate, this you?

I click on the link Darren's sent me and it takes me to the *Daily Mail* website.

TikTok 'detective' arrested for disturbing the peace.

A self-declared 'TikTok detective' has been arrested for breaking and entering a property where a missing British woman was last seen partying.

Jamie Finn, 25, posted a video of himself being arrested by Dutch police officers on his TikTok channel Crime_Tok_Detective after they apprehended him at the property belonging to a well-known art dealer, located on one of the city's most famous canal belts.

Since Georgie Taylor-Johnson went missing on New Year's Eve, Finn has posted a number of videos to his 206,000 followers on his social media platform under his alias, investigating possible explanations for her disappearance.

Finn is the latest in a disturbing trend of amateur detectives interfering with crime scenes to garner an online audience. The nature of this 'sleuthing' is largely seen as exploitative and harmful, a cynical trend in which people know they can easily get views and followers by posting unsourced theories.

Social media reached new heights of

ghoulishness last year in response to the disappearance of teenager Elena Brookes, who went missing on a night out clubbing with friends in Ibiza. Elena died from accidental drowning and her body was tragically found washed up on the beach two weeks later. But in that time, the hashtag #FindElena racked up nearly 300 million views on TikTok and nearly 150 million views on Instagram reels, with influencers making money off videos dedicated to speculation around her disappearance.

During the intensive search, detectives say they were 'inundated with false information, accusations and rumours', which was damaging to the effectiveness of the ongoing investigation. They had to issue a dispersal order to break up groups of amateur sleuths filming in the area.

Finn's popularity appears to be snowballing, as does the amount he's generated to crowdfund his search. His appeal for help from the public has raised almost £20,000 at the time of going to press. The Dutch police are not treating Ms Taylor-Johnson's disappearance as suspicious.

I'm speechless.

I'm famous. Fucking famous. And I've raised twenty grand! I fire off a quick message to Aaron. He'll be on the building site with the boys so he can pass on the news.

Nice one bruv, he replies immediately. We're all rooting for U back home.

They've changed their tune, I'm not the dipshit they had me pegged for after all. But this is just the start – wait till they see me on *I'm a Celeb*. Soon I'll be on every talk-show couch and reality TV series going. Except *Strictly* – I got two left feet, so that's not going to work out.

A sudden stab of guilt.

I haven't called Nan yet. Hope she's OK and hasn't had another fall. *Don't go soft now, Jamie*, you got to keep your head on. I make a promise with myself to check in on her later. Until then, I push her right out of my mind and focus on myself. Switching the camera on, I spin it around, stick my thumb up and grin, snapping a selfie outside the cop shop.

Crime_Tok_Detective shows the Old Bill how it's done.

Then I upload it and post it.
My new profile picture.

THE FRIEND – BECCA

I stare across the canal at Schmidt's place, with its triangular jutting roof and tall sash windows that appear like hooded eyes, feeling sick with worry.

What secrets lie behind those walls? I pray to God whatever this TikTokker found in the attic turns out to be nothing. But my ears are still ringing from watching his video. The image of those words – *HELP ME* – scratched into the hard wood keeps flashing behind my eyes.

She's going to be OK. Georgie will be fine. The marks could be centuries old. There's nothing to say they're connected to Georgie's disappearance.

And then I think about the secrets they were keeping that night and what Rami told me, and—

I take a shuddering breath.

There are a few journalists hanging around outside taking photos, which is attracting the attention of passers-by. A crowd is forming and I instantly recognize the man in the army-green anorak skulking nearby, filming on his phone, and duck out of sight.

God, he's odious. Stalking me, intimidating me, making

up stories. He's blackening Muse's name before it's even opened. Worst of all, he's making Nathan doubt me. But what if he can make the police sit up and listen and finally *do* something? Now the press is interested, the police can't be seen to be doing nothing. Surely?

As if he can sense me watching, the TikTokker swings around, angling his lens across the water. I slip behind a parked car, my heart skittering. I can't be caught on film, not again, Katya's warning is ringing in my ears. If I upset her, she'll tell Nathan about our secret and I dread to think how he'll take the news. Nathan already thinks I'm losing it; knowing I've been spying on Katya will only bring them closer together. The image of her comforting him. Running her hand across his arm, touching *my husband* . . . Anger reaches for my throat, my thoughts becoming darker and darker.

Bitch. The word rings out like a fire alarm.

Thinking about Katya pawing my husband drags the memory of New Year's to the surface. The image, fuzzy and tangled and just out of reach. But who – *who* did I scream *bitch* at?

No one.

It's my imagination, my head is all over the place.

It would help if I ate something, but I don't have any appetite. I've gone so long without a proper meal now, it hurts to put food in my stomach; and I'm doing it again. Abandoning myself. I was up all night worrying about Georgie and replaying my argument with Nathan and then things went from bad to worse when Nathan came home at 3.30 a.m.

Instead of coming straight to bed, he fell asleep on the sofa watching TV. The rational part of my brain knows he was too knackered to move, but still, I stayed awake until dawn, watching the light creeping through the curtains, panicking. *He doesn't want to be near me. Did something happen with Katya after I left?*

I inhale sharply, filling my lungs with icy air. It's getting colder, the air's becoming thicker, harder to breathe. I turn away from the sight of the police, a frown settling between my brows. There's a call I need to make, but I'm trying to summon the courage.

I tracked down her number from her old cleaner, Marta, who still works for Nathan's dad at the pub.

She's moved to a village nearby. She's downsized, she reverted to her maiden name after the divorce. My mouth turns bone-dry as I dial her number.

The landline rings and rings and I feel a twitch of relief she's not home. I can put off the conversation for a while longer.

'Taylor residence. Hello?'

I fall silent.

'Yes, hello?'

The shock of hearing Georgie's mum down the line steals the air from my lungs.

'Who's there?'

The familiar sound of her formidable voice, whisking me back in time.

Summer was turning into autumn, the branches on the trees were drooping under the weight of the ripened apples, but all I could think about was Georgie and if she'd come home from London for the weekend.

'What are you doing down there?' Mrs Taylor-Johnson hollered at me. I'd been caught spying on their house again, desperate for a glimpse of my old friend.

'Well?'

A rabbit in headlights, I couldn't get a word out.

'Have you forgotten how to speak, dear?' A small shake of the head as she said: 'You better come inside then.'

Wading through the long grass, I clambered over the stone wall and followed her into the shade of the house. She poured me a glass of her freshly squeezed lemonade, the ice cubes bobbing, mint leaves swirling, while she sipped on a gin and tonic. I remember thinking how much quieter the kitchen seemed without Georgie, and how much drunker than normal her mother appeared. Georgie leaving home had clearly left a hole in her life as well as mine, and I'll never forget the pity in her eyes. 'It's for the best that you didn't follow her to London.' She nodded gently, topping up her drink. 'You really are very different people; you'd have fallen out sooner or later.' I could tell she was getting a small thrill from bringing me down. From reminding me I came from a council estate.

I left via the front door feeling humiliated and lower than ever and I cried the whole way home, my heart breaking wide open all over again.

I feel a painful lump stick in my throat.

'Damn cold callers.' Her voice fades as she pulls the receiver from her ear, about to hang up.

'Mrs Taylor-Johnson,' I say loudly. 'It's Becca!'

'Who?'

'Becca Peters, I mean, Banbury. Rebecca Banbury.'

A pause. Several beats passing. Then:

'Becca from the village?'

It feels like a shove to the chest. Of all the ways to categorize me.

'Georgie's old friend,' I correct her, but my voice is shrinking already.

Silence. I can hear her thinking. I can picture her – the former catalogue model with her thick highlighted hair sprayed stiff around her neck, a pashmina shawl draped around her shoulders. Her drawn-on eyebrows pulling together with disapproval. Her mouth hardening into a line.

'What do you want?' she says eventually. Her tone ice-cold.

'I, well I . . .' I falter. 'Um. I was wondering if you've heard from Georgie?'

A heavy sigh. 'We're not starting that again, are we?'

'Um . . .'

'Goodness, dear, it's been, what, almost a decade since the last time I caught you pining after my daughter.'

'It's just . . .' I grit my teeth and continue. 'Well, the thing is, Georgie came to stay with me on New Year's Eve and we went to a party together—'

'Really?' she interrupts, sounding like she doesn't believe me.

I glance back across the canal. The crowd around the house is swelling. I don't want to worry her unnecessarily; the TikTokker's discovery might be nothing, it could be another of his sick publicity stunts. I feel like a teenager again, timid and uncertain under her scrutiny. Am I doing the right thing? Should I alert her to how serious this is?'

Of course you should, Becca. She needs to know. And I can't keep doing this alone. As soon as you tell her the full story, she'll want to help.

'I'm really worried about her.'

'What do you want, Rebecca?'

I hear the faint *glug* of liquid being poured from a bottle.

'She's missing!' I blurt out.

The *clink* of ice hitting the sides of a glass.

'I beg your pardon.' She breaks into a laugh, as if such a thing were preposterous.

'I'm so sorry to have to tell you like this over the phone, but I thought you should know. And I hoped Georgie had been in touch by now.' I force the words out hurriedly.

'Don't be ridiculous. Georgina isn't missing.'

And now I'm listening out for it, I can hear the slight slur in her words.

'It's hardly unusual not to hear from her. Georgina only gets in touch when she wants something, and since the divorce, I don't have an awful lot to give.'

It's 10 a.m. and she's already drunk.

'I think something might have happened to her.'

'Oh, don't be a drama queen, dear, I have one of those in the family already. She'll be off having fun somewhere. Where's hot this time of year? St Barts? The Caribbean – there, that's a good starting point, no?'

'But she was just in Italy for her great-aunt's wedding anniversary—'

'What are you talking about?' she says impatiently. 'Are you sure this isn't her way of getting attention?'

My mouth falls open.

'Do you know my daughter at all?'

'I – um . . .' I swallow. 'I think this is more serious than that.'

'This sounds like a very Georgina thing to do.'

'Sorry? What does?'

A theatrical sigh. 'To get everyone running around her. Oh, there'll be a boy involved, no doubt. Someone she wants to chase after her. It's not the first time she's done something like this, dear.'

I'm speechless. How can she think her daughter would fake her own disappearance for attention? And I thought *my* family was unpleasant. Mrs Taylor-Johnson really is a cold-hearted bitch.

A wave of heat flares through me, I'm getting mad on Georgie's behalf. And in a strange way it helps me understand my friend a little better – it explains why she treated me so callously when we were young. If you come from a home like that . . .

'She hasn't been answering her phone since New Year's Eve and all her things are still at my flat,' I go on in vain, hoping something might trigger her mum to care. 'There's also her diabetes medication . . .'

Another sigh. 'Georgina gave herself diabetes from all that drinking. Purely self-inflicted. It's type 2, so she could reverse it if she mended her ways. But oh no . . .'

Jesus. Am I hearing this from the woman who has G&Ts for breakfast?

'Have you been to the police?' Her tone softens a touch. A vague note of concern coming through.

'Yes,' I tell her. 'I've reported her as missing.'

'Oh, she'll love that.' I can hear her smiling down the line.

As if Georgie would go through all this to get attention and sympathy. I could imagine Mrs Taylor-Johnson doing something like that though, which is probably how she came up with the twisted notion.

She asks a few half-hearted questions about what the police are doing, sounding increasingly disinterested at my replies, and then veers off on a tangent, talking to herself, muttering about how hard things have been since the divorce. I feel my temper starting to fray. I don't want to know about her terraced garden or how much she's struggled with the budget for the renovations on her new property. I want to talk about Georgie.

I can't bear it any longer.

'Should I let Mr Taylor-Johnson know?' I say, to shut her up.

A hollow laugh.

'Oh, he won't care, he's just had a baby. He's busy with his *new* family.'

The bitterness trickles through the phone line and leaves me cold.

'Well, I guess I'll just keep you updated as and when I hear news.'

'It's OK, dear, I'm sure Georgina will be in touch soon enough when she needs something.'

'Well, um, bye then.'

The line goes dead.

THE TIKTOK DETECTIVE – JAMIE

I'm so busy checking my phone for likes and new followers, I don't see the black transit van pull up.

It rams onto the pavement, knocking me sideways. The back doors fly open and two men dressed in army camo gear leap out in front of me.

The next thing, I'm being grabbed by the arms, lifted up off my feet and dragged into the van. I'm thrown into the corner while the tyres screech. We jerk forward, taking off at speed.

'What the hell are you playing at?' I look up. Three guys in balaclavas peer down at me and one of them's holding a baseball bat. 'Hey, stop the car NOW or I'm gunna fucking do you in!'

The one with a neck as thick as my thigh steps forward, towering over me. He winches back an arm. I raise my hand to ward off the blow but his fist smashes into my stomach.

'Ughhh.'

An explosion of pain across my abdomen. I fold in two, retching. A trail of saliva joins my mouth to the van floor.

'What the fuck do you want?' I wheeze. The coppery taste of blood fills my mouth. 'I ain't got no money on me – check if you like.'

They swap looks and laugh.

'Go on, have a look, you wankers.'

The driver takes a sharp left, sending me flying. I roll, knocking into the metal side wall and my skull feels like it's been cracked in two. I touch where it hurts. What's that? Gross, it's all slippery. When I pull my fingers from my temple they're soaked in blood. I look up and notice how the guy on the left has swapped his bat for something else and I feel a lurch of fear. I read it wrong. These boys aren't messing around.

The van stinks of diesel and sweat and old leather boxing gloves – but not for long.

'This'll shut him up,' the gorilla with the thick plastic bag grunts while the other two pin me down. We've parked up, but fuck only knows where because there's no windows in the back of the van, just plastic sheeting spread out across the floor.

'No, wait!' My last breath is sucked out of me like a vacuum as the plastic hood is pulled over my head and tightened around my throat.

'Not so clever now, are you?'

'HELP!' I scream, but the plastic sticks to my mouth like a suction airlock, blocking my airway. I can feel my lungs spasm, my eyes enlarge and my insides turn to liquid.

'Now listen carefully, because we're only going to tell you this once.'

My eyes flick between them, my vision blurring through the opaque mask, my lungs shrinking.

'You have no idea who you're messing with. OK?'

Moisture mists in front of my eyes. The air in my chest is shrinking.

'You need to stop what you're doing.'

I try to fight back but my hands and feet are secured tight. I stretch, reach for the ligature, but their grip on me tightens, my left arm is twisted so high up my back it feels like it's about to snap in two. Pain sears, so hot and burning it brings tears to my eyes. The fuckers.

The big guy with the tree-trunk neck crouches, meeting me at eye level.

'Mr Schmidt has asked me to pass on a message . . .'

I wheeze, sucking the plastic right inside my mouth.

'Tsk tsk.' He clicks his tongue. 'He's not happy with you. Not happy at all. Sticking your nose into things that don't concern you. Drawing attention to his business.'

I bite down, trying to chew my way out of this, but it's too slippery. The plastic sinks further down my throat and I can feel it tightening around my face like I'm butcher's meat in a vacuum bag.

'But Mr Schmidt is a fair man, which is why he's letting you off with a warning for breaking into his house. But there will be no second chances, do you understand? If he sees you anywhere near his property or sticking your nose into his business again . . .'

The ligature tightens, cutting into my throat.

'Well, you're a bright enough lad, I think you can guess what will happen . . .'

Something slices my skin. My vision blurs, white spots appearing like snowflakes.

'So let this be your first and last warning.'

I'm seeing stars. Is this the end?

'Do we have an understanding?'

The light is fading and my final passing thought is of Nan. Who will look after my beloved nan if I croak?

And then, there's a wash of white like I've shot to heaven and all I can see is *her*. That blindingly beautiful face of hers.

Georgie Taylor-Johnson.

THE TIKTOK DETECTIVE – JAMIE

I rub at my neck. Luckily, the pain from being almost throttled to death has dulled to a constant ache now I've had a few beers.

It's left an ugly red mark and bruising though, which has caught the eye of a few people in the bar opposite my hotel. I raise my pint and cheers the pot-bellied baldy staring over at me. Ha. That made him look away.

I feel a bit shaky and I'm still wheezing, sucking air into my lungs, and I've been shitting blood but I'm alive and kicking, that's the main thing.

Tossers dumped me on the side of the motorway. They made me hitch a ride back to the city centre, which took up nearly half a day. It's 9 p.m. I'm way behind schedule now, which is annoying, to say the least, but I've got some good news to make up for it.

I read over the message again from the Sky News reporter requesting an interview. Each time it feels less real. They want to interview me. *Me*. A strange feeling rises in my stomach. I'm light-headed and giddy and it's not just the beer. Jamie the security guard, who nobody gave a crap about four days ago, is now a somebody.

So fuck those goons for trying to intimidate me. Nobody tells me what I can and can't do.

I'm a hero.

My followers have doubled since I arrived in Amsterdam. The GoFundMe money has risen to £32,000. Who can say they've achieved that in their life, hey? Exactly. All those people with their limiting beliefs and their opinions about TikTok detectives. Those morons who leave comments on the *Daily Mail* website. Who's having the last laugh now?

I am.

Had a few more beers to celebrate and now I'm feeling horny.

Watching these girls in the window will do that to ya. They keep giving me the eye, calling me over with a sultry look it's hard to resist. Some of them look really fit. Not quite OnlyFans, but with a bit of slap on their face they could be a doppelganger for some of those models.

I move outdoors, grab a seat beneath the bar's outdoor heater and have a smoke of some weed I bought earlier. It feels good to relax after what went down. I order another beer and settle back into the warmth, going through my messages. The conspiracy theories about Georgie's disappearance have been flooding in since my discovery in Schmidt's gaff, and the fundraising amount has shot up again. I post a thank you, reminding them that all the money will feed straight back into finding Georgie.

I feel a twitch of guilt.

But I push it to the back of my mind when the lady serving asks if I want another drink. Does a bear shit in the woods? Course I bloody do. This lad is celebrating being famous. I buy her a drink and ask if she wants to join me. She turns her nose up at my offer but four sambuca shots later, I couldn't give a shit. My head is spinning, I'm on my way to getting smashed.

I need to let off some steam.

I drink this pint quicker than the last, plus one final sambuca for the road, then get up to leave. I'm unsteady on my feet and stumble. Oi-oi, nearly had me in the canal there, but I make a recovery. SAVE! Better use the street urinal while I'm here, though it's filthy, even by my standards.

Jesus! I hold my breath as I step inside the metal cage and then stumble back onto the street, trying to get my bearings. Is it left or right to the hotel? I blink. The red lights and flashing banners all look the same. I walk past a shop called HAPPY DREAMS, its window filled with dildos, handcuffs and gimp masks. There's a knocking shop next door. I lurch to a stop, gawping at the brunette in the window. I don't realize I've been staring until she taps on the glass and knocks me back into life.

She gives me a cutesy wave.

She's gorgeous.

I think about Gemma back home, that's my missus, we've been on and off since school and she wouldn't be happy with me for staring at another bird, but I'm only human. A man can look, for fuck's sake. And with my beer goggles on, this one could be a model in her red lacy underwear and platform heels. She has a tattoo on her right leg. A unicorn or a dragon or something like that wrapped around her thigh, with wings reaching right up there, tickling her you-know-what, which has now got me thinking about her you-know-what. And these urges, I can't control 'em. Not this time.

I tap on the window and she opens the door, giving me that same sultry look, inviting me inside.

It's more functional than sexy and I try to block out the strong smell of disinfectant. I make a slow turn, taking in the bed with the plastic-covered mattress. There's a rail running along the back wall with all sorts of equipment hanging from it – handcuffs, horse-whips and stuff I've never seen before. I stare at some truncheon-looking thing. What the hell would you do with that? Not sure I want to know. Look, I'm not really up for any of that kinky shit, I just want a straightforward shag.

She pulls the curtain across the window, shutting out the street, and shows me her cutesy look again, all innocent eyes, but I'm no fool.

I stumble and reach a hand out to steady myself. The wall is damp and cold as ice. Ew, this place is rancid. Never mind. I won't be hanging around. Just a quickie and then I'm out of here.

'Would you like to wash first?' She points me towards the tiny handbasin and paper towel dispenser.

'I need to sit down,' I tell her, almost tripping up on my way to the bed.

I fall flat onto my back. She undoes my belt and

straddles me, playing with her hair, twirling it around her finger.

'How old are ya?'

'How old do you want me to be?' She leans forward, showing me some cleavage.

I feel myself grinning.

'I can be anything you want me to be.' Her voice goes even higher. 'Do you want to tell me what you like?'

I push up onto my elbows and the sudden exertion makes me dizzy. I immediately fall back onto the hard plastic mattress, which smells like it's soaked in disinfectant.

'What's your name?' I slur.

'Sapphire.'

I laugh. 'Your real name?

'Sapphire,' she says coyly.

'Don't believe ya.'

'But it's a pretty name.' She curls her hair, wrapping it around her finger and pulling a strand across her face. It's covering her lips as she says: 'Don't you like it?'

'Where you from, *Sapphire*?'

'What do you like?' She unzips me.

'You sound English.'

'I'm an expert with my tongue.' She parts her lips and I notice the flash of silver from her piercing.

'You from Blighty then?'

She lowers her head, looking at me through her falsies.

'I'm from wherever you want me to be from,' she says in her sexy voice.

There. Again. Unmistakable. Leeds? No. Northampton? Oh, I don't fucking know, but she's English all right and that's got to be unusual for here. These girls are mostly eastern European, and I feel slightly cheated. A bit of a let-down, if I'm honest. I was after some wild Russian pussy.

'How about we get these off?' She tugs at my jeans, trying to get them past my hips. I push up onto my elbows but the room is spinning like a carousel, my head tips and I fall back onto the bed with a *thwack*.

I feel her hand reach into my boxers.

'You like this?' she whispers, her voice now husky as she grabs hold of me. 'Tell me what turns you on.'

She touches me but I can't get hard. It's happening again. It's not just with Gemma.

She keeps going anyway, a smile fixed on her face, but I can't control my anger and frustration. I feel a surge of rage and sit up suddenly, knocking her off balance.

She scrambles to one side, eyeing me warily as I swing my legs off the bed, my jeans bunching around my ankles.

My fingers feel fat and useless and I fumble with the zip, leaving the buckle, my belt hanging loose as I stagger towards the exit.

'Hey, relax, mister.'

I lunge for the door but miss my step, grabbing onto a chair before I hit the deck. The feeling of humiliation intensifying.

'HEY! Where's my money?'

Stumbling the final metre to the door, I yank back the curtain onto the canal. Passers-by stop and stare, gawping at the spectacle behind the glass. A group of lads point and laugh. I give them the finger, but their cackles echo and I feel as impotent as I did five minutes ago.

'Get the fuck out of here, asshole!' she screams after me, but she can't keep the fear from her voice.

I glance back and she's wrapped the curtain around her body, clutching it to her with one hand while the other is gripping some sort of alarm. And that's my cue to bounce, before the Old Bill come. I can't be arrested, not again.

THE TIKTOK DETECTIVE – JAMIE

The ferry ride across to Amsterdam North is choppy.

A white-knuckle ride as I grip the steel railing to steady myself, gulping mouthfuls of cold air to stop the urge to chunder. The rolling waves are making my stomach flip over like a pancake and it's taking all my concentration not to lose my lunch to the deck.

A very long fifteen minutes later, I stagger off the ferry, following the stream of cyclists as they disperse and then disappear into the industrial estate. Tall windowless industrial units tower over me. There's a twenty-foot wall of graffiti running the length of a warehouse. In the distance are modern high-rise flats with wrap-around balconies promising views over the water with a poster saying *enquire now*.

I take a sharp left, retracing my steps, looking out for the familiar signposts. The boarded-up cafe. The homeless guy sleeping in a doorway. The charity shop whose window someone threw a brick at. I stop in front of the cracked glass, swaying. Backlit by the moon, my reflection is broken into pieces. The hood of my coat is tucked behind my shoulders. My hair sticks up at random angles. A strip of milk-white belly flab is on show above my belt, which swings around my hips like a serpent. I'll be honest – I've looked better.

Pulling my jumper down to cover my waist, I stagger on, leaning into the wind. Silence crowds around me as I move further and further away from the redevelopment, checking over my shoulder every now and then to make sure I'm not being followed.

It's eerily quiet out here in the city's wasteland, except for the creepy *ting ting* of a sign being smashed about in the wind. A final glance behind me and then I enter the deserted shipping yard.

It's a maze, with hundreds of multicoloured shipping containers stacked on top of each other like a game of Tetris. I scratch my head, trying to remember which way to go. I take a right, then immediately left, snaking through the industrial labyrinth. I stop, double back on myself and veer right instead.

It's creepy AF out here with the towering rows of containers blocking out the moon. The wind howls through the passageways, the corrugated-iron blocks rattle, they clang and tremble, threatening to avalanche down on me. I pick up the pace, tucking my face into my coat, driving my legs into the ground.

I carry on for another hundred metres or so, fixating on what's waiting for me at the other end. Not long now. Almost there.

Turning into the final wind tunnel, the briny smell of the sea rides the air. Hang on, what's that? I think I hear something coming from the other direction.

I slow down. Trying to listen in above the noise of the wind.

Swish swish.

A faint sound, behind me.

I hesitate before the next corner. Listening.

Swish.

The distinct sound of feet on wet gravel.

Oh fuck – someone's followed me.

I stop dead and twist around, peering into the darkness.

'Hello?'

Silence.

'Hello? Who's there?' I peer into the darkness. The moonlit night shifting and moving like a ghost dance. 'Come on, show yourself!' I blink and blink again, my vision blurring in and out of focus. It's as quiet as a grave-yard except for the haunting *ting ting* and clang of metal on metal.

I listen for sounds. But there's nothing.

Fucking hell, mate. I give my head a little shake. *You're getting paranoid. Pull yourself together, lad.*

Spitting out a glob of phlegm, I wipe my nose and plough on. *Nearly there.* Excitement kicks in my chest like a wild animal.

Number 2079, number 2079. I repeat the numbers like a football anthem, closing in on the shipping container like a heat-seeking missile. Red then orange then green then—

BINGO. A grin spreads as I stare at the yellow hunk of metal bookending the row. It's scratched to shit, covered in dents and colourful overlapping stickers. FRAGILE – LOL.

I stand taller, trying to get a handle on myself and control my growing excitement. I stare at the padlocked door, my body swaying as if I'm still on the ferry's deck. The brisk walk has done nothing to sober me up.

I fish out the keys from my pocket, only to let them slip through my fingers.

'Fuck's sake!' I bend over, but a sudden gust of wind sends me flying and I land hard on my elbow, the same arm those goons nearly snapped in two. My eyes water with the pain.

Now I'm really mad and frustrated. I stare at the padlock with determination, it takes all my concentration to insert the key. I probably shouldn't have come here like this, when I'm pissed out of my skull, but I couldn't keep away. How could I?

The padlock springs open. I toss it to the ground and let out a groan as I inch the corrugated iron door open. It squeals on its hinges like a pig in a slaughterhouse.

I shine my phone torch into the pool of black.

'Sorry I'm late,' I slur. A lazy grin on my face.

The light catches her. A tiny disembodied voice, from deep inside the container. A pair of glassy eyes staring back at me.

THE DAUGHTER – GEORGIE

'Where the bloody hell have you been?'

Jamie staggers towards me, kicking over an empty Coke can, shoving my sleeping bag to one side.

'WELL?' I demand.

He pulls a face, wobbling to a stop, and all my hairs stand on end. My entire being is instantly repulsed. This is not what we had planned.

'We have a problem. The torch battery's dead. There's no gas left for the heaters.' I rub at my arms. 'It's fucking freezing in here!' I narrow my eyes. 'I thought you were coming back with supplies?'

'I've been busy.'

'And I've run out of water.'

He belches.

For the love of God.

'Jamie, are you listening? I have no heating; no water. I'm literally dying of thirst.'

Swaying on the spot, his eyes begin to glaze over.

'Jamie?

'Yeah?'

'What was the hold-up? You've been gone for hours.'

'Said I was busy.'

I eye him warily. 'Doing what exactly?'

'Fuck's sake, you sound like my old man.'

Has he spoken to someone he shouldn't have? Has he given away too much information? I need to know everything, and immediately. His motormouth better not have landed us in trouble.

'Don't you trust me any more?'

I ignore his impertinent question. What the hell has got into him? This is not the affable Jamie Finn I knew just a week ago. All this TikTokking is clearly going to his head. Bathing in all the attention from my disappearance is feeding his enormous ego and I'm not certain that's a good thing. I need someone I can manage.

'Like I said, filming content.' He pulls another face, like I'm crazy for asking, but I don't believe him. I don't trust him an inch, not with the way he's staggering around, propping himself up against the side of the container. How did he let himself go so quickly? His jumper rides up, exposing that revolting belly of his. His eyes are half closed; a lazy smile fixed on his face. I feel a prickle of unease.

Oh, good God. What have I done?

He blinks, forcing his eyes open, and I notice that his flies are undone, his belt hanging loose. The stench of beer fills the confined space that's been my home for the past three days. I knew it – I should have listened to my gut, I knew he wouldn't be able to hold it together.

'Not my fault,' he says. 'It took forever to get here.'

'Well, this was your idea.' I look around in disgust.

'It was all we could afford, remember.'

'We could have got something better.'

'Nah, not out the way like this.' He grins. 'No one's gunna find you here, princess.'

Something spidery crawls down my neck. *Don't panic, keep calm and carry on.* It's too late to back out now, the wheels are in motion, things have gone too far. I've got to see this through. I scare away frightening thoughts by focusing on the end goal.

The GoFundMe money.

If you'd asked me twelve months ago whether I'd fake my own disappearance to rinse the public of their money, well, I would have laughed in your face. And I would have felt horrifically guilty committing such heinous fraud. But that was then, before everything changed. Before things got, well, a little desperate. And let me tell you, desperation makes you do the stupidest of things.

You see, wealthy socialite Georgie Taylor-Johnson is a facade. A performance I've been putting on. The truth is, my life in the fast lane has led to me developing an unhealthy relationship with recreational drugs. A dependency, if you like, and now I owe a few important people rather a lot of money. Fifty-two thousand pounds, to be precise, which is quite terrifying really. Especially knowing what's going to happen to me if I can't pay off my debt.

So there you have it. A fall from grace if ever there was one. But as I said, when you're desperate, you stop worrying about the little things and slip into survival mode, which is what I've been doing.

Surviving.

Just about.

And I'm utterly exhausted.

My eyes flick around the revolting space, reflecting on the process I went through to end up here. Because it was a process, starting with the disappearance of Elena Brookes. The public hysteria after she vanished on a night out while on holiday with her friends was what gave me the idea for my master plan.

Mystery and suspense – it's the cornerstone of every great work of fiction. Think Agatha Christie. She faked her disappearance – leaving her abandoned car by a chalk quarry.

The first rule of the Georgie Taylor-Johnson school of faking your disappearance: make it convincing.

Choose a seedy location abroad, known for its criminal underbelly, to make your disappearance plausible and drive conspiracy theories. Elena vanished in Ibiza; I've gone one better. Amsterdam.

Second rule. Single out a friend who you've not seen for years, who will know nothing of your downfall, your addictions and the eye-watering sums of money you owe to sketchy drug dealers. An old friend, living a sheltered life, who will vouch for you being a wonderful person and will appear devastated by your disappearance. Someone who will draw attention to your disappearance, who will do anything for your safe return. Enter silly, gullible Twiggy.

Next – choose a stage for the disappearance. A party that will create mystery and intrigue. A louche crowd that will leave open-ended questions. My connections really paid off here. Hearing about Schmidt's afterparty was a stroke of luck. Thank goodness I was able to talk my way in after they refused me an invite. I've still got it, no matter what they're saying about me.

Fourth rule. Make it dramatic. Leave confusion-slash-mystery surrounding your disappearance. This took some careful engineering.

Fifth rule. Switch to a burner phone so nobody can track your whereabouts. Leave passport and belongings at gullible friend's house. A suitcase containing designer outfits (a few items I hung onto to keep up appearances after pawning the rest for money). And, most importantly, leave behind a pouch full of medication. Diabetic Georgie will not be able to survive long without her insulin. Result – stakes increased.

Rule six. Spend weeks learning the plan inside out. There must be no holes. There can be no mistakes. The public must panic, seeing you as the next Elena. They must believe something truly awful has happened to you, so they will do anything for your safe return – i.e. contribute to a search fund. The sense of there being a race against time to find you is essential.

And finally. Pick an accomplice so desperate for fame he will do *anything* to fulfil his side of the arrangement. I look at Jamie, a useless hulk of a boy who I met while I was in rehab last winter.

He was patrolling the corridors at The Sanctuary, an eye-wateringly expensive clinic my father sent me to last year in a last-ditch effort to clean up my life and get me off the drugs. Almost without knowing it, I'd slipped into a dark place. All my partying and socializing and trying to keep up with the in-crowd had left me breathless and discombobulated and unaware that my white-powder habit and my grubbier crack cocaine smoking had got out of hand. It was a miracle I still looked OK on the outside when my insides were taking such a godawful battering.

Anyway, Jamie gave me an earful for wandering around after lights out and I rather liked that. Him telling me off. It was refreshing, and we started chatting immediately. Most of the things he said were nonsensical, unrefined, just like his appearance. A rough diamond, if you will. I could see he was attractive beneath the layers of scruff though, and he made me laugh. And I couldn't remember the last time I'd genuinely done that.

As the days dragged on, I looked forward to our little chats. We'd meet in the grounds and stroll around the estate, the chilly November cold a welcome relief from the overheated clinic rooms. I could tell he liked me, of course, which gave me a little boost of self-esteem when I was feeling particularly low, stuck in the countryside with nobody to talk to or flirt with.

But it was when Jamie started opening up about his TikTok sleuthing that I really began to pay attention. At first, I wondered if he was as troubled as some of the people I was stuck in The Sanctuary with. But no, he was a streetwise Londoner with a healthy dose of imagination and I could instantly see the potential to make money from filming true crime.

I filed the idea away and we stayed loosely in contact when I came home. My life was a million miles away from his. Outside our rehab bubble, we didn't have anything in common really.

Then Christmas Eve happened.

I'll never forgive my father for what he did.

And then my life really started to fall apart.

Slowly at first, but things quickly gathered pace, snowballing, and nine months later I was in rather a lot of trouble. I'd burnt my bridges with everyone who cared about me, and as it turned out, the bulk of my friendships had been superficial. I did tentatively reach out to Twig, but even she ignored my friend request. It was a rude wake-up call, realizing I had no one. Jamie had become the only person left I could turn to.

And together, inspired by Elena Brookes' genuine disappearance, we hatched a plan.

Although – I stare at him – I'm now wondering if I need to make a few adjustments to what we agreed.

He won't mess this up, he's too hungry for fame. Jamie will do anything to be a star. I calm myself.

Anything.

The word echoes and I try to breathe through the rising cloud of fear.

NOW

5 January

Inspector Van den Berg watches as they slowly winch the body out of the canal.

One jerky movement after the next. Limbs dangling and swinging from side to side like a rag doll. Water gushing down like a rainforest shower. Inspector Van den Berg lets out a sigh of relief that the child's witness statement was incorrect. She was dreading having to deal with a decapitation. At least now she has something to work with, so to speak, although she can't yet tell if it's *her*; the dive team are too far off to see properly.

A white forensic tent is being built by the water's edge. The officers behind her are speaking in low voices. Everyone's talking about Georgina Taylor-Johnson and it's putting her on edge because the inspector knows she's facing an absolute rollicking from her superiors for not taking the disappearance seriously enough.

Prickling with irritation, she turns suddenly, exploding on two officers standing nearby.

'I thought I told you to clear the area,' she snaps. 'The minute the podcasters and TikTokkers get their hands on this, our investigation is desecrated!' She looks up at the tall uneven houses lining the canal. The inquisitive faces pressed up against the windows. The glare of a phone screen catching the light.

It's impossible to stop them all. She's fighting a losing battle.

The light that used to burn so brightly inside her fades a little more.

'Inspector.' The officer who took the eyewitness report approaches. 'I think you'll want to see this.'

Inspector Van den Berg turns her back on the body and moves towards the street, the snow rushing at her horizontally.

'I spotted something under the car,' he says proudly. 'I didn't want to touch it in case it was evidence.'

She squints at the green Vauxhall Corsa, reluctant to remove her hands from her pockets where she's been keeping them warm. She lowers to one knee, groaning as she tilts her head to one side, ear scraping the cold ground. She peers beneath the undercarriage where the snow hasn't yet reached.

A mobile phone.

She looks back at a pair of hefty black boots.

'It's evidence. Bag it,' she instructs the officer waiting behind her.

Her hand ploughs into ice mush as she levers herself back to standing. A small twinge as she straightens. The inspector massages her lower back and makes a mental note to book an appointment with the chiropractor for later this week. Her body is starting to crack under all the added stress.

'You think it could belong to . . . ?' The officer stops,

glancing back at the police boat heading towards them with the body on board.

'Let's get this to the team for analysis immediately. Whatever is on that phone, I want to hear about it.'

THE FRIEND – BECCA

Do you really know Georgie? Her mother's words echo and I wake up with a start.

My heart is thumping and my head swimming in where I've just been. I dreamt it was summer and I was back at Waverley, and it takes a moment for my body to catch up with my brain, to pull the pieces of myself back together and reconnect with my bedroom. I reach a hand across the bed, relieved to find Nathan's warm body beside me. The faint whistle of his breathing breaks the cold hard silence.

Rolling over to the bedside table, I check my phone again. I kept it on all night in case Georgie got in touch, or the police, or anyone who might know something.

There's nothing.

I check my social media to see if anyone has replied to my plea for help.

Nothing.

Just a few teary-eyed emojis and hugs. Then I scroll back through Georgie's Instagram posts, opening and checking each one in turn to see if someone has left a new comment, searching her pictures for clues, searching her face for answers. Even though I've been here dozens of times over the past few days, I'm suddenly convinced the answer must lie there somewhere.

It doesn't.

Where are you, Georgie?

A groan from beside me. I glance across to where Nathan's stirring from his sleep. Poor Nathan, he looks exhausted. Dark circles beneath his eyes, puffy skin, a patch of angry red eczema on his neck that always flares up when he's stressed.

He rolls over to face me, his cheek marked with lines from the pillow. Cracking open his eyes, he blinks several times, as if he too is acclimatizing. I wonder what he was dreaming about.

'You're up,' he croaks.

'Sorry, did I wake you?'

'I need to get up anyway.' He stretches one foot out of the duvet. 'What time is it?'

'Six twenty-five.'

A heavy sigh. 'Only four hours' sleep. Kill me now.'

'Can't you have a lie-in? You're going to make yourself ill.'

'One more day and then it's over. Well, sort of.' He presses the heels of his hands over his eyes. 'Oh sweet Jesus, what have I signed up to?'

I don't know how to answer that and he props his head up on his hand and looks at me. 'What are you thinking?'

'What do you mean?'

He brushes the hair from my eyes, tapping my temple softly. Affectionately. 'I can hear the cogs turning.'

I smile. Relieved the storm between us has calmed a little. Then my smile falters as I remember my dream.

'I spoke to Georgie's mum.'

'O-kay. And, how did that go?' he says carefully.

'She thinks Georgie's faking it. That she's making the whole thing up for attention, which is crazy. I can't believe her mother would say something like that.' God, I feel guilty for voicing it, for breathing life into it.

Nathan looks back at me kindly; he's doing his best not to bring up Rami since our last fight. He's coming around to the idea that it's the TikTokker who's sabotaging our relationship for views. Things are a little better between us, and I need it to stay that way.

'I know her mum is a bitch, but still,' I go on. 'That's a despicable thing to say, even by her standards.'

He strokes my arm.

'Seriously, Nathan, you don't think she would be capable of something like that, do you? And why? It doesn't make sense. What would be the point? Her mum implied it would be over a guy, but Georgie gets enough attention as it is. Jesus, men fall over themselves to be with her.'

I feel a surprise lump in my throat. A twitch of jealousy at how life has come so easily to her. Georgie's never had to struggle or fight for anything. Resentment over the past rears its ugly head again. I close my eyes briefly, pushing it to the back of my thoughts, because in the past is where it should stay. Right now, finding Georgie is all that matters.

When I open my eyes, Nathan is still gazing at me, his expression unreadable. He's trying his best to be open-minded and I suddenly feel grateful for how fiercely loyal he's been over the years. He must be the only man not to have fallen under Georgie's spell, and I love him for that.

'Can you think of a reason she would fake her disappearance?' I ask tentatively.

Nathan continues to look at me, a silence sitting between us. Finally, he asks, 'Do you really want me to answer that?'

'Only if it doesn't cause an argument.'

'Well . . .' He shrugs. 'This is Georgie you're talking about. She always was a prick-tease – she lives for male attention. So yeah, I can see her doing something like this to wind a guy up.'

'OK.' I lower my gaze. 'Maybe we shouldn't talk about this.'

'You did ask.'

'I know I did . . .' I take a breath and thread my fingers through his. 'I know,' I say softly.

A flicker of doubt is creeping up on me now that Nathan's echoed what Georgie's mum said. I give myself a mental shake. There's no denying Georgie can be selfish, but she wouldn't have orchestrated something as calculated as her disappearance. I'm her friend, I would know. Wouldn't I?

Nathan seems to register the look of disappointment on my face.

'I'm sure she'll turn up soon,' he says soothingly.

I nod, swallowing the painful lump in my throat.

'Have you tried reaching out to her father? Could he help?'

'Georgie said they hadn't spoken in a long time.

Apparently, he's just had a child with his new wife. Poor Georgie, she must feel so forgotten about. Anyway . . .' I change the subject before I start crying. God, I *hate* how my default reaction is crying. 'How's it going at Muse? Are you all set for opening night?'

He blows air into his cheeks.

'It is going OK, isn't it?'

I think back to what Katya said. How the renovations had taken a backwards step. I feel a pinch of guilt at how little I've been there for Nathan. Is he struggling more than I realized?

He runs a hand through his hair and sighs. 'I can't believe the launch is tomorrow.'

'It's going to be brilliant. I'm so proud of you.'

He smiles but the smile doesn't reach his eyes.

'Can I help out?' I rub my thumb over his finger. 'Please. I want to be there.'

Even though I need to spend today looking for Georgie, I have to offer because I can see the stress in the way he's holding himself. His neck is stiff, his features are strained. The red patch of skin below his ear is flaring pink.

'I wish you would rest and feel better.'

'I'm not sick, you know.'

He plants a kiss on my nose.

'You're going through a lot. With Georgie and everything else . . . Just leave the rest to me.'

'But I want to be there for you.'

Nathan looks pleased. He kisses me again and then shrugs off the duvet, takes the dressing gown from the back of the door and wraps himself in it before disappearing into the bathroom. I hear him whistling a tune, and my heart lifts. Even in the face of adversity, my husband always has a way of brushing himself off and picking himself up. Like flicking a switch.

I think about Georgie again and wish I shared that superpower. Her disappearance has left me near paralysed. My thoughts are becoming darker and the more people suggest it's a hoax or nothing to worry about, the more I'm convinced otherwise.

People don't just vanish. You'd have to be a really twisted person to make up something like that.

THE TIKTOK DETECTIVE – JAMIE

'Jamie Finn, they're calling you the next Sherlock Holmes. How are you feeling about being the latest true crime TikTok sensation?'

'Yeah, I mean, it's nice and all, but being famous ain't why I'm doing this. I'm here to find Georgie.'

The Sky News reporter nods and smiles with admiration. 'The public are seeing you as something of a good Samaritan. Putting your neck on the line to find answers. What made you want to do that?'

'There're so many missing people out there in the world that get forgotten or overlooked, and when I heard about Georgie's disappearance, I just felt a connection, ya know? I knew I had to try to find her. The police ain't interested, so it was up to me to step up.'

'That's incredibly selfless of you, Jamie.'

I shrug. 'Nah, it's nothing really. Anyone else in my shoes would do the same.'

'And do you have any leads?'

I think about Georgie hiding out in the shipping container, about our scam, and put on my best sad face. 'Got a couple of theories I'm working on but' – I look directly into the camera – 'if there's anyone out there who knows something, please get in touch. Even if you don't think it's important . . .'

'Are you concerned for her safety?'

I chew on my lip and furrow my brow.

'Don't want to alarm anyone, but yeah, I'm really worried.'

'That's terrible. What do you think could have happened to Georgie?'

'Like I said, I don't want to speculate, but these theories my viewers are putting forward, well, there could be something in it.'

'How long are you planning on staying in Amsterdam?'

'As long as it takes. I ain't going home until I find her.'

'And what would you say to anyone who wants to follow in your footsteps? TikTok sleuthing is becoming increasingly popular – how do you feel about being at the forefront of an emerging trend?'

I shrug. 'Dunno really. Guess it shows you don't need no qualifications or a degree to do what you love. Get out there and start speaking your truth!'

'That's brilliant advice, Jamie. And how can people get in touch with you?'

'You can find me on TikTok at Crime_Tok_Detective for live crime analysis and on-the-ground live updates. Get in touch, people, love to hear from ya. Let's find Georgie and bring our girl home.'

I'm buzzing from my interview but reeling from my last convo with Georgie. I think she's about to mug me off because last night there was talk of moving the goalposts. Now she's saying it would be better if she stayed missing, cos that way the drug dealers she owes money to would give up looking for her.

Georgie's not happy with how much I've crowdfunded. It's not enough money. I'm tired of her games. I swear, there's no pleasing that woman. She wants to take her share and leg it. But that's not what we agreed. The whole point of faking her disappearance was so I could find her alive. Me, Jamie. The hero.

The double-crossing bitch.

We spent hours working on our story. The plan was to spin this out for another ten days, then I'm supposed to find her stumbling around the docklands close to death.

Sound good? I thought so. The police would think her drink was spiked at the afterparty. Georgie would tell them she couldn't remember much other than she was grabbed from behind, blindfolded, bundled into the back of a van and driven out of the city. She was held hostage in a dark basement by some eastern European gang who wore masks the whole time. They planned on selling her on to some sex traffickers in Belgium but got cold feet after seeing how much press she was getting, so they dumped her in the docklands instead, which is when I came along. An anonymous tip-off leads me to Georgie.

Not the most original of stories, admittedly, but nevertheless, convincing. I'd be crowned a hero for rescuing her and the coppers would have egg on their face.

Georgie even suggested I knock her about a bit, give her some bruises and suchlike to make the story more convincing. I told her I'm no wife beater, and that's the first time I saw her turn. And when I say turn, I mean she went batshit crazy, questioning my loyalty, said I'd never be famous because I'm weak and too afraid to take things to the next level. She said she'd give herself the bruises if I wasn't man enough. Then she pulled out a knife.

WTAF.

I swear, I've never seen so much blood. She cut open her arm and collected the blood in an ice cream tub and handed it to me. Like, what the fuck was I supposed to do with that? Then she came up with the idea of planting it in Schmidt's place, spattering it across the attic right before the live feed. Said it would drive the conspiracy theories.

I told her, that's one step too far. I could be arrested for murder! We settled on me carving some scratches and sketchy words into the floorboards instead.

Man enough? What the fuck is she on about? It was me who risked everything, breaking into the house. It's all been me – there would be no money if it weren't for my videos and my sleuthing. Georgie's confused about who has the power. She's forgetting who the star of the show is. *Me*. I'm the hero of the story. And I'll throw her to the wolves if it suits me.

You know what? I'm fucking fuming.

The more I think about it, the more wound up I'm getting. I don't know what I ever saw in that stuck-up bitch. Yeah, OK, maybe I did fancy her when we first met – I mean, who wouldn't; she's fit and has this sexy thing going on, the way she tosses her hair and looks at you with those fuck-me eyes and speaks all posh like. I always thought she was out of my league, but after last night, forget it. She looked filthy, and not in a good way. Even though I like a dirty bird, seeing her like that was a huge turn-off. I had her down as girlfriend material, but now, I can't wait to get rid of her. I've worked out who she really is – how she uses people.

Just look at how she treats her so-called bezzie, Becca. Poor girl. Georgie didn't hesitate to throw her under the bus, and now Becca's having a breakdown, blaming herself for what happened that night. That's cold, even by my standards. Reckon I should ease off a bit, give the girl a break. I'm not a monster, ya know.

Georgie better not destroy our plans, because if she does, I won't be held responsible.

I glance down; my hands have rolled into fists without me even knowing it. I've got a short fuse; I've been done for GBH on top of the other stuff I was nicked for, so it's no secret – I can't control my anger. Fighting my way out of corners, it's all I've ever known. So Georgie needs to understand, there is no change of plan. I've got my nan to look after. I've been working up to this moment for years. Fucking YEARS. I'm not going back to being invisible Jamie. Becoming a world-famous detective is all I've ever dreamt of and there ain't nothing I won't do to anyone who stands in my way.

Nothing.

THE DAUGHTER – GEORGIE

I'm itching to switch on my phone, I'm never been without it for very long. I'm desperate to know if he's been in contact.

Sitting alone in the dark gives you a lot of time to reflect and unfortunately all I've been able to think about is last Christmas and how I ended up in this rather pitiful situation. I blame him entirely. My father, that is. Dear Papa. He really showed his true colours that night.

It was Christmas Eve. 'Deck the halls with boughs of holly, fa-la-la-la-la, la-la-la,' I quietly hummed to myself as we drove away from that lunatic asylum of a drug re-habilitation centre. Calling itself The Sanctuary – ha! It was anything but that with its overheated rooms and their flat-pack furniture and their nauseating group bonding sessions. Good God, I got backache sleeping on the cheap mattress. I suppose the location was OK, a Georgian house nestled in the heart of a sprawling estate. And I did enjoy strolling around the grounds with Jamie, but that was about it. The rest was *hell*.

The only reason I agreed to go there was because Papa

had given me an ultimatum, or rather, his new wife – Mummy's much younger replacement – Verity, had told him it was either *her* or *me* if I didn't stop using and drinking. I could see the spell she'd cast over him – she has Papa wrapped around her finger – and I couldn't risk losing him to her.

I must admit, I did feel an awful lot better after going six weeks without booze and drugs. My skin had improved dramatically, I had my glow back. I looked fresh-faced, at least four years younger and, best of all, Papa was pleased. He had that proud look in his eye, which I hadn't seen for the best part of a decade, since being sucked into my Chelsea party vortex.

'Deck the halls with boughs of holly . . .' Ah, I really did intend to stay clean and put my best foot forward. There was even talk of me finding a job of sorts, away from social media and events – and I was certainly warming up to the idea of a digital detox.

But things quickly went downhill after we arrived home. I say home, but it was really Papa's love nest with a woman young enough to be my sister. As soon as I stepped through the door of their mock mansion, Verity rolled her eyes at me and then proceeded to drape herself like a wet rag over Papa's shoulder in a blatant exhibition of ownership.

That was the first trigger.

And then, as I was unpacking my suitcase in my so-called bedroom, which felt as cold and unfriendly as a night in a hotel, Papa knocked on the door with a strained expression. Instantly, I knew whatever he was planning to lecture me about was Verity's doing. He'd become a mouthpiece for that vulgar *child* who was clearly only with Papa for his money. I'm not sure which school of witchcraft she was attending but he'd become enslaved to her, unrecognizable.

I wanted to shake him, to scream: *Wake up!* I felt frustrated, hurt and angry all at the same time as he reeled off a list of new *house rules*, as if he had been lobotomized and someone was speaking directions in his ear. The flat in Chelsea was to be sold. I was to remove myself from my friendship circles. Verity had a terrific recommendation for a Pilates and wellness coach who would help me turn around my life. My allowance was to be reduced. Significantly reduced. Under no circumstances was I to return to drugs, even for medicinal purposes. And if I brought them to his door, he would cut me off altogether.

'We're doing this with your best interests at heart, Sparkles,' Papa said to me while the rage quietly swelled inside my chest.

They were treating me like a child again, at twenty-nine years of age. My entire social life was about to be obliterated, but that wasn't to be the final trigger.

'We have some news,' Papa said sheepishly. 'Verity is desperate to become a mother and so we've decided to try for a baby.'

'Sorry, what?' I shook my head in bewilderment. 'But you're nearly sixty!'

'You'll have a little baby sister or brother. Won't that be wonderful?' He smiled. Then, looking at me critically, he added: 'I never thought it was a good idea you were an only child – that was your mother's doing.'

Boooom.

It felt like my heart had detonated inside my chest. My insides instantly turned to mush.

'I'll leave you to get unpacked.' And with that, Papa retreated, closing the door quietly behind him.

It didn't take long for me to locate the little pouch of white powder I'd hoarded away for a rainy day. Hidden at the bottom of the cupboard in one of my designer shoeboxes. *Silly Verity forgot to look there.* I smiled triumphantly as I gave it a shake, my eyes feasting on the contents. Within seconds I'd gone from feeling satiated to ravenous. I felt like I hadn't had a proper meal in weeks and I tore open the bag, tipping the entire contents onto my dressing table.

I used Papa's now redundant credit card to cut the cocaine into lines, the whole while thinking about what this baby meant for me. I already felt invisible; a baby would create an even bigger gulf between us. I'd become irrelevant. Obsolete. I bet he wouldn't even notice if I disappeared.

Recentring, I focused on what would make me feel better. Briefly catching myself in the mirror before diving my head down to meet the neatly drawn lines of white powder.

I inhaled sharply.

The hit of ecstasy was instantaneous.

Six weeks off drugs made it feel even more magnificent. This could become a thing – depriving oneself to reach a greater high. I giggled to myself, and that's when I felt it. Someone was in the room with me. I could feel their eyes drilling into the back of my skull. Slowly, I turned around to face my future. I'll never forget the look of disappointment on my father's face. The corners of his mouth were pulled down with sadness.

'Where did I go wrong?' he whimpered. 'I should never have bought you the flat in Chelsea. Too much too young, everything handed to you on a plate – you never learnt to fight for anything.' He shook his head. 'You never learnt the value of anything.'

I dabbed my nose, wiping the powder away.

He was glaring at me now. 'That horse, what was his name again? The one you begged and begged for, for your tenth birthday. How many times did you ride him before you got bored? Three times? And then he was discarded, like all your other toys.'

'Oh come on!' I rolled my eyes at him. The only reason he bought me those things was to make himself feel better for abandoning us.

'Where did I go wrong?' he quietly echoed.

Eugh. His pathetic diatribe was making me nauseous. Self-pitying arsehole. After the number of times he cheated on Mummy, how dare *he* lecture *me* about where I went wrong.

'Mummy was right about you!' I spewed at him. 'You do realize Verity's only with you for your money? Why else would someone in their right mind want to marry you?' A crooked smile. 'I suppose that makes Verity no better than a prostitute.'

Booom.

His features darkened. I'd seen that look before, when

he would lash out at Mummy during one of their explosive drunken rows, but he'd never ever directed it towards me. I was always his angel. His *Sparkles*.

It all happened so quickly, the speed with which he raised his hand and slammed it across my face. It felt like a kettle full of boiling water had been poured across my cheek. I held the side of my face, my entire body feeling as if it was on fire, while Papa looked at me in astonishment.

We stared at one another for what felt like an eternity, neither of us knowing what to say.

Then I grabbed my things and I left, knowing I'd never be back. I'd never accept *anything* from him again because everything my father touches turns to shit. Even if he offered me a million pounds. Even if I was destitute. Even if I entered into an arrangement with a deranged TikTokker that made me feel like I was being kept in a dungeon.

I look around the cramped shipping container littered with empty ready meal cartons and bottles and drink cans and I break into laughter. A delirious desperate laugh, and I feel the tension of the past few days lifting instantly. I should laugh more. When did life get so bloody serious? I glance at the needle marks on my arms and my heart sinks. That's when.

THE TIKTOK DETECTIVE – JAMIE

It's 1.45 a.m. and deathly quiet, like a town shut down for winter.

I've been hanging around outside Schmidt's place. Nah, not the party house, his other place. Turns out he owns five more canal houses plus a dozen properties around Europe – Belgium, Germany, Switzerland. And then there's the ski lodges in Val d'Isère and the holiday homes in the Caribbean which he rents out to Russian oligarchs for eye-watering amounts. How the other half live, eh. And going by how his boys roughed me up for snooping, it doesn't take a genius to work out that most of it's funded through illegal income streams.

If I were a betting man, I'd say Schmidt's using his gallery and connections to clean dirty money. Works by famous artists sell for millions on the open market, making it easy to clean substantial amounts of dirty cash in one go. And the seller can make up whatever price he fancies because art's wanky and subjective like that. Hundred to one that's why Schmidt did his nut in when I poked my nose around his business.

Unless – I squint through the whirling snowflakes – I'm barking up the wrong tree and he's involved with something else entirely.

Whatever criminal activity he's up to, I'm not getting any content from freezing my balls off out here. There's been no movement for the past hour, nothing that will drive the conspiracy theories. He's probably sleeping, which is what I should be doing too. I'd be better off back at the hotel plotting my next move. I'll bring Georgie what she needs in the morning. Whatever it is, it can wait, I can't be doing with another argument, not on this hangover. Jesus, my mouth's still as rough as sandpaper and my head feels like someone's stuck an axe through it.

I stifle a yawn and start making my way back towards the red-light district. It's about a twenty-five-minute walk from where I am in the Jordaan – that's the posh part, for anyone who's scratching their head wondering. If I take the back streets, I might be able to cut that down by a third.

The snow is seeping into my trainers, making a sick squelching noise. I zip up my coat and lean into the wind, the icy air stinging my lungs. I slow, holding a hand to protect my face from the onslaught of snow. Is it straight ahead or do I turn right?

There's a neon sign up ahead – *Euphoria* – and it's open twenty-four hours. Fuck it, I could do with warming up and then I'll be on my way.

I walk down the concrete steps into the underground coffee shop where a guy with a bird's nest hairdo and chunky framed glasses nods to welcome me. I browse the menu, choosing something strong to get me to sleep, and then I change my mind about heading back to the hotel, might as well have a quick hit while I'm here.

It's dark and gloomy inside, the walls are painted black giving off dungeon vibes, and it's deserted except for a few stragglers and insomniacs like me. A woman with dreadlocks down to her waist peers at me through a cloud of smoke. I overhear a couple of Americans in the corner chatting shit. I head towards the back, sliding into a leather booth that smells of old socks and weed, and get to work on rolling a joint.

Placing my mobile on the table, I watch it flash like a disco ball with notifications. I scroll lazily through the latest conspiracy theories: same sort of crap I've been getting all week. I can't be arsed to read them tonight. Pushing the phone away, I sit back heavily and take a drag on my joint, the first go hitting me like a punch to the chest.

Oooff, that's strong, I almost cough up my lungs. But I immediately go back for more and it doesn't take long for the euphoria to kick in. Soon I'm feeling light-headed and relaxed and not giving a fuck about anything.

My phone blinks with new alerts and I stare at the screen numbly. Thoughts, coming and going like trains at a station. I take another drag and, as the smoke clears, I notice something out of the ordinary.

Someone's sent me a video.

Hello. What's this? My curiosity spikes.

I swipe it open. It's from some bird called Maria. She's fit. I sit up, wondering if this could be my lucky night. A fan who's sent me a filthy video? Then comes the message:

Hi Jamie. I was about to send this to the police but after watching you on the news I knew you'd be able to help. #FINDGEORGIE.

Instinctively I look over my shoulder because this feels like something I need to keep secret. The woman with the dreadlocks stares back at me, unblinking. Has she been watching me this entire time? I feel a prick of heat on my neck and return to my phone but within seconds the sensation is back.

I snap my head around. This time, I catch the eye of the guy selling weed. The American in the corner peers at me under his baseball cap then whispers to his mate. Jesus, why's everyone watching me?

Deep breath. Keep your shit together.

I stub out my joint; probably best I ease off, I tell myself, remembering the last time I got high and paranoid and imagined people were following me home. That night ended with a punch-up in the street, five hours in A&E and seven stitches sewing my cheek back together.

So yeah, back to that video.

I press play and I'm immediately pulled into a room gloomier than the one I'm in. Everything's steeped in darkness, it's impossible to work out what's what. I squint, peering at the grainy footage, watching shapes move about, the silhouettes of people outlined by candlelight. I can't be certain, but it looks like a party of some sort.

I skip forward until I'm peering into a room with high ceilings, jam-packed with people partying hard. Anorexic-looking birds quaffing champagne and snorting coke off sideboards. Hang on – I recognize this place.

The penny drops. It's Schmidt's gaff. It's the afterparty.

But whoever this girl behind the camera is, she's making me feel like I'm in *The Blair Witch Project*. She's swinging her phone around like a trapeze artist and I'm getting motion sickness, especially with my hangover. Thankfully, one of her mates takes it out of her hand as they group together for a selfie.

But it's not the birds I'm eyeing up.

My eyes are drawn to the flash of movement in the background. A blink-and-you'd-miss-it moment. I rewind a few frames.

Play.

Nah – come on, that can't be right.

Stop. Rewind. Play.

But it is right, I'm not imagining it. And I recognize her immediately.

Again. *Stop. Rewind. Play.*

My eyes are pulled into the screen, while my arteries flood with adrenaline. I feel as dizzy as a junkie who's had a hit of heroin.

I look up, staring into the middle distance.

Shit.

Who would have thought it, hey? My heart's thumping against my ribcage, excitement breaking into every part of my broken, hungover body.

Because this is the plot twist that's gunna make my name.

Shrugging off my tiredness, I grab my gear and head back into the cold.

I need to record a video ASAP, get Maria's witness

footage uploaded, along with my expert analysis. I can already imagine the speculation that'll feed off this. The fresh conspiracies that the armchair detectives will be spinning in the chat groups.

This will probably ruin her life, no doubt about it, but what can I do? There're always casualties when you enter a profession like this, and if I allow myself to get bogged down in shame and guilt, how will I ever rise to stardom? I replace her face in my thoughts with Nan's, imagining the life I'll be able to afford for *her*. A new home, somewhere warm and safe, where she'll have a carer who'll check in on her.

Don't let them put me into a home. Promise me, love.
I promise, Nan.

Picking up the pace, I fight against the shrieking wind and the cold. The snow's seeping into my trainers, turning my toes into blocks of ice. Weather reports said the canals would freeze over tonight and I imagine how different the city will look in the morning, a winter wonderland filled with ice skaters.

But right now – with nobody around and the snow in my face, it's creepy as fuck.

A quick glance over my shoulder, because I'm getting that weird sensation again – as if someone's following me. Jeez, that guy wasn't kidding about his gear being strong. Hopefully the paranoia will wear off soon because I can do without a bad trip. I need to stay focused.

Crossing over a bridge I head onto the Brouwersgracht, where it's even quieter, but it will shave off a few minutes. As I walk, my hot breath mists in front of me like a steam train.

I'm halfway along the canal when I feel it again.

I spin around, stand stock-still, ears pricked, listening. My eyes skim along the buildings, searching between the parked cars. A dog barks in the distance and I nearly jump out of my skin.

'Fuck's sake!' I mutter, cursing myself for getting so stoned. I turn and carry on, but in no time the paranoia is back with a vengeance and I'm imagining I can hear footsteps. The muted *squeak squeak* of someone creeping up on me.

I turn sharply.

'Who's there?'

Holding my hand up, I struggle to see through the onslaught of snow.

'Come on,' I growl, squinting to make out if that's the shape of a person behind a BMW. 'Show yourself, ya pussy!'

Silence.

Nothing. Ha, I could have sworn someone was there. No more weed for you, Jamie.

I'm about to move off when the sound starts up again. Only much closer this time. The crunch of snow under a boot and from out of the darkness emerges a figure. It takes me a few seconds to work out who it is.

'Oh, it's you,' I sigh. 'What do you want?' The tension easing.

Silence.

My gaze drops to their hand and I blink. The whoosh of excitement I felt earlier suddenly turns to fear.

THE DAUGHTER – GEORGIE

'Jamie?'

The noise starts up again. The sound of footsteps, pacing back and forth.

'Jamie?'

What on God's earth is he doing? Just open the door, for heaven's sake, I'm dying of thirst. Things are not going my way. The GoFundMe money isn't nearly enough to pay off my debt. Jamie's drinking is out of control and threatening to ruin our plans. He needs to remember, *I'm* the one in charge. All I need to do is tell the police he's behind the kidnapping. That *he* held me hostage. Just take a look at my bruises. Who will they believe? Me, of course. But even more disappointing is my father. Why hasn't he shown any interest in my disappearance? I wanted him to suffer. To teach him a lesson for hitting me. I wanted Papa to be riddled with guilt. I suppose he's too preoccupied with Verity and with making money to even notice. Some things never change. I should have known he wouldn't give a shit.

I pick up the empty bottle of water, crush it in my hand and throw it to the other side of the container.

The footsteps stop.

Silence.

I hesitate. 'Jamie?'

A weighted silence.

Someone is there, just outside. But what are they doing?

The noise starts up again and I listen carefully, because I'm feeling a little uncertain. Jamie's clumsy. A great hulk of a boy. Whoever this is, is lighter on their feet, nimbler.

And now a new noise. The clunk of the padlock being moved around. The scrape of a key in a lock. Then, the drawn-out groan of the door being winched open. The hinge squeals and my pulse trips up.

More silence.

My heart leaps into my throat when light spills inside.

A dark figure steps into the container. Dressed head to toe in black, a balaclava hiding their face, a torch in one hand, a three-inch serrated knife in the other.

'Jamie?' I squeak.

THE FRIEND – BECCA

What have I done?

I'm morphing into an entirely different person. It's like there's two of me and I have no idea which Becca I'm going to meet in the mirror next.

But strangely, I feel better. A weight has been lifted. A release. Maybe I can get to sleep now. I'd do anything to be able to fall asleep.

I turn the key, the front door whines and I feel the muscles around my neck seize up. I hold my breath, wait a few seconds, then inch it open, slipping into the hallway like a thief in the night.

The heating went off five hours ago, it's so cold in the flat I can see small puffs of my own breath. I leave my boots by the welcome mat and hang up my coat next to Nathan's. My fingers are white from the knuckles and I can't even feel my toes, they're so numb from being outside in the cold.

I turn up the thermostat to 22 degrees, the faint hum of the boiler kicking in breaks the eerie silence. Placing my keys in the ceramic bowl and my handbag on the kitchen table, I cross over to the worktop where I notice Nathan's half-eaten midnight snack. I take a bite out of the cold pizza, tidy the rest away into the fridge and then pour myself a glass of water, downing it quickly. I rinse the glass, place it upside down on the draining board and then I creep towards the bedroom, the LED motion sensors in the skirting board lighting up the strip of hallway like an airport runway.

God, I'm so exhausted I feel like I've flown in on the red-eye.

Blinking away tiredness, I move silently from one side of the bedroom to the other, anxiously glancing over in Nathan's direction to make sure I don't wake him. He stirs, letting out a small groan, and then rolls over, hugging the duvet into his chest. I wait for him to start snoring again before making my move. I lock myself inside the bathroom and breathe out a sigh of relief.

Now I know he's fast asleep, I run the shower and strip off. I'm desperate to wash the night off me.

The hot water stings like a burn but within seconds my body adjusts and I close my eyes and tilt my head back, welcoming the sensation, the heat slowly bringing me to life. I stay in the shower for longer than I should and when I finally get out, the bathroom is thick with condensation and the mirror has steamed up. I have to rub a hole to find myself but when I do, I'm horrified by my reflection.

I look like I've been in hospital for weeks. Pale, chapped lips; my face has become gaunt in such a short time. I quickly turn my back on who I've become, reaching for a towel. Once I've rough-dried my hair, I tiptoe into the bedroom, lift up the corner of the duvet and, without making a sound, slip beneath the covers. Ordinarily I'd reach out for Nathan, I'd wrap my arms around him, I'd hug his back or thread my fingers through his, desperate to feel his skin on mine, but tonight I don't want to be close. Tonight, I watch from a distance, noticing his eyeballs flicker and his lip twitch. He must be dreaming. I wonder if he noticed I was gone?

Rolling over to the bedside table, I plug in my phone to charge. The screen lights up, reminding me how it's the next day already. It's 4.47 a.m.

NOW

5 January

It doesn't matter how many dead bodies she's seen over the years; it never gets easier.

In fact, it's becoming more difficult. There's no such thing as desensitization, not in her experience, anyway. Inspector Van den Berg steels herself as she boards the police boat. Two forensic officers follow closely behind carrying a metal stretcher. They set it down at the far end of the deck next to the body, which is hidden under a protective sheet.

It's the British girl. It has to be.

Discovered not far from where she was last seen alive.

'It's her, isn't it?' she asks one of the divers who helped winch the corpse from the water.

He stands back, making room for the inspector as she approaches the mound beneath the navy-blue tarpaulin sheet. She lowers herself, crouching beside the body, her nostrils filling with the stench of stale canal water.

The inspector shivers as an icy breeze whistles past. The snow continues to fall relentlessly, pausing for no one, not even for the dead.

It's now or never.

She grabs hold of the sheet, breathes in hard and

folds back the corner, revealing what's left of the victim's face.

Mouth gaping.

Eyes frozen wide open in a milky death stare.

NOW

THE FRIEND – BECCA

It seems like it was only yesterday Georgie and I were getting ready to go out, that I was rifling through my cupboard, searching for something to wear.

Nathan's anxiously watching the clock, doing his best to hide his frustration, while Georgie's voice rings in my ear. *'Not that one, Twiggy, for goodness' sake. Stop hiding yourself.'* In the end, I pick out the red dress she gave me on New Year's Eve – as if wearing it will somehow bring her closer to me.

Twenty minutes later and we're in an Uber, crossing Amsterdam. Nathan's staring at the road ahead, lost in thought, while I'm doing my best to hide my exhaustion. I stifle a yawn, realizing I'm very tired, which makes sense considering I barely slept last night. I shouldn't have gone out, that was a mistake.

I pack away my guilt and concentrate on putting on a performance for tonight. Which is difficult since I've spent most of the day crying. Every half an hour or so I've been hit with a tidal wave of despair and before I know it, I'm in a heap, sobbing. It's opening night, I'm meant to be sparkling with happiness, so what's wrong with me?

I'm struggling to process my feelings. I can't get Georgie out of my head. From what I can see, the police have lost all interest and her parents don't care, so it feels like the pressure is on me to do something. That I'm her only friend. That I'm the only person who cares about her. But I'm crumbling by the minute.

Biting down on my rising anxiety, I pull out my compact mirror and reapply my red lipstick – the one Georgie picked out for me. But my hand is shaky, I'm making a meal out of it, so I fish out a tissue and rub it all off. By the time I'm finished, my lips feel bruised and the tissue looks like it's stained with blood.

I take a shuddering breath, and another, as we pull up outside the restaurant. The dark sky is lit up with spot-lights, there's a red carpet with VIP rope strung between brass stanchions and a line of very beautiful people queuing around the corner. It's as glamorous as the Oscars. A woman with a clipboard is manning the door, checking names off a guest list, and I notice the disappointed faces of people being turned away.

What resembled a building site only a couple of days ago has transformed into something you'd see in the pages of a society magazine. I don't tell Nathan nearly often enough how proud I am of him. I'm speechless, in fact. He must have worked miracles to get the investors to come around because this would have cost a small fortune to pull off.

'Nathan!' I let out a gasp. 'This is unreal, how did you—'

He looks back at me nervously.

'Fuck, fuck, I hope it goes OK tonight.' He blows out a quick breath, appearing far too stressed. 'If anything goes wrong . . .'

'Why would it go wrong?'

He presses his palms against his eyes and for a split second I think he's about to cry, which is making me want to cry again.

'Brad Garcia has flown in from New York; he's investing over a million in Muse and . . . a lot is riding on this, nothing can go wrong, that's all.'

I pull his hands away and kiss them, because it feels like he's on the verge of a breakdown. Where is this coming from?

He looks worried and confused, and it's making me feel confused. Nathan shakes his head. 'Forget what I said, it's a done deal, I'm just panicking. It's Dad – I can hear his voice in my head, criticizing me, and it's not helping.'

'Forget your dad, this is about you.'

He kisses my hand. 'I know, I know, you're right. This is a new chapter, for both of us.' His face fills with fresh determination. 'Come on, let's do this.' He suddenly opens the door and springs out of the car. Cold air swoops in where he's just been. It's a clear night, just like on New Year's Eve. Nathan holds the door open for me; I grab his hand tightly, as if my life depended on it, and I step into the bright strobing light.

There's a swarm of photographers crowding around the entrance, taking photos of people posing against a wall of flowers with the word *Muse* looped in electric blue lighting. Mostly influencers, local celebrities and food critics. Smiling. Pouting. Then I hear someone shout out my name.

'Becca!'

I'm hit with a blinding light.

'Over here, Becca. It's Willem de Koning from the *NL Times*.'

Flashbulbs – all going off at the same time.

'Becca, did you kill Georgie?'

I turn my head sharply.

'Was it you?' The photographer's voice lifts with excitement. 'Did you murder your best friend?'

SNAP. SNAP. SNAP.

I'm momentarily blinded, the flash bleaching out the night, and for the briefest of moments it feels like I'm reliving the nightmare of being drugged. The fear, the confusion, until Nathan steps out in front of me. He shoves the photographer to one side, points a finger in his face. 'Do that again, mate, and you won't be able to hold that camera.'

I'm taken aback. I've never seen Nathan behave this way, with such violence. He's usually even-tempered, never raises his voice. But once I've gotten over the shock, I'm flooded with affection for him and grateful he's here protecting me. I'm not sure I could manage alone.

'I'll call security. Wait here.'

'Nathan, I feel sick,' I whisper.

'What are they expecting us to say? It's not like we know anything.'

'I'm going to be sick.'

'Did he hurt you?' He cradles my hand, holding me

upright. 'It's going to be OK, ignore him, he's trying to provoke a reaction.'

'Why are they saying I killed Georgie?' My voice rises in pitch. 'She's not dead!'

Nathan turns abruptly, peering down at me, his eyes creased with concern. 'Becca, I need you to focus.' He lowers his voice. 'Listen, we'll deal with it once this is over. I promise, we can figure this out together, but right now' – he sucks air into his cheeks – 'right now, I need your help to get us through tonight.'

It pains me to see him like this – begging me to be there for him on the most important night of his life. I feel wretched, I have never disliked myself more than I do right now. And when this is over, I want Nathan to know how sorry I am for letting him down.

'OK.' I nod weakly. 'You can count on me.' Even though my head is spinning and the thought of putting on a smile feels insurmountable, I look out into the crowded restaurant.

'Oh Jesus, he's here.' Nathan turns abruptly, pulling me along in a new direction. I peer over his shoulder at the man standing alone at the bar. It's Dean, Nathan's dad.

'I can't deal with him right now,' Nathan says.

'Why did you invite him?'

'What choice did I have?'

'You *always* have a choice.'

'He's here to gloat, I can tell.' Nathan scratches his brow nervously.

'He doesn't deserve an invite, not after the way he treated you.'

Nathan's eyes are on my face but I can tell he's not really listening to what I'm saying. What's eating him tonight? Is he worrying about what his dad thinks? Even after everything Nathan's achieved, is he still seeking Dean's approval? It's heartbreaking to watch.

'Be yourself, you've got nothing to prove . . .'

'Teagan and Mark, glad you could make it!' Nathan lets go of my hand to greet a couple I don't recognize and I find myself suddenly alone in a room full of people. I straighten out my dress and cross my arms, unsure where I should stand or what I should be doing. I feel like a spare part, which is ridiculous considering this is as important a celebration for me as it is for Nathan. When did I become so small and insignificant? I grab a glass of champagne from a passing waitress, even though I promised myself I wouldn't drink again, not after what happened last night.

'That dress looks great on you, love.'

I wheel around, startled.

'Hiya, love. How've you been?'

'You made it OK then?' I force out a smile for Dean and search for Nathan. But my husband has drifted towards the corner of the dining area, where he's lost in conversation with Katya.

'How's about this,' Dean lets out a low whistle, scanning the room. 'My boy's all grown up, hey.'

'It's incredible, isn't it?'

He scratches his stubble absently but says nothing. Dressed down in jeans and a jumper, he's barely made any effort. I bet he can't stand that Muse outshines his pub in every way and that Nathan made it happen without his help. I glance back at Nathan and my chest tightens at the sight of Katya playing with her hair while laughing flirtatiously.

'So Nathan says you've been through the wringer.'

'The wringer?' I frown, dragging my gaze back to Dean.

'With that girl from Waverley Hall. What's her name again?'

'Georgie.'

'That's it. *Georgie*,' he echoes. 'Didn't realize you two were still mates.'

'Of course we're still friends,' I say defensively.

'Is that so.' He gives me a strange look. 'And now she's missing?'

'Since New Year's Eve. But you probably already knew that?' I say more sharply than I intended, and Dean blinks at me in surprise.

'What are the police saying?'

'The police are a waste of time,' I murmur. 'I've been doing everything—'

'Poor girl, growing up with parents like that,' he interrupts. 'It's bound to mess you up. Turn you into a bit of a wrong'un.'

'She's not messed up.'

'If you say so, love.'

'She's missing!'

'OK, calm down. It was just an observation.'

'And I'm the only one who seems to give a shit.'

His brow wrinkles. A silence slides between us as he studies me intently.

'It's a lot of responsibility, running a restaurant.' He changes the subject. 'A shedload of hidden costs, things you wouldn't even think about. Nathan should have come to me for advice.'

'Nathan's doing a great job,' I say protectively, feeling triggered again.

Dean's eyes flash. 'All the same, it wouldn't have hurt him to reach out to his old man. I could've taught him a thing or two.' He drains the last of what's in his glass. 'You look after my boy. He needs a strong woman by his side now he's taken this on.' He looks at me in a way to suggest he thinks I don't fit the bill. 'Anyway, I'll be over there if anyone needs me.' He gestures towards the bar. 'Good to see you, love.'

And then I'm alone again, feeling even more unsettled than I did five minutes ago. Why does everyone have it in for Georgie? Dean's wrong about her. I frown. Isn't he? I have that cold creeping feeling again. I search for Nathan but he's disappeared and so has Katya. I finish off my drink and immediately replace it with another.

THE FRIEND – BECCA

The room hushes to a silence and Nathan clears his throat.

He smiles nervously at his audience. Family, friends, investors, reviewers. Everyone who is anyone in the restaurant business has turned up for the launch, and I feel nervous for him. I take another sip of my drink; it slips down my throat far too easily. I'm self-medicating with alcohol. I'm on my fourth already and everything's feeling a little hazy. A little numb. A touch more bearable.

'Thank you all for being here tonight. I know some of you have travelled a long way.' Nathan looks to his father. I hear the catch in his voice, the emotion spilling over. His eyes find mine and I smile encouragingly.

'As many of you know, this has been a journey. I still can't quite believe what began as a few sketches in a notepad has blossomed into something beyond my wildest dreams. But I couldn't have done it alone. It's with the help of so many of you here tonight that we've been able to make it happen, so thank you.' Nathan sweeps his gaze across the sea of faces. 'Thank you from the bottom of my heart.'

A sound. Coming from the back of the restaurant.

The doors slide open, the noise of the city breaking in. The interruption makes Nathan stumble over his words. He clears his throat, replaces his smile while I peer around to see who's been so inconsiderate to arrive this late.

I'm too far away on the other side of the room to see. The air is thick with heat and cooking smells. While Nathan continues to explain the inspiration behind Muse, my mind drifts, returning to New Year's Eve, because there's something about that night I'm missing, something vital.

I close my eyes as if that might shut down my obsessive thoughts and when I open them, I feel more drunk than I was before. Someone next to me whispers to her partner; I catch both of them staring and my cheeks heat up with shame.

I look behind me and this time I see something. A flash of movement. A face I recognize.

What is *she* doing here?

Inspector Van den Berg whispers something to the officer she's arrived with. They linger at the back of the room, their eyes scanning the crowd.

What are they doing here so late at night? That can't be a good sign. Oh God, they've found Georgie. I feel my stomach sink to the floor. I look back at my husband anxiously.

Katya's moved to be by his side. They're sharing the microphone. They're sharing a joke. Everyone's laughing, but the only sound passing in and out of my ears is a whooshing noise, much like a raging wind in a storm. And now the room is collapsing. It's the champagne, of course. It's really not helping that I've had so many glasses.

I turn towards Nathan in despair but he's staring at Katya. I look over my shoulder and the inspector is whispering to her partner. Heads bowed together, speaking urgently, like they're about to run out of oxygen. What are they saying?

Maybe it's not bad news. They've come to tell me they've found Georgie, that she's in hospital recovering. The inspector looks up, catches my eye, and a lump lands in my throat.

'Thank you to everyone who has believed in us and this dream of ours.' Nathan smiles at Katya and the room erupts into applause. Meanwhile, the inspector has inched closer. The crowd parts as she carves a path towards me.

I turn back to Nathan. Has he seen? I don't think so, not yet.

'Most of all, I'd like to thank my wife, Becca, who's been behind me every step of the way.'

I feel the shadow of the inspector looming.

Nathan raises his glass and a room full of people all turn at the same time, searching for me.

'To Rebecca.' He smiles. 'Baby – I couldn't have done it without you.' He raises a toast while I feel a firm hand land on my shoulder.

'Mrs Peters,' the inspector says in my ear.

'To Rebecca!' the room echoes.

It's like I'm outside of my body.

'We'd like you to come to the police station.'

An out-of-body experience – yes, that's it. I'm floating, while the alcohol swishes around inside me. My stomach heaves.

'What's this about?' I swallow bile. 'Have you found Georgie?'

'There are some questions we'd like to ask you. If you could come with us now.' Her eyes flash and suddenly this feels like something else entirely.

'Is this about Georgie?'

She keeps her gaze fixed on mine.

'Can't this wait?'

'I think you'll feel more comfortable doing this at the station.'

'Doing what?' My mind is spinning, because this isn't making any sense. If they've found Georgie, why not tell me here? Heads are turning. Eyes are being pulled from Nathan towards me. I look back to my husband nervously.

What's going on? he mouths.

'Please,' I hiss to the inspector. 'This is my husband's launch party. It's important.'

'So is our investigation.'

'Surely this can wait until tomorrow?'

'I'm afraid not.' She stares me down.

'At least tell me what this is about.'

'If you refuse to come with us voluntarily, we'll have to arrest you.'

'Arrest?'

More heads turn. The entire room slowly stills into silence.

'Arrest me for what?'

'For the murder of Jamie Finn,' she says, loud enough for everyone to hear.

'Murder?' I murmur, searching around me for help. 'Is this some joke?'

'His body was found in the canal this morning.'

Now everything is happening all at once, the room is tipping, the floor wavering beneath my feet, while my head is bloated with champagne. 'I can't help you, I don't know anything.' I back away.

'I won't ask you again.'

'Look, you've made a mistake.'

I feel the grip on my arm tighten.

'I don't even know Jamie Finn!'

The inspector reaches for her handcuffs and I panic. Blind panic.

I stare around, squinting, shrinking under everyone's gaze. A hush descends over the room. People are whispering, throwing me looks. Dean is watching, open-mouthed, while Katya shakes her head at me. And then, all of a sudden, Brad Garcia gets up from his table and walks out of the restaurant. Oh no. No, no, no. I glance back at my husband, crestfallen. His face is creased with disappointment and my heart cracks in two.

The restaurant is silent, so quiet I can hear everyone's thoughts, their eyes following me as the inspector marches me towards the exit. The sight of the police car parked outside makes my knees buckle, almost toppling me. They haul me back onto my feet, gripping my arms so tightly I might as well be in handcuffs.

This can't be right; I'm being treated like a criminal. As I near the door, I slow. A final glance back at Nathan. But my husband won't even look at me.

THE FRIEND – BECCA

I volunteered my DNA. I allowed them to swab my mouth, I gave them my fingerprints, but as I continue to wait in this cold sterile interview room, I'm starting to wonder if I've walked into a trap.

The shock of being taken to the police station has sobered me up and I'm desperate to change out of this skimpy dress. I've got goosebumps and I feel exposed, like a specimen being studied under a microscope. My gaze flicks to the CCTV camera mounted on a bracket in the corner. I know they're watching and I cross my arms, holding myself tightly as if that will somehow protect me from what's coming.

Don't panic, this will be over soon.

They can't seriously believe I'd murder someone? The quicker I answer their questions the sooner I can get back to Nathan. Then I think about where I was last night and how that will look if they find out, and my stomach sinks further.

'How are you feeling?' The inspector looks at me earnestly. 'Do you want some water?'

I shake my head.

'Is there anything I can get you?'

I look back at her, surprised. Half an hour ago she was threatening to arrest me and now she's wanting to take care of me? The change is so dramatic it's like I'm suffering from whiplash, but maybe that's the idea.

'I need to get back to my husband,' I say.

'Just to remind you, you're here voluntarily, you can leave at any time.'

I rub my eyes, trying to push the last of the champagne haze away, while she returns to her notes. The sound of paper being turned fills the room. The police station is in the bustling city centre, but this feels more like an echo chamber buried deep underground. Scuffed walls and peeling beige paint. A strip light buzzing overhead. I want to reach up and smash it off the ceiling.

'Mrs Peters, can you tell me where you were last night?'

'I was at home.'

'All evening?'

'That's correct.'

'And your husband can confirm that?'

I swallow. 'Yeah, of course he can.'

Inspector Van den Berg notes that down on her A4 pad of ruled paper. Even though this interview is being recorded, she's taking notes of almost everything I tell her, and when she's not writing, she's staring me down. Carrying herself with a quiet but intimidating authority. I'm starting to feel a little frightened. Maybe it's time I asked for that lawyer?

'And how would you describe your relationship with Jamie Finn?'

I frown. 'We didn't have one.'

'But he thought he had one with you? From his TikTok videos we can see he was watching you closely.'

'You could say that! He's been stalking me!'

'Did you report him?'

I go quiet.

'Mrs Peters?'

'No. I didn't.'

'Why not?'

'I don't know. You didn't take me seriously when I reported Georgie missing – I thought the same would happen again, that I'd be wasting my time.'

She jots that down and underlines it.

'Did he attack you?'

'Not attack me as such, but . . .'

'Did you lash out in self-defence?'

'Me? No, I—' I stop, suddenly wary of where this is leading. 'Why am I here?'

She puts down her pen and folds her arms, leaning into the table.

'Mr Finn's body was discovered earlier today in a canal. And we have reason to believe his death was not accidental.'

I swallow. 'He was murdered?'

'The news is going to get out quickly and I'm hoping you might be able to clear up some unanswered questions.'

My hand moves involuntarily to my throat. 'You don't really think this has anything to do with me?' Then, panic, as my thoughts boomerang to *her*. My eyes flick between the inspector and her sergeant. 'Does this mean you've found Georgie?'

'I'm afraid not.'

'You do know that Jamie was searching for her? What if he found out something?'

'There's nothing to suggest there's a connection at the moment.'

'But there has to be.' My voice rises. 'Are you even looking for Georgie?'

'Mrs Peters, if we could return to why we've brought you here.' Her eyes flash.

Jesus, why won't she answer me?

'What happened to him?' My voice sounds unsteady.

She opens her file, removing a series of photographs and lining them up in front of me. One, two, three. I don't know why, but it takes me a few seconds to register who they're of.

I've never seen a dead person before – I don't suppose many people have. It feels a little surreal, especially as I knew him. My mouth feels suddenly dry as I take in the ugliness of death. The mottled skin that's taken on a wax-like sheen. His lips are blue, almost grey, the same colour as the bruising ringing his neck. But it's the dead-eyed stare that leaves me cold. I turn my head away, but she leaves the photographs in my line of vision.

'When did you last see Mr Finn?'

'I . . . I can't remember.' I keep my eyes fixed on the floor. 'Maybe a couple of days ago.'

'What time was that?'

'I don't know exactly. I need to think . . . He was filming outside the house.'

'Whose house?'

'The house where Georgie went missing.'

'What were you doing there?'

'I went back to try to jog my memory. I keep thinking, if I can only remember what happened that night, it might help find Georgie.'

'Did you kill him?'

'Sorry, what?' I cough with shock.

Her expression remains neutral, as if she's asked if I'd like a cup of tea.

'Is that a joke?'

She doesn't say anything.

'NO!' I shake my head in disbelief. 'I didn't kill him. Why would you even ask that?'

More silence. The room feels like it's shrinking while my temperature soars. It's like I've been struck down with the flu: the back of my neck, my palms, they're suddenly clammy.

'I didn't like him much,' I say eventually. 'He frightened me. But I wouldn't do anything to harm him. Why would I?'

'Because he was accusing you of being involved in the disappearance of your friend.'

'But . . .' I swallow. 'I'm not, so—'

'And he was damaging the reputation of your husband's establishment.'

'Nobody in their right mind would believe what he was saying.'

'He had proof you were involved in the disappearance of your friend.'

'Proof? What proof?'

'Was he blackmailing you, Mrs Peters?'

'Blackmailing me about what?'

'Was it an argument that got out of hand?'

'Wait – what argument?'

The inspector holds my gaze and then notes down whatever she thinks I've said. Then she gets up suddenly and leaves the room.

I look at the sergeant, bewildered. The woman's eyes flicker to mine, giving nothing away. My head is spinning, I feel the muscles around my neck and shoulders tightening. Should I stop the interview?

But before I have time to put my thoughts in order, the inspector reappears with a laptop and a transparent ziplock bag with something small and dark inside. Her eyes find mine, she sits back down, without breaking eye contact.

'Showing article seventeen, found at the scene of the crime.' She removes the midnight blue iPhone from the bag and places it on the table.

'What's that?' I stare at it.

'Mr Finn's mobile phone.' She watches me closely. 'We discovered it beneath a car after what looks like signs of a struggle.'

Then she opens her laptop and enters a password. Moving her finger across the trackpad, she frowns with concentration while peering down at the screen. There's a sense of something building, in the same way air becomes charged before a thunderstorm. I chew at my fingernails anxiously.

'We've downloaded the information stored on Mr Finn's phone, which contains footage of the afterparty you attended on New Year's Eve.'

'Is Georgie in it?'

'Rather than contacting the police, the witness sent the video to Mr Finn.' A hint of bitterness enters her voice.

A witness to what? I'm a deer in the headlights, uncertain whether to run or wait for whatever force is steamrollering towards me.

She angles the computer screen towards me and presses play.

It's a room full of beautiful people, their outlines silhouetted by an electric blue glow. A sickness is growing in my stomach as I'm dragged back to New Year's Eve. The camera jerks around and I see a flash, a face I recognize.

'That's him! That's the guy Georgie was with!' I fall over my words, I'm trying to get them out so quickly.

But the inspector ignores what I'm saying. Her eyes flick from me to the computer back to me again. I feel the heat of her gaze, the temperature soaring, the moment I appear on the screen.

I barely recognize myself.

I'm stumbling around. I appear drunk and agitated. I'm like a bull in a china shop. I throw an arm around Georgie, hugging her too tightly. I glance down, a flash of something sprints across my eyes and then . . . then I lunge at her.

The inspector freezes the video as my hands reach for Georgie's throat.

I stare at the still as if I'm looking at a stranger for the very first time. It is me, it's definitely me, but I don't recognize this *thing* I've become. I look up sharply and swallow.

'That is you, isn't it, Mrs Peters?'

My hand shakes as I lift a finger towards the screen and touch her face.

'Yes.' I pause. 'But—'

'What are you doing?'

'I . . . I . . .' I shake my head.

'You're attacking Miss Taylor-Johnson, isn't that correct?'

I look again at the frozen image. My eyes are wild, I appear almost possessed. It's me, but it's not me.

'Why did you attack Miss Taylor-Johnson?'

Again I shake my head.

'Mrs Peters?'

My body is beginning to tremble.

'Can you speak up for the tape, Mrs Peters.'

I blink, trying to prise open the memory. The music, the darkness, the heat. The party to end all parties, I can picture it all except that moment.

'Mrs Peters,' she presses.

You bitch, the words ringing out like a tuning fork. 'I don't know.' I continue to peer into the computer screen as if the answer is waiting for me there, but I'm as clueless as I was two seconds ago. 'I'm sorry, I can't remember.'

'You can't remember?'

'I was drugged.'

'You were drugged,' she echoes.

'You've seen my blood results!'

'You could have dosed yourself with Rohypnol.'

'What? Why on earth would I do that?'

She presses play, the video continues but I can barely

watch. Georgie scrambles to get away from me, she trips, she falls, wincing in pain as her knees hit the hard wood floor. She loses her handbag, the contents spilling out while two men I don't recognize pin me back by the arms. Georgie looks up at me, her face full of fear.

The inspector pauses the video.

I stare into Georgie's eyes, my fear reflected back at me.

Oh dear God, what did I do?

THE DAUGHTER – GEORGIE

My heart is beating too fast. I've not gone this long without insulin before, what will happen next? I feel panicky, a little woozy and light-headed, all at the same time.

'JAMIE!' I cry out. 'Fuck you, Jamie!' My throat is so dry, any vibration, even the smallest sound I make, hurts. It's like I'm being force-fed tiny pieces of broken glass. I'm desperate for water to wash the sensation away.

What time is it? It feels like hours, possibly days have passed since I last had something to eat or drink. I sink back against the cold metal wall of the shipping container, trying to come to terms with my new reality.

I'm being held prisoner.

I knew I shouldn't have trusted him, the double-crossing bastard. Jamie must have struck a deal with one of his Neanderthal friends. They've agreed to screw me out of my share of the money, rob the public for as much as they can get before releasing me. At least I was doing it out of desperation. I had no choice. Doesn't the idiot realize – I can't last without my medication. His grand plan to become a famous detective will backfire if I don't survive.

Stop it, Georgina, you're overthinking this. He's taken my supply of meds and both my phones to frighten me. It's obvious, Jamie's trying to get back at me for threatening to change the plan. He's teaching me some sort of lesson, but oh boy, he'll be sorry for crossing me.

A new sensation takes hold. My fingertips and toes are beginning to tingle. That'll be the blood pressure dropping. I lower myself horizontally onto the cold metal floor just in time. I feel my eyes roll into the back of my head.

A cold breeze on my face. Footsteps approaching. I think I'm dreaming until I hear the sound of someone breathing next to my ear.

My eyes snap open.

The dark figure in the balaclava is bending over me. He shines the torch into my eyes, it's momentarily blinding.

Panic seizes me. Adrenaline surges. I grab at his wrists but he pulls my arms apart, twisting them behind my back. Pain sears, a hot sharp sensation shooting into my shoulder blade, bringing tears to my eyes.

'HELP ME!' I scream into the darkness.

He binds my hands behind my back. A rope? No, something thin and wiry. The cable ties bite into my skin.

'Jamie! STOP! What the bloody hell are you doing? I'm sorry, OK!'

Two holes for eyes peer down at me, unblinking. The grim reaper, come to collect the dead, and I'm struck by the same feeling as when he was last here.

'Jamie?'

A new noise. A high-pitched ripping.

'No, no, stop!'

Something thick and sticky, smelling strongly of chemicals, is pressed over my mouth. My voice vibrates against the gaffer tape, my screams instantly silenced. I start to hyperventilate, shunting air in and out through my nose, my lungs tightening, and then the last of the light is cancelled out. Something is pulled over my head. A hood of some kind that's rough against my skin and smells of dirt, like fresh soil. Coughing into my chest, I inhale dust. Tears stream from my eyes.

I can't see.

I can't breathe.

My body trembles with adrenaline but I barely have the energy to move. Without my shot of insulin, I'm growing weaker and dizzier by the second. Of all the stupid things I've done, this is the worst. What have I got myself into?

I'm pulled to my feet but my knees give way. I hear him breathing heavily, wet and whistly in my ear. Through the smell of earth and chemicals, I pick up on something else. What is it?

It doesn't smell of Jamie. There's no nauseating stench of sweat and cooking fat. I feel dread rise up through me, because if it's not Jamie, who is it? And what do they want with me?

My mind scrambles through all the people who might have it in for me but there's too many to count if I include past lovers and jilted exes, and I'm painfully aware I'm wasting the last of my energy rehashing old grievances, but I suppose I'm going into shock.

A blast of cold air.

The wind screeches past me and I hear the clang and rattle of the shipping containers. The crunch of snow under my feet. I'm outside. I'm being moved. Where's he taking me?

I twist around, trying to wrench myself free, but his grip tightens. Then comes a flurry of sounds. Feet scuffling, a low groan as he pulls on a lever. The creak of a van door opening.

Panic seizes me, the hood sucks into my nostrils, blocking all airflow, and I think I'm about to pass out when my feet lift off the ground.

I'm flung through the air.

God lord, I'm flying.

And then I'm not.

I land on my side, my head knocks into something hard and cold, and pain shoots from one side of my temple to the other, shaking everything in between.

Another rip of metal.

The clunk of the van door closing.

Silence.

Then the rattle of an engine starting up.

Where is he taking me?

THE FRIEND – BECCA

I can't quite take it in.

Jamie is dead. *Murdered*. Georgie is missing and they think I might have something to do with it.

I stare numbly into the middle distance. Inspector Van den Berg's voice sounds a million light years away as I continue my attempts to unscramble what happened that night. Am I involved in Georgie's disappearance?

'We've spoken to Georgina's mother.' The inspector's voice snaps me back into the interview room.

'Why, what's she said?' Just the mention of her name triggers me.

'She doesn't like you much, does she?'

'I wouldn't believe anything she says. She's an alcoholic.'

'Mrs Taylor was concerned about your friendship with her daughter.'

'She's a snob. A narcissistic, neglectful excuse for a mother,' I say bitterly, thinking back to all the times she dismissed me.

'Is that so.' The inspector chews the end of her pen thoughtfully, then makes a note.

I try to calm my breathing, forcing myself to focus. *She's baiting you; she wants you to break.*

Inspector Van den Berg glances down at her file. 'Mrs Taylor described you as' – an eyebrow arches – 'besotted and obsessive. Is that a fair interpretation of your relationship with her daughter?'

I clear my throat. 'I come from a council estate, which makes me nothing in her eyes.'

'Apparently you didn't take the news well – that Georgie wanted to put an end to your friendship.'

I look down at my hands. The bruising is still visible and I feel a rush of guilt but I don't know why.

'She said you used to spy on their house. She found you' – she glances at her notes – 'creeping around in the orchard behind their home.'

'I walked there every day. That was something I did to get away from home.'

'For some time, she worried you had feelings for her daughter that went beyond friendship.' The inspector leans across the table. 'Were you in love with Georgina?'

'What?' I say incredulously.

'It's not something to be ashamed of. A beautiful woman like that.'

'No.' I match her tone.

'Then you were jealous of her?'

'Why would I be?'

'From what her mother says, you had a lot to be envious of. You come from a deprived home, a violent upbringing. Georgina had everything. You had nothing.'

'It wasn't like that.'

'She looked down on you.'

'Georgie hated her parents.'

'You planned to live together.' She refers to her notes. 'But then Georgina changed her mind. Her mother said she'd become afraid of you.'

'No.' I shake my head.

'That you were clingy.'

'Her mother brainwashed Georgie into thinking her London friends would abandon her if she was seen with me.'

'Obsessive.' She carries on: 'Georgie was frightened of what might happen if you lived together.'

'That's not true.' But I feel a sharp pain in my sternum as the words leave me.

'Georgina tried to let you down gently but she knew you wouldn't take the news well.'

'I was upset, as anyone would be. But I got over it.'

'She broke your heart.'

'We were kids.'

'This whole time you've been harbouring feelings of hate towards her. She destroyed your life.'

'I have a good life. I wouldn't swap it for anything.'

Another stab of pain hits my insides.

'So when Georgina met with you, twelve years later, you finally took the chance to act out your revenge.'

'That's absurd. She was my friend.' I stumble, clearing my throat. 'She *is* my friend, and I would never, ever do anything that would deliberately hurt her or cause her pain.'

'You killed her and Mr Finn found out.'

'No.'

'He was blackmailing you, wasn't he?'

'No. No.' I shake my head.

'So you killed him too.'

'I would never hurt Georgie, I, I—' I stop and look up. My eyes fill with tears.

The inspector meets my gaze.

'Love her?' She smiles. 'Is that what you were about to say, Mrs Peters?'

I stare back at her. My head is spinning and I have no way of slowing it down. I feel so muddled, like I might pass out. I've never lost my temper; anyone who knows me knows I wouldn't say boo to a goose. If anything, I'm the doormat everyone wipes their feet on. So what happened on New Year's Eve? Was it the drugs? Did they make me lose my mind?

You bitch.

It doesn't make sense. Why would I have said that to Georgie?

You bitch.

Was I jealous? I can remember feeling so miserable that night, recovering from the grief of losing the baby, and with Nathan being away in London with Katya.

'Mrs Peters . . . ?'

And envious of how Georgie turned heads everywhere we went. I felt invisible next to her. Small and irrelevant.

'Was New Year's Eve your chance to get even with your old best friend for breaking your heart?'

BITCH.

I look up sharply.

'I want a lawyer.'

The inspector sits back in her chair heavily, scowling. She has to turn off the tape.

THE DAUGHTER – GEORGIE

We're on the move again. But it's impossible to know where they're taking me with this hood over my head. All I can see is splinters of light through the rough weave of fabric. Music blasts from an old speaker. Some Dutch band on the radio. I can feel tyres bumping over uneven ground. A dirt track? Are we in the countryside?

At first, I tried making mental notes on where we were going, listening out for sounds. At one point we were travelling so fast I could feel the floor heating up, which told me two things: the van was extremely old and we were not in Amsterdam any more. I thought about the plethora of motorway routes bleeding out of the city, the multitude of directions we might have been headed in. We could have crossed over to Belgium for all I knew, and I quickly became disorientated. My eyelids grew heavy and I must have drifted into sleep.

Now my stomach is churning, I feel like I'm about to throw up and I've never been so thirsty in my entire life. I know it's the diabetes, this wretched disease I brought upon myself. I also know I'm experiencing the advanced stages of hyperglycaemia and, without insulin, it won't be long until I lose consciousness. I experienced something similar after a weekend at Ascot, boozing and partying on an empty stomach; as you'd imagine, it didn't agree with me. And if dear Seb hadn't found me slumped in a corner, perhaps I wouldn't be here today.

I say *here*, but I'm fading by the second.

It's not only my body that feels like it's been put under anaesthetic; my mind is feeling the effects too. I'm trying to rack my brains but I can't think clearly. I force myself to stay calm. *Think, Georgie, think*. Who are these people? Jamie said he'd been threatened by thugs. It has to be them – who else? The moron must have led them right to me. But what do they want? The GoFundMe money? Or . . . I swallow. Is it *me* they're after? I shake the distressing thought from my mind, I've watched *Taken* too many times – that's Hollywood, it can't be what's happening to me, can it?

I slam my hands against the van door in a final burst of adrenaline.

The van lurches to a stop. The engine suddenly cuts out.

Oh God, oh God. I've angered them. Now what? I tell myself to stay calm, but my body does the opposite. The very last of my energy is used up by bucking and kicking. The harder I fight, the deeper the cable ties bite into my wrists. My mouth floods with the bitter taste of chemicals as I hyperventilate against the tape.

The door creaks open, a burst of cold hits my skin. The air smells of rotting fish and seaweed and brine. I can hear waves breaking, seagulls cawing in the distance. No, please no. My heart starts beating so fast it feels like it's about to jump out of my chest. A terrifying certainty leaps into my head.

They're going to dump my body in the ocean.

THE FRIEND – BECCA

She's inside my head.

A worm, burrowing holes in my already fractured memory; implanting her version of the truth. I can't be sure of anything any more. Is the inspector right? Is there a whole other side to me I don't know about? Was it an argument that got out of hand?

Did I kill Georgie?

No, no. Oh God. I don't know.

I've been released without charge, which means they don't have enough to go on. What they've got on me is circumstantial; but I've had to surrender my passport. I'm not allowed to leave the country. How long until they find some piece of evidence that will put me behind bars?

But what that will be, I have no idea. My sinkhole of a memory opens, I'm losing purchase, I feel myself sucked back inside. *Bitch*. The bruises on my hands. Passing out in the street. The darkness. The cold biting at my cheeks. The pulse of music, fading.

I wipe my eyes. I give my head a little shake.

Focus.

Peering through the windows into the deserted restaurant, I take another shuddering breath. There's a figure at the bar. Hunched over, his head buried in his hands. The familiar outline of my husband, it's unmistakable, and I'm trying to work up the courage to go inside and face the music. What am I going to say to him? He'll want answers. I have none.

All the lights have been turned off except for the drink fridges. The soft indigo glows around the bar like a halo. The pulse of music grows as I cautiously make my way towards him.

Staring into space, his shoulders rolled forward, Nathan reaches for the bottle and pours himself another whisky.

I hesitate. Was this a mistake? He's drunk and miserable and doesn't appear in the mood for talking. I stand stock-still, trying to think of something to break the ice. But I'm also exhausted. I'm frightened and all I really want is a hug. But more than anything, I need Nathan to reassure me that I'm not a murderer. He's known me my whole life, he knows I wouldn't be capable of hurting someone. I need him to tell me it's going to be OK.

I swallow my sob and dry my eyes.

'Nathan?' I say eventually.

He half turns to me. A lazy stare, his eyelids lowering.

'They let me go in the end.'

He returns to his whisky, knocking back what's left in the glass in one.

'Nathan?' I say quietly.

He stares ahead. His shoulders rise and fall. I can't tell

what he's thinking. His expression is unreadable but his jaw is tight.

'They think I killed . . .'

As I tail off, he considers me for a moment.

'Did you?' he says, without even looking in my direction.

Oh no. No, no. That's not what he's supposed to say. I'm confused by what's happening. I came here looking for reassurance, not more uncertainty. Several agonizing heartbeats pass while I silently beg him to say something, anything, to make me feel less guilty.

'Do you really think I could do something like that?' I say eventually. I feel my heart taking off as I wait for his answer.

He shrugs.

I bite my lip, fighting back tears.

'We lost Brad's investment tonight,' he says.

The memory of the businessman standing up and walking out in the middle of Nathan's speech when I was being arrested feels years old, not hours. So much has happened in between.

'He's pulled his funding,' Nathan goes on. 'It's a disaster, the launch was ruined.' His voice is still muted. Unnervingly quiet.

'I don't understand why it all hangs on Brad.'

'Dad was right, I have no idea how to run a business.'

'What?' I look around. 'Muse is a triumph; you should be so proud.'

'It's the hidden costs. A year of delays and false starts. The builders and contractors, the suppliers, the staff. Do you have any idea how much it costs to keep a restaurant afloat?' Without Brad Garcia's level of investment, Muse won't survive.'

'If he's that successful, he'll be able to see past this, he'll know what a great thing he has in you.'

A hollow laugh. Nathan shakes his head. 'Brad's a success *because* he knows when to walk away. He's seen it all before, how one bad story can ruin a business. We'll be front-page news any minute now.'

I swallow back tears. 'I can fix this.'

'First the conspiracy theories, and now my wife arrested on suspicion of murder. He takes another slug of whisky. 'This is the end for Muse.' His voice breaks.

'It's just the beginning.' I take a step towards him.

He shoots me another glance, warning me off with his eyes, and I slow to a stop.

'Don't.' He shakes his head. 'Please, just—' His voice cracks.

'I'm sorry,' I whisper.

'I don't want to hear it, Becca.'

'Let me help.'

He turns his head away. 'I can't do this with you now.'

A sharp sour smell comes off him and I notice the shot glasses lined up in a row. He's been at it for hours. Beside the whisky, there's a bottle of sambuca, two thirds drained.

'What happened tonight shouldn't be enough to put Brad off,' I say. 'Not if he was serious about a future with us.'

Nathan exhales heavily through his nose. 'Would you do business with anyone linked to money laundering, kidnapping and – what was the other thing that TikTokker accused us of? Oh yeah, trafficking, that's right.'

'They're just stories; nobody will take them seriously.'

'Did you read the comments? Did you see what they were saying about us? All it takes is one bad review.' His eyes widen, his jaw pulses. 'It's Katya I worry about. She's put all her savings into the business. If it goes under, she's lost everything.'

Katya. Why does it always come back to her? I glance around the dining room. 'Where is she?'

'Gone for a walk to clear her head.' He flicks me a look. 'What is it between you two?'

'Look, you don't need to worry about that TikTokker. He won't be spreading any more lies about us . . .'

Nathan looks up sharply and I don't recognize his expression.

'They found Jamie Finn's body.'

He goes silent.

'The police think it's murder.'

Nathan presses a button on his phone and the music stops abruptly. The room is plunged into an echoey silence except for the sound of ice cubes clinking in his glass.

'He can't hurt us any more.'

'Do they know what happened?' he says eventually.

There's a three-second pause while I deliberate whether to tell him that I'm the prime suspect in this murder enquiry.

'The damage is done,' he continues. 'We won't be able to get Brad back on board now. If this guy's been murdered, it will only draw more attention to the rumours he started.' He pours himself another shot, the liquid spilling over the sides of the glass and across the bar. 'And now everyone suspects my wife of being a killer.' He knocks it back, winces and wipes his mouth. The *glug-glug* sound of him refilling his glass is painfully loud in the otherwise silent room.

'I'll fix this,' I whisper.

His eyes meet mine. There's concern in them but mostly hurt and anger.

'It too late for that.'

His voice is cold and I feel my whole body start to shake.

'Nathan?'

He won't look at me. I've never hated myself more. I bring my hands to my face; I wipe my eyes but new tears quickly replace the old ones and I can't bear it any longer. My world feels like it's crashing down around me.

I turn and walk.

I grab Nathan's coat and I walk out of the restaurant and into the cold, crying harder than I've ever cried. I can't go home; because I don't want to be alone. I feel lost and bewildered and desperate to make things right. If I can clear my name, if I can find Georgie. That will fix things, won't it? I need to find out what really happened between us at the afterparty. And I know who can give me the answer. I have to force him to tell me the truth this time.

Hunching my shoulders to my ears to keep out the cold, I retrace my steps to where I was in the early hours of this morning.

THE FRIEND – BECCA

'What are you doing here?' he whispers. 'I told you not to come back.'

'I'm sorry.' My face crumples. 'I didn't know where else to go.'

I stare at Rami, my eyes searching his, and he lowers the baseball bat he's gripping tightly in his hand. He glances nervously around the boat and then his face softens. He can see I'm desperate.

'Did anyone follow you?'

'I-I don't think so.' I check behind me and I'm hit with a blast of freezing air. It's a clear night, with only a few specks of snow and the sky is pricked with stars. The frozen canal glimmers in the moonlight. Like a magnet, my gaze is pulled towards the house opposite. *Number 34.* Only five days ago, music and light poured onto the street. Now dark and abandoned, it feels like a ghostly face might appear at the window at any moment.

I take a shuddering breath.

'OK. You can come in,' Rami says.

I dry my eyes.

'But only if you're quiet.'

'Thank you.'

'Be careful, it's steep.' He holds out a hand but I stubbornly refuse, making a meal of lowering myself down a stepladder in my party dress and heels. I wobble, missing the final step and falling forward. Rami grabs me just in time, my face planting into his chest. Slowly, I lift my head, looking up into his almond-shaped brown eyes, and I feel a prickle of heat.

He's been on my mind since last night. Since I turned up on his doorstep in the early hours of the morning after I'd been wandering the streets with a head full of unanswered questions. He was kind, he listened to me, Rami made me feel heard and— I quickly push away the feeling; it would be dangerous to allow it in.

Now I'm cocooned in the warmth of the cabin, I notice he's dressed for bed in pyjama bottoms and a T-shirt. I'm so consumed with myself, I've lost all track of time. He tells me to get comfortable while he climbs up to where I've just been. Poking his head above deck, Rami scans the canal, checking one final time that no one's followed me.

Who is he so afraid of?

Pushing a pile of clothes aside, sweeping up plates and cups and leftovers, Rami makes a space for me on the sofa. Barely noticing the mess, I sit down heavily, elbows sinking to my knees. Head in my hands, I burst into tears again.

He looks anxiously across the cabin to the end of a narrow corridor, pressing a finger to his lips.

'Hans is asleep.'

Rami starts to come towards me. I think he's about to give me a hug, but then he stops by my feet.

I look up at him. I can imagine my tear-stained face, my eyes, puffy and bloodshot. God, I must look so desperate and pathetic. What am I doing here?

'I'll get you a glass of water,' he says.

I focus on my breathing, trying to keep my mind anchored to each breath. When he returns, I've composed myself. Drying my eyes on my coat sleeve, I manage to lift my gaze, taking in the cosy living space as if I'm seeing it for the first time.

It's much smaller than it appears from the outside and reminds me of my granny's house, with messy stacks of books and mismatched furniture – an untidy mix of styles, textures and eras. The walls are made of teak wood, creaking with every blast of wind. In the corner, a small wood burner glows red with the dying embers of a fire. The sitting room bleeds into a galley where there's a stove, fridge and a washing machine. Rami opens a porthole to rinse away the stale air.

'Two blokes cooped up in a boat doesn't smell great,' he says apologetically, and now I'm also blushing, wondering why he cares so much what I think. He hands me the glass and sits down next to me. Our knees touch. Tension fizzes between us.

'Want to tell me what's happened?' he says eventually.

I take a sip of water, staring into the middle distance.

I came here looking for answers but now I've arrived, I can't seem to speak.

'You OK?'

I shake my head.

'Becca?'

I shut my eyes tightly, saying nothing.

'Wasn't tonight your restaurant opening?'

'I'm in serious trouble,' I murmur.

'I can't help if you won't tell me.'

'The police think I killed that TikTokker, Jamie Finn – the one who's been spreading stories about us.'

He stares at me.

'And they think I murdered Georgie.'

'Oh-kay . . .' I watch him hunt for words.

'They're saying I was jealous of her. That I wanted to settle some old score.'

'But you're the one who's been trying to find her. That doesn't make any sense.'

'Nothing makes sense.' I clamp my hands against my temples. 'Why won't my stupid brain let me remember?'

He shunts air through his nose. 'Fuck, they're idiots. I hate the authorities.' His jaw tightens.

'My husband, he . . . um . . .' I falter.

'The police are under pressure; the morons didn't take your friend's disappearance seriously when they should have. Don't let them rattle your cage.'

'Nathan thinks I might be involved.'

'Your husband?'

I shut my eyes again, fighting back more tears.

'You realize this is bullshit? How could someone as

sweet as you do something like that,' he says defensively. This expression of kindness, the reassurance I needed from Nathan but didn't get, sends me soaring over the edge. I burst into sobs.

'I can't remember what I did.' I turn, facing Rami square on. 'The police have a video of me at the party, I look deranged. I attacked Georgie. Something happened between us that night . . .' I say, searching his eyes for comfort, for further reassurance.

Rami looks away.

'Oh God.' A pause. '*You know.*'

He chews on the inside of his cheek.

'You saw us, didn't you?'

He stands up.

'Why didn't you tell me?'

He begins pacing the room.

'Rami, why didn't you say? You swore you didn't know anything.' My voice grows in volume, in ferocity. 'You lied to me!'

He stops pacing and crouches by my knees. 'Shhhh. Please. Don't wake Hans.'

I stare at him with hurt, angry eyes.

He takes my hands in his. 'I told you; I can't get involved. I warned you.'

I feel more muddled than ever. 'But if you'd just told me the truth.'

He swallows, unable to meet my gaze.

'All this time I knew something was wrong, I *knew* I was involved . . .'

'I'm sorry. But I can't see how telling you would change anything.'

'What?' I look at him, uncomprehending. 'It changes *everything*.'

His features soften. Gently, he pulls my hands away from my face.

'Listen, I found you unconscious in the street, so how could you be involved?'

'*Anything* could have happened before then.' I start to tremble, remembering the look on the faces of the people at the party. Fear. *Terror*. What did I do in that unaccounted for time?

He rubs my hands urgently, the same way he did the night he found me in the snow. 'Shhh, it's OK.' He's doing his best to soothe me. I can tell he wants to help; he's a good person and I feel my heart swell with emotion.

Someone cares about me.

Then I think about my husband and all the things I've done to destroy our marriage.

'Nathan hates me,' I say. 'I ruined the most important night of his life and he'll never forgive me.'

'Yeah, but what sort of husband doesn't defend his wife?'

'When the video leaks to the press, when Nathan sees what I did, what will he think of me then?'

Rami's expression darkens. 'Seriously? He sounds like an arsehole.'

'I'm so confused.'

'Maybe you had good reason? Have you considered that?'

'You're not making any sense.'

'What if your friend provoked you?'

'No,' I insist, 'you've got this all wrong. There's nothing Georgie could do that would justify me behaving like that.' I stop crying and look up at him. 'There's something wrong with me. I'm *damaged*.'

'When was the last time you had some sleep?' he says gently. 'You should go home and get some rest.'

'How can I go home now?' My face creases in distress. 'Rami, I'm scared.'

Rami's brow wrinkles as if he's struggling to decide what to do. I can see he wants to help me, but something is holding him back. What is it? Do I frighten him?

He looks at my glass of water.

'Want something stronger?'

I nod and he stands up, crossing the narrow cabin into the galley. He opens the cabinet below the sink and roots around, positioning himself in such a way I can't see what he's doing. For a fleeting moment, I wonder if he's trying to hide something. But then I let go of the thought as Rami pulls out a bottle of whisky.

I chase one gulp down with another, the burn warming me up from within.

'Feels a bit weird, drinking alone,' I say. 'Will you have one with me?'

He shakes his head.

'Because you're Muslim?'

'I just don't like whisky.' He grins at me and I smile back. He's looking at me so intently, I forget to breathe for a second.

311

'Do you miss them?' I change the subject quickly.

'Them?'

'Your family?'

Last night while we were chatting, he opened up a little. He told me about the war in Syria. How he fled to Europe after his mum and dad were killed. Since then, he's been struggling to make a new life for himself. He doesn't feel welcome in Amsterdam; it's been eight years but he's still lonely and lost. Rami mentioned something about a sister, that she was stuck in a refugee camp in Athens and he was trying to find a way for them to be together again.

'I miss her every hour of every day,' he says.

'What's your sister's name?'

'Samira.' Rami smiles sadly. 'She's my twin.'

'Do you look alike?'

'Not really.' He laughs. 'But I know what she's thinking, what she's feeling, without ever having to ask. When Samira's hurt, I feel her pain, even though she's thousands of miles away.' Another small laugh. 'I know that sounds strange, I mean, it's not something that can be explained by science, but it's there, I believe it exists, some sort of connection joining us together.'

'I believe you,' I say.

'Samira's putting on a brave face for me. She's got her own tent, which is something, because some of the women are being forced to share with men. And she has a phone, so we can video call. Now that our parents are dead, all we have is each other. I'd do anything for her, even if it meant sacrificing my own life.'

His words are so powerful, we both fall quiet.

The silence bleeds.

The boat creaks.

The wind picks up.

Something's scratching at the window, trying to get in.

Tap, tap, tap.

Like a fingernail on the glass.

Tap. Tap.

Rami suddenly looks worried. He pulls back the curtain covering the porthole, but then the tension evaporates and he laughs with relief.

It's only a branch. An elm tree skeleton finger, tapping on the glass.

'Living on a boat turns you into a crazy person.' Rami tries to make a joke of it but I'm left with that feeling again. He's hiding something.

I'm torn between wanting to needle the truth out of him and wanting to forget.

I take another sip of the whisky and he sits down next to me again.

'I know it doesn't compare, but I miss my friends back home,' I tell him. 'And I miss the kids at the school where I used to work. They were such sweet children. Here in Amsterdam, the people are nice and everything, but I feel like an outsider. I don't know, perhaps things would be different if Nathan would include me in the restaurant. I'd be busy, at least. There'd be people to talk to. Life is about having a purpose, isn't it?'

More whisky. More confessions of the heart.

Before I know it, I'm leaning against him, resting my head on his shoulder. This is wrong, I know it is, but I don't mean anything by it. I'm just so confused and tired, *so very tired.*

'Tell me something . . .'

He looks at me sideways.

'Talk to me.'

He frowns. 'I don't know what you want me to say.'

'It doesn't matter, it can be anything. Please, help me forget about what's going on for a minute.' I exhale into his chest but my heart begins to beat faster. Things are moving quickly, picking up where they left off last night, when I arrived on his doorstep in the early hours of the morning, complaining of not being able to sleep and needing to talk to someone. Not someone, *him.*

Rami makes me feel heard. He understands my loneliness. He knows what it's like to be a foreigner, never fitting in, never quite belonging. Two lonely souls colliding. Both in need of reassurance. Both in desperate places. It's a dangerous combination. *Christ, I shouldn't even be here!* But I can't stop leaning into the feeling. I sit back, putting some distance between us; but, in doing so, I notice his eyes journey down to my cleavage.

He closes the gap between us.

Rami regards me silently, running a hand over my arm while I'm caught somewhere between desire and intense guilt.

THE DAUGHTER – GEORGINA

I can feel them watching me. I can hear him, right next to me.

'HELP!' My scream vibrates against the tape. 'HELP ME!' But it comes out as one long muffled noise. *I don't want to die. I don't want to die.* Tears stream down my face, the damp fabric scratching at my skin. *I'm sorry for what I did, I take it all back. Please make it stop.*

I'm still in the van and I think there's more than one of them with me but I can't be certain. I strain to listen, but the roar of my heart is deafening. Panic tightens my chest and reduces the amount of air I can fit into my lungs, and I'm already dizzy without my meds. Of all the stupid things I've done in my life. Why didn't I just swallow my pride and ask for help?

I want to go home. I want my papa.

The hood is whipped off and a bright light sears my retinas. It's pointed directly into my eyes, bleaching out everything around me. For a moment, all I can see is stars. Then I can make out a dark shadow, moving restlessly back and forth. Feet thudding across the steel floor. I squint, peering into the light, trying to see who it is, how many of them I'm up against, but the glare is blinding. Oh dear God, this is my worst nightmare come true.

The figure is dressed in dark clothes and he's holding a knife in one hand. Immediately I focus on the blade, picturing all the ways he might use it on me. And then I notice a phone clamped into a tripod pointed directly at my face.

No, no, no. I buck and twist. A hand grabs the back of my neck, holding it firm so I'm facing straight ahead.

'Repeat everything I tell you – understand?' a voice says from behind me. It's distorted, robotic. Monstrous. Almost as if it's been pre-recorded to disguise its identity.

The figure leans across me and I catch a whiff of that scent again. Sweet and stale, like alcohol breath.

Then the tape is ripped off. My lips and face are burning, like a layer of skin has been torn off. I pull oxygen deep into my lungs. I cough, choking on the cold air.

'Understand?'

I can't stop coughing.

'Do you understand?'

I think I'm going to throw up.

A sharp smack to the back of my head.

'Yes,' I splutter. 'I understand . . . but please . . .'

The grip around my neck tightens.

'State your name and that you are being held prisoner. If they tell the police, you will be killed.'

'Please, I feel sick. I need my medication,' I plead.

'If they don't comply with the demands, you will be killed.'

'I need my insulin. It was in the blue rucksack with the rest of my things. I beg you.'

My head jerks back as they grab a fistful of hair. It feels like they're going to pull it out by the roots. I cry out in pain and the grip tightens.

'Say your name.' A growl in my ear. Only this time it's a real voice. A man's voice.

'Georgie,' I croak.

'Your full name.' The robot is back.

I can barely swallow.

'Your full name.'

'I'm Georgina Taylor-Johnson.'

The pressure on my hair releases and I drink in the air. Big mouthfuls as if it might run out at any second.

'Let me go, please!' My voice shakes. 'I haven't seen your face; I promise I won't tell anyone. But if I don't have my injection I'll—'

A hand over my mouth, then intense pressure, forcing my lips apart. I try to scream as something's rammed inside. Rough against my tongue, stripping all the moisture from the roof of my mouth, the cloth is shoved right the way back. I gag, tears leak from my eyes.

I can't speak.

I can't breathe.

The room begins to spin as I lose consciousness.

THE FRIEND - BECCA

I feel his arms loop around my waist. But I don't try to stop him.

I came here tonight searching for the truth. Did I kill Georgie? But a couple of whiskies in, all I can think about is Rami's body pressed up against mine.

A gathering weight in my chest.

A yearning for him to touch me.

Gazing up at him, I can't see beyond his lips. All this time, I've been wanting to remember, searching for a missing piece in the puzzle, but right now, in this very moment, I don't want to think about anything but Rami. I'm exhausted. I want to forget that there was ever an afterparty. I need Rami to clear my head. Just for tonight.

I sense a hesitation. He pulls back a fraction, looking at me anxiously. Something's on his mind and it's eating him up. What is he hiding?

Or am I reading it all wrong again? There's five years between us but I barely notice the age gap because Rami seems so mature. I suppose living through a war will do that to you – force you to grow up quickly. I can't even begin to imagine the horrors he's seen or the pressure he's under to make a new life for himself. He can't be earning much from waitering. Then I find myself wondering whether he does more than serve drinks to these rich women he meets at the parties and I feel a prickle of jealousy. Which is ridiculous because I have no right to be jealous. After all, I'm married.

Whatever's been weighing on his mind seems to lift when he sees the dress I'm wearing. *Georgie's dress.* His eyes run over me, while my thoughts reach places they shouldn't go, turning over fantasies, imagining what sort of kisser he is, what he's like in bed.

Oh God, I'm drunk.

Or maybe I'm just drunk on tiredness.

I blink, but it doesn't stop the cabin swaying. The room is moving in and out of focus. Jesus. What am I doing?

'You OK?' His hand slides down my back, skin brushing against skin, because Georgie's dress is so bloody skimpy.

'I need a moment.'

Rami immediately pulls away. He looks injured – no, fearful. What's going on?

This is a mistake. I should never have come here.

I look over my shoulder at the ladder that leads up to the deck. It's not too late to leave. Then I turn back to face him and, without thinking, I press my lips on his.

He looks taken aback. For a moment he does nothing except stare at me. What have I done? This is embarrassing, I feel such a fool. A married woman throwing herself at a younger guy who wouldn't ordinarily give her a second glance.

Not much is making sense right now. I stand up to leave, although I have absolutely no idea where I'm going. It's as if the world is spinning a little too fast.

The next thing, I feel his hand around mine. Gently, carefully, he pulls me back down so I'm next to him. I feel his warm breath on my collarbone. His hands encircling my waist. An intense flashback to when he rescued me on New Year's Eve hits me head-on, leaving me dazed.

This is wrong, I shouldn't do this . . . But then I think about all those months, no, *years*, of feeling trapped, left with no choice but to share my husband with Katya. Always feeling second best. I don't know what's in this whisky but it's like a truth serum.

I've been lying to myself.

Rami looks at me as if to say *Are you sure?* I lean into the moment. The shameful truth detonates in my chest: *I've wanted this since the night I first saw him.*

His mouth is on mine. The warm pressure against my lips. He cups my face in his hands, slipping his tongue inside my mouth. I shut my eyes and the room spins a little faster.

I'd be flying if he wasn't holding me down.

He pushes me back onto the sofa, his chest pressing on mine. I run my hands over his back, feeling the strength in his hand as it slides up my thigh, pushing my dress to my waist. It's been so long since I've done this. It's become so mechanical with Nathan, like he's lost all interest in me.

Oh God, this is wrong. I've never slept with another man. I lost my virginity to Nathan in one of the B&B

rooms at the pub when I was seventeen. We were so young. It was sweet, Nathan *is* sweet.

Even if Nathan and Katya make me feel like a third wheel sometimes, that doesn't justify me behaving like this, does it?

Rami's hand moves across my breast, sliding the fabric from my left shoulder, then from my right, pushing the dress lower.

I'm not wearing a bra.

He smiles with delight and I arch back, falling into the sensation of what he's doing with his tongue.

Falling. Falling.

Shutting my eyes, free-falling. Until Nathan's face swims into view. Jealous. Hurt. *Heartbroken.*

I snap my eyes open. But Nathan's still there.

Oh God, this is SO WRONG. What am I doing? Risking my marriage for a cheap thrill. This is a mistake. As if I hadn't made enough of those already. Nathan would never betray me.

A flash of panic.

Sitting up with a start, I push Rami off me. The rush of blood to my head makes me dizzy, like I'm on a carousel, spinning around the room. *Make it stop. Please make it stop.*

'Hey,' he says softly in my ear. 'We don't have to do this.'

Our eyes connect, I'm cringing, I feel so utterly foolish.

'Is it something I did?'

'No.' I clear my throat. 'You're lovely, it's just, I . . . I, um.'

'You don't need to explain.'

The silent word *married* hangs between us.

More silence.

More tension.

'Will you be OK getting home?'

I glance around, the cabin's still spinning and showing no signs of slowing down. But it's not my drunkenness deterring me from going home – ordering an Uber would be easy enough – it's the knowledge that I can't face Nathan. Especially not now.

'Is it OK if I leave first thing?' I ask tentatively.

He hesitates. That look again. Something's eating at him.

'Sure.' His brow furrows. 'Do you want to come through to my cabin?'

'Mind if I sleep out here?'

He looks hurt. Then he recovers his smile.

'I'll grab you a blanket and pillow.' Rami tiptoes along the hallway, disappearing into another room. He reappears moments later with his arms full.

'Will the guy you share with mind?' I whisper, helping him with the bedding.

'Hans gets up early. He takes his boat out in the morning. As long as you're OK with being woken up?' He hands me one of his T-shirts to sleep in.

'But will he have a problem with me being here?'

A small laugh. 'He'll be relieved I've finally got a girl-friend.'

Rami looks away quickly and I feel my cheeks heat up.

'Obviously, you're not my girlfriend,' he recovers. 'But

Hans is old-fashioned, he's always on at me, saying it's time I got one. He was married for thirty-seven years so he thinks every man needs a good wife.' He stops. 'Anyway, you've got everything you need?'

I respond with a smile.

'OK. So . . .' He looks at me awkwardly. 'I'll be through there if you need me.'

'Thanks.' I hug the pillow into my chest, feeling more naked than I did five minutes ago.

He leans in.

I freeze.

He plants a kiss on my cheek.

'Night then.' He takes one last look at me.

I open my mouth to say something and then let the words die in my mouth. But I feel his kiss warming my skin, long after he's left.

I wake up in a room that feels as hot as a sauna.

A much larger room than the one I fell asleep in and it's full of people. A painfully beautiful crowd, elegantly dressed in designer clothes. Dancing, drinking. The dull thud of the bass echoes in my ears. I turn my head and Georgie looks back at me. A strained smile. Something flashes across her features. And then, then a hand wraps around my heart and squeezes. A dark fury descends and I lose all control.

Bitch.

I lurch awake.

Properly awake this time.

I grope around, trying to work out where I am. My

tongue is dry, my mouth tastes sour like I've been drinking for days on end, and I'm wearing someone else's clothes.

Rami's clothes.

My heart slows as the memory of a few hours ago catches up with me. I place my head back onto the pillow and make myself small, curling into a ball. Rubbing my tummy, I try to nurse the burning sensation while another memory flashes my way. It's as dark outside as it is in my head. I turn over and face the small circular window, gazing at the moon. I make a wish.

Make it stop.

No.

Make me remember.

My head lolls back onto the pillow and eventually I manage to doze off. A fitful sleep, until I'm woken again. A creak. The sound of a door opening. Then the muted *pat pat* of bare feet coming towards me. I peel open my eyes, expecting an old man, but it's Rami. He tiptoes around the galley, doing his best not to wake me. Instead of pouring himself a glass of water, he drops down onto one knee, opens the cabinet beneath the sink and roots around inside. There's a brief rustling before he pulls out a plastic shopping bag. He stands up, a troubled look on his face.

He glances in my direction and I quickly shut my eyes.

He crosses the room, his footsteps fading. I listen for his bedroom door closing, but the creak comes from further away – he's climbing the ladder. I hear the whine of a hinge, then a cold breeze sweeps towards me. I sit up and crawl to the corner of the sofa just in time to see Rami's feet disappear out of the hatch.

My phone tells me it's 5.15 a.m. Where the hell is he going?

I hesitate, a sinking feeling in my stomach. Then I slip my feet into Rami's trainers and follow him.

THE FRIEND – BECCA

I see footprints in the snow, but no sign of Rami.

I turn in a circle, but there's no movement. I strain to listen for any sounds. Nothing.

He's vanished.

Did he go for a walk? He seemed distracted, like there was a lot on his mind. But clearing his head, in this weather? That seems most unlikely at this time in the morning.

Then I think about him sneaking around in the kitchen and an uneasy feeling grows in my tummy. I try to slow my thoughts down, to think rationally about my next move. I should probably go back inside and wait for him.

Sliding around in shoes three sizes too big for me, I shuffle to the other side of the boat, across the wooden gangplank and onto dry land. I try following Rami but his footprints have been swallowed up by the fresh layer of powdery snow.

Where now?

As I make a start towards the bridge I hear the roar of a car engine behind me. So loud and powerful it makes me jump. I turn into the blinding headlights, stumbling away, half falling backwards; instinctively taking cover behind a row of parked cars just as the glossy black four-by-four drives past.

The Range Rover continues a few hundred yards before the brake lights come on. A blurry red glow like a flare in a storm. The engine hums. Exhaust fumes plume like factory smoke. Why are they stopping?

A dark figure emerges from the alleyway that cuts through to the neighbouring canal. Shoulders rounded, cowering from the wind. A plastic bag swinging from one hand. Rami opens the back door of the Range Rover, a nervous glance in both directions before he gets in.

All my alarm bells are clanging. The smart thing to do would be to turn back. But what if Rami needs help? He warned me about bringing trouble to his door. Maybe someone followed me to his boat? I'm so toxic right now I could be glowing fluorescent. The thought I might be destroying someone else's life is too much to bear.

Working my way along the line of parked cars, I inch closer, my heart in my mouth.

My balance is slightly off as I navigate in oversized shoes with toes that have frozen into solid blocks of ice.

As I draw nearer, I can just about make out the men in the front. They don't look like the sort you'd want to run into in a dark alley. The driver has a shaved head, a silver hoop in his left ear and is wearing a tight-fitting T-shirt that shows off his bloated biceps. The guy beside him is older, skinnier; leathery. Their heads are twisted around to face Rami and, judging by their frowns, the conversation has already turned sour.

Panic.

I feel guilt, combined with a desperate sense of urgency and helplessness.

The driver reaches a hand up, presses a button, and the inside of the four-by-four lights up like a lantern in the dark. The stubble on his chin glistens under the reading light. I get a better look at the men; at a guess, I'd say they were eastern European. There's every possibility they are carrying weapons. Rami hands over the plastic bag. The man in the driver's seat reaches into the bag and pulls something out.

I edge closer, craning to get a better look.

What is it?

He lifts it up, examining it beneath the light.

My heart almost stops.

I'd recognize it anywhere. Made from the finest leather. *Chanel*. It's unmistakable.

Fear crawls up my throat.

Why does Rami have Georgie's handbag?

THE FRIEND – BECCA

I'm a house of cards in a hurricane.

The storm in my head is growing louder and louder. My head is whirling, nothing makes sense. Rami kidnapped Georgie? Are the people he works for also involved? Who were those men? Jesus, how could I have been so stupid to trust him? How could I have done *those things* with him? My thoughts are spiralling, getting darker and darker as I leap to the conclusion that my friend is *dead*.

I'm fighting with myself not to scream at the Uber driver to go faster. I'm also fighting with myself to stay positive, but how can I, now that I've seen her handbag. It's been six days since Georgie disappeared and, without her bank cards, without her phone and her emergency supply of insulin, how can she have survived?

I'm going to call the police. They'll arrest Rami. Finding Georgie alive is all that matters now.

But as we pull up outside my apartment building, I see two police cars parked outside. Oh God, am I too late?

There's also a small group of reporters and photographers hanging around. On seeing me arrive, a couple of them walk purposefully in my direction. I sprint from the Uber, reaching the main entrance with only seconds to spare. I slam the door behind me, leaning my weight against it.

'Becca?' There's the clatter of metal as one of them forces open the letterbox. She calls my name repeatedly while I look around in a kind of daze. 'Becca Peters?' The sharp drill of knuckles against the door. The dull throb of a headache gathering behind my eyes as I try to work out what the hell I'm going to do next.

Stop wasting time. I hear my own voice commanding me into action like a drill sergeant. I race up the stairs, taking them two at a time. My chest has swollen to bursting, I've never felt so desperate, so full of urgency, so grubby. And at the same time, all I want to do is crawl into my bed and pull the covers over my head.

I'll tell the police about Rami, explain that they've got the wrong person.

Finally, I'm on the third floor. I take in a shaky breath and let myself into the flat.

I hear voices in the living room. Inspector Van den Berg and a uniformed officer stand up on hearing me approach. Her expression is cold and sombre. Nathan perches on the edge of the sofa, nursing a cup of tea in his hands. He looks up, his face ashen.

The air feels heavy, thick with grief. What's happened? They look at me expectantly. It's as if the very room is holding its breath, waiting for me to say something.

Nathan blinks rapidly. His eyes are troubled and full of questions.

'What's happened?' I say hoarsely.

'Where the hell have you been?' he asks.

'Is it Georgie?'

'Do you want to tell me why you didn't come home last night?'

The inspector steps towards me and my stomach lurches.

'Mrs Peters . . .' she begins.

'It's Georgie, isn't it? Please tell me she's not dead?'

'There's been a development. We've come by evidence linking you to the murder of Jamie Finn . . .'

'No, wait!' I cut in, my voice trembling with hysteria. 'I know who did it. You've got this all wrong. It was the waiter at the afterparty, he's—'

The inspector and the officer share a look.

'We have CCTV footage that places you near the scene of the crime,' she says.

'What? No! That's not possible.' I try to sound firm and assertive.

'You were spotted on Brouwersgracht at 3.45 a.m. on the fifth of January.'

'Wait, I need to think, I-I went for a walk that night, Nathan had gone to bed but I couldn't sleep. I was staring at the ceiling for an hour – no, longer than an hour. You have no idea—' I stop, feeling suddenly hot and then cold. 'I haven't been sleeping properly for weeks.' My eyes flick to my husband for help. 'Nathan knows, he can tell you I've been struggling.'

'Oh God, Becca.' Nathan looks at me with horror.

'You went for a walk in the early hours of the morning to clear your head?' the inspector says incredulously.

I shift from one foot to the other, my chest tightening with guilt. How can I admit I went to see Rami two nights in a row? Nathan will never forgive me.

'Are you admitting you lied in your statement when you told us you were home all evening and your husband could vouch for your whereabouts?' she continues.

'You told them that?' Nathan stares at me in astonishment.

'It's Rami – it's the waiter from the party, he's behind all this.' I look between them urgently.

'Becca, what are you saying?' Nathan shakes his head in disbelief.

'I was with him last night. I saw it with my own eyes. Rami has Georgie's handbag!'

'You were *with him* last night?' He stands up.

'Please, Mr Peters.' The inspector holds up a hand, stepping between us. 'Let us deal with this.' She turns back to me.

'I know this isn't making much sense,' I tell her, 'but you have to listen to me. He'd hidden her Chanel bag. Why would Rami have Georgie's handbag, unless he was involved somehow? Then two men in a Range Rover came to collect it.'

'So there is no handbag any more?' The inspector looks at me like I'm crazy.

Nathan runs his hand back and forth across his face. 'You were with him last night?' he repeats.

I can feel my heartbeat in my throat. My words are tangling. I'm digging an even bigger hole for myself. I look from Nathan to the detective then back to him again.

'Becca?' His voice breaks.

The sickness in my tummy grows.

'You spent the night with him?'

I want this conversation to stop right now.

'Tell me you didn't spend the night together.'

I feel the inspector watching, evaluating, but saying nothing.

And I can feel my hands trembling. I try gathering myself. If I can just explain . . .

I turn to Nathan: 'Look, after I saw you at the restaurant, I was feeling desperate, I needed to fix things. I . . . I went to see Rami . . . to ask him about New Year's Eve. I wanted to know if he saw me attack Georgie, if he could tell me what I did next. I *knew* he was hiding something.'

'And this is the same guy that TikTokker caught you with in the cafe?' Nathan says.

'It's not what you think.'

'But you *did* spend the night with him?'

'Not in that way—'

The inspector is staring, looking at me closely now.

This is going horribly wrong. *Make it stop.* I'm frighteningly aware of how I'm coming across. How unhinged I must sound. I look to Nathan with pleading eyes, but he shakes his head and turns his back on me.

'You won't have long to find Georgie.' I try to reason with the inspector. 'They're behaving recklessly, they're covering their tracks.'

'Covering their tracks?' She frowns.

I feel like I'm going to throw up at any moment.

'And who are *they*?' she says. 'I thought you said it was Rami?'

All that whisky from last night is sloshing around in my stomach. I raise my hand to cover my mouth and the inspector steps forward.

Her expression changes to one of concern and there's a split second where I think she's about to help me. To tell me to sit down and catch my breath. Then she stands taller, her features hardening. She reaches around, unclipping the handcuffs from her belt.

'Mrs Peters, I'm arresting you for the murder of Jamie Finn and the suspected murder of Georgina Taylor-Johnson. You have the right not to answer questions. You have the right to the presence of a lawyer before and during the interview. You have the right to a translator.' She holds my gaze. 'Do you understand?'

THE DAUGHTER – GEORGINA

Hours, maybe days have gone by, I've lost all sense of time and I haven't eaten or drunk anything for so long my insides feel scooped out.

It can't be days, that would be impossible without my medication, so perhaps it's only a matter of minutes, although I know we've moved again. I have a vague recollection of the rumble of the engine, the hiss and boom of the radio rattling through the old speakers.

I shut my eyes, longing for sleep.

There's a moment of enormous relief as I find myself drifting into the past. I'm thirteen again, it's Christmas at Waverley and I'm in the drawing room, my bare feet planted on top of Papa's soft leather loafers as he twirls me in circles, teaching me to ballroom dance. Around and around, I'm spinning and giggling.

I crack open my eyes and shut them again, drifting into another time. Another place.

There are tears of joy or perhaps sadness on my cheeks when I come to in the back of the van.

A sudden flash of silver.

My kidnapper holds up the knife. I flinch, thinking he's about to use it on me, but instead he slices through the cable ties.

I feel a sudden release of pressure, a moment of calm, before he drags me across the van by my wrists. My eyes open and close; above me a masked face is breathing heavily, grunting in frustration. I can smell alcohol. I open my mouth to beg him to stop but I can't get a word out.

I've lost the ability to speak.

I'm paralysed.

How am I still breathing?

The sky opens up above, pale blue, the winter sun hitting my face. It's like I've stepped into a different climate. It's other-worldly. Then I come crashing to earth. A sharp pain in my lower back as I land on hard ground. I'm dumped like a bag of rubbish put out for collection. The smell of soil and hedgerows rides the air. My eyes move lazily from side to side, taking in the vastness. An endless sky and field upon field of ploughed earth. On the horizon sits a windmill.

Come spring when the tulips flower, it will be magnificent. A sea of vibrant lemon yellow and tomato red. I muster a smile; I can't help but laugh at the irony. Of all the glamorous places I've visited in the world, this is where I'm to take my last breath? In a heap of mud and worms.

I shut my eyes.

A silent movie begins playing in my mind, a grainy black-and-white one. I see myself, just turned sixteen, back at Waverley. This time the drawing room is filled with impossibly beautiful people as Mother celebrates her fiftieth birthday. She's wearing a floor-sweeping Komodo gown over her rather inappropriate party dress. Twirling drunkenly, spilling her martini over the priceless Persian rug. The guests looking on awkwardly. Daddy's face is a picture.

Twiggy and I are sniggering. Dear Twigs, we used to have an awful lot of fun. What a sad little life she leads now, she deserves so much better than Nathan, if only she could see her worth. I feel terrible about what I've done, using her like that. I do hope she'll forgive me.

I feel achingly tired. Just breathing is becoming an effort. I close my eyes and think of Papa. I'm seven now, sitting at the top of the stairs in my pyjamas and slipper boots, waiting for him to return home from his 'business trip'. I'm anxious, I'm excited, I know he's been to see one of his lady friends, and I can hear Mother clunking around in the kitchen, followed by the sound of a glass shattering. But I also know that when he gets home, no matter how explosive things become, his eyes will light up on seeing me. He'll give me one of his bear hugs and pretend nothing is wrong. *Tomorrow is another day, Sparkles*. I hear his voice, soothing, in my ear.

Tears find their way into my eyes as I think about the last time I saw him. The disappointment in his eyes. The hurt. The anger. I was convinced that my disappearance would make him sorry. That he'd realize how much he missed me. That he'd come to rescue me, like always.

I smile sadly. He really doesn't give a shit after all.

I mean nothing to him.

I am nothing.

The words keep repeating as I slip further into a deep sleep.

TWO HOURS LATER

THE FATHER – DUNCAN

'Where is she?'

The hospital receptionist startles.

'Tell me where my daughter is!'

She searches around for help. 'You need to calm down, mijnheer!'

'I got a call from the police saying she's been rushed in here.'

'OK. What's your daughter's name?'

'Georgina.'

'I'm going to need more information—'

'Georgina Taylor-Johnson.' His voice rising, he tries to get his breathing under control. He can feel his heart rate accelerating and his temper is at boiling point.

She returns to her computer, her eyes skimming over the admissions on the screen while a doctor appears behind them.

'Are you the father of the woman who's been missing?'

Duncan Taylor-Johnson spins round. 'Yes! Is she OK? Where is she?'

'She's in intensive care,' the doctor says carefully.

'But she's OK? I want to see her!'

The doctor's brow wrinkles. His expression is sombre. 'Please follow me.'

'She's going to be all right, isn't she, Doctor?' Duncan calls after him but the doctor doesn't answer. Instead, he leads the property developer away from the busy accident and emergency reception, through two sets of swing doors and along a narrow corridor. The noise of the hospital – the buzz of heart monitors, the hiss and pump of machines – grows from a murmur to a roar.

Nurses rush past while the smell of antiseptic and over-cooked vegetables funnels towards them. The doctor takes a sharp right, flashing his key card against a reader. He holds the door open, ushering Duncan into the family room.

His chest balloons with dread. It's always a bad sign when they need to speak to you in private. The doctor closes the door behind them and a heavy silence fills the room. Duncan doesn't like the way he's looking at him, or the way he's nervously adjusting the stethoscope around his neck.

'I must prepare you,' the doctor says eventually. 'Georgina is very unwell. She's in a coma.'

'A coma?' Duncan blinks, unable to process the words.

'A diabetic coma.'

'How? I don't understand. What happened?'

'Without insulin, her blood sugar rose to extremely high levels. She was severely dehydrated too, which contributed to her diabetic ketoacidosis.'

'But she will wake up?'

The doctor looks at Duncan with concerned eyes.

'Once her glucose levels are back to normal, she'll recover?' Duncan reiterates, his voice quivering. He's feeling suddenly overwhelmed.

'There have been some complications. Georgina suffered a stroke.'

Duncan starts crying. 'A stroke?'

'It can happen when the body goes through something like this. The blood pressure rises too quickly and—'

'But she *will* wake up?'

'We can't tell at the moment whether there's brain damage, or how serious it is.'

Duncan blinks through the tears. He stares at the doctor in disbelief.

The man places a gentle hand on Duncan's shoulder. 'I wish I had better news.'

Duncan Taylor-Johnson reminds himself to breathe. He crosses to the window that looks over Amsterdam. The family room is on the third floor with sweeping views across the city. The sky is dark and unruly, much like his mood. In the wall of glass before him he finds a ghostly apparition of himself. Greying hair, his face sun-worn from summers on his yacht and winters skiing in Courchevel. He's ageing quicker than he'd like and he wishes he could turn back time, revisit those early years when things were less complicated.

He wishes he could go back to Christmas Eve, the night that put a chokehold on his life. If he had a second chance, he would do it all differently.

He wouldn't have lost his temper when he found Georgina taking drugs. He wouldn't have taken the tough-love approach. He wouldn't have put his new family first.

When Duncan eventually heard the news his daughter was missing, the very first thing he assumed was that it was a ploy to get his attention. Why, WHY hadn't he taken it seriously?

'Is this really happening?' Duncan whispers.

'I'm so sorry. We're doing all we can.' The doctor glances towards the door. He lowers his voice. 'The police are here; I think they want to ask you some questions.'

'Where is she?' Duncan looks around.

'She's in intensive care. Your daughter is in a critical state, but she's stable.'

'I need to see Georgina!'

Duncan senses a presence outside, looming in the corridor. A shadow, blurred through the frosted glass door. Immediately, his stomach tightens and the muscles in his neck spasm as his anger surges and spills over. This is *their* fault. Why didn't they react sooner? He grabs the handle, his face flushed with rage.

The police officer looks up. A woman with short hair steps into his path, flashing her ID.

'Mr Taylor-Johnson? I'm Inspector Van den Berg.'

The detective is tall, almost the same height as him, and she looks him straight in the eye.

Duncan glares at her, blood heating with rage.

'Can we talk?'

He reaches out and takes hold of her ID, examining it closely. Finally, when he's satisfied, he hands it back, closes his eyes briefly, exhaling and counting to five. It's taking every fibre of his being not to lose control. The horror of today is relentlessly rushing towards him like a bullet train.

It began in the early hours of the morning when Duncan was woken by a WhatsApp from his daughter. Only it wasn't Georgina sending the video message.

Someone had her phone.

Someone had her.

Bound and gagged, eyes bulging from where they'd rammed the cloth so far down her throat, Georgina was crying. She was terrified. A dark figure disguised in a balaclava loomed behind her, two slits for eyes, an arm wrapped tightly around her body and a knife at her throat. He was pressing the blade so firmly against his daughter's jugular, blood was trickling across her skin.

It was worse than any horror film. At the memory, Duncan's body starts to shake, his hands tremble. The ghastly images will be forever seared into his memory. His poor baby girl.

He didn't hesitate, not for a second. Duncan did as he was asked – he emptied the contents of his safe into a sports bag and headed to the study where he collected his passport, laptop, chargers and European adapter plugs. He gently kissed his wife and his newborn baby goodbye, careful not to wake them, and left his sprawling estate via the garage, having selected the Jaguar F-Type. Gunmetal grey with tinted windows, its supercharged V8 engine packed, making it the ideal choice for the long-distance journey ahead.

It was nothing short of a miracle that he wasn't stopped for inspection at the LeShuttle border control.

'I don't have to answer your questions,' Duncan snaps at the inspector.

'We won't take long,' she insists.

'This will have to wait; my daughter needs me.'

Registering the grief and strain in his face, the inspector's eyes soften.

'It's important. Don't you want us to catch whoever did this to her?'

More than anything. Rage claws inside him. Duncan spent the entire journey trying to work out who these criminals could be, and how Georgina came to be mixed up with them. He's considered the possibility of a disgruntled former employee, but nobody came to mind. It must be connected with drugs. An unpaid debt, perhaps. Why didn't Georgina ask him for help?

A crushing guilt descends as he remembers *why*. Duncan swore he'd never end up like his bully of a father: a respected army brigadier, a loyal husband in public, and a monster behind closed doors.

'What do you need from me?' he murmurs, his anger dissipating into grief.

'We believe your daughter was abducted on New Year's Eve by a gang involved in trafficking. We suspect they murdered a social media influencer after he discovered their identity. Have you received any strange messages? Were you contacted by anyone out of the ordinary?'

The horrific images of Georgina being tortured flash before his eyes. Duncan hesitates, then admits: 'I was sent a ransom demand.'

She looks taken aback. 'Why didn't you bring this to the police immediately?'

'They would have killed Georgina. They warned me: *no police*.'

'When?'

'This morning.'

She's writing this down. He notices her underline something.

'How much?'

He swallows. 'Three million.'

She shakes her head. 'And you paid the full amount?'

'They promised Georgina would be there when I handed over the money, I-I didn't know what else to do.'

'Did you meet with them?'

'They told me to go into the underpass at the Rijksmuseum. I was instructed to put the cash in a sports bag, leave it next to the bin and walk in the other direction. It was crowded with people, a tour bus arrived moments later.'

'Are you able to describe them?'

'It was all done through messages. By the time I realized that I'd been tricked, the bag had gone and they had vanished.'

'But you have the phone number?'

'It's been disconnected.'

After they sent Duncan the video using Georgina's mobile, they switched to a new number, most likely a burner phone, no doubt untraceable. These were career criminals, far too clever to be caught. His wealth meant he was always going to be a target for ransom demands. He should have prepared better. This was his fault. *He was to blame.*

The inspector lets out a heavy sigh. 'Mr Johnson-Taylor, you need to come to the station and be interviewed formally as a matter of urgency.'

'No, not until I see Georgina!'

'We'll need your phone, and anything else that can help us track the perpetrators. We can trace their last known whereabouts via the masts.'

He hands her his mobile without even thinking.

'It was a man.'

'What makes you say that?'

'A hunch. I don't know for certain, but – could a woman do this to another woman?'

'You'd be surprised.' The inspector continues: 'I don't think her captors realized she was diabetic. They probably panicked when she fell unconscious.'

Duncan feels tears building and looks away.

'You did what any father would have done.'

'If I'd come sooner, if I – if I'd done something . . .' His voice breaks. 'My wife, she's just given birth. I'm a father again, at fifty-eight. I've got a baby daughter.'

'It sounds like you have a lot on your plate.'

'That's no excuse.' Duncan shakes his head. Why hadn't he swallowed his pride and picked up the phone to his older daughter to tell her he was sorry? If he had, he'd have known Georgina was in trouble. 'It's my fault.' He chokes on the words, remembering how he raised his hand, recalling the force with which he struck her across the face. He's a monster and that's all there is to it. He turns towards the next set of double doors with a heart so heavy he can barely lift his feet.

The inspector steps out of his way.

The doctor who has been observing the tense exchange returns to Duncan's side, his expression even more strained than before. Dropping his voice to a whisper, he says: 'I think you should prepare yourself. It's not easy seeing someone you love on life support.'

Oh dear God. Duncan swallows to keep himself from being sick. The urge to turn and run is overwhelming. He's not sure he's ever felt this frightened, this helpless, or less ready to deal with a crisis. The *bleep bleep* of the heart monitors, the hiss and pump of the ventilator fill his head. In something of a daze, he stumbles towards the noise, towards the machines keeping his daughter alive.

'I'm sorry, Sparkles,' he murmurs, his voice choked with emotion. 'Please forgive me.'

'Mr Taylor-Johnson—'

Duncan slows, taking a breath. Fighting back the tears, he turns to face the inspector.

'We'll find out who did this to your daughter.' She looks at him earnestly. 'I promise.'

THE FRIEND – BECCA

I want Georgie to be the first to know.

Nathan had already left for work so I didn't get the chance to tell him, but as I sit here, cradling my friend's hand in mine, it feels right that we share this moment together.

The news has come as a shock. I'd given up all hope of it ever happening, and now it is happening, I can't wrap my head around it.

Georgie will give me the confidence and reassurance I need, I think, as I gently rub her hands, trying to warm them up. Her fingers are ice-cold and her skin's so pale I can see her veins. It feels like there's no blood there at all.

The nurses have explained it's to do with her circulation – lack of movement combined with her diabetes means the blood struggles to reach her extremities. God, it's heartbreaking seeing my Georgie like this, with tubes feeding into her nose and arms, reliant on the life support machine forcing oxygen into her lungs. And she's lost a dramatic amount of weight. Her cheeks are hollowed out, the bed linen drowns her tiny frame. Biting my lip, I quickly look away before I break down.

We'll find out who did this to you, Georgie.

Though after two months, it feels as if we might never get there.

The police are still pursuing the theory that Georgie was abducted by an eastern European gang who held her for ransom after discovering how wealthy her father was. They think Jamie was murdered when he tracked them down and threatened to reveal their identity. Conspiracy theorists suggest Jamie might even have been blackmailing the gang. They say Dieter Schmidt is involved with the traffickers, laundering their profits through his gallery. But these are just theories. Without any proof, new leads or momentum, the police have scaled back their search. It's clear they're losing interest.

When the inspector released me, having finally taken seriously my suspicions about Rami, it was too late: he'd vanished. The old man he lived with claimed he had no idea of Rami's whereabouts, but I know he's lying – they're all lying, they're covering up for someone, I just don't know who. It all leads back to the afterparty, I'm certain of it. I feel so helpless, so utterly frustrated about not being heard. I wish I could do more.

I try to stay calm, forcing myself to look past the bottles of medicine and the machines. There's a fresh bouquet of pink and white lilies by her bedside.

Georgie's father must have been here earlier. He travels to Amsterdam twice a week while he prepares to bring her home. He's spent the past two months constructing a purpose-built annex fully equipped with all the latest medical technology. Soon she'll have round-the-clock private care; he hasn't given up hope of her waking from the coma.

I haven't given up either. Because without hope, what is there?

I bite my lip, losing my battle to hold back the tears. As I squeeze Georgie's hand, I force myself to remember the good times, those summers at Waverley, soaking up sunshine by the pool. Sharing stories beneath the shade of the apple trees. Spying on Georgie's mum's friends at her outrageously glamorous parties. I try to see past the shell of a woman on the bed and remember Georgie how she was: beautiful and magnetic, I'll never forget. *Never.*

Georgie has a sister now, and I hope she'll meet her one day soon. I was shocked to see how Daisy had grown in only a few weeks. As I recall the baby photos Georgie's dad showed me, my mind turns to what lies ahead and I take a deep breath, preparing to tell Georgie my secret.

'There's something I need to tell you,' I say quietly.

It feels strange, speaking out loud when I'm not sure Georgie can hear me. I carry on regardless, suddenly desperate to tell her.

'I'm pregnant!' I say into the silence.

More silence.

'I'm going to be a mum; can you believe it?'

Watching her closely, I search for a sign. Something, anything, a flicker of an eyelid, a twitch of her hand. *Nothing.*

Drying my eyes, I carry on, my voice choked with emotion.

'I know what you're thinking.' I smile sadly. 'You're

worried for me, aren't you? You'd say I was doing this for the wrong reasons, that a baby won't fix my marriage, but I want to reassure you: things are better with Nathan now. Everything feels calmer, in fact.' I pause. A small smile. 'In fact, it's the best it's been in years.' I stifle a sob. 'God, I feel so fucking guilty saying that, with you in here like this. I'm so sorry, Georgie.' My voice cracks. 'I know you'd be happy for me, though, wouldn't you? I know you can hear me.'

Unable to hold back the tears, I get up and walk towards the window. The sun is shining, the snow and the darkness feel like a distant memory.

'Me, being a mum!' I shake my head. 'It's wild, isn't it?'

I turn back to face my friend and immediately feel wretched again. How far apart our lives have drifted. For the first time in our friendship, I'm the one with something good happening. It feels wrong and I can't cope.

'The restaurant is doing well,' I say, quickly changing the subject. 'We're fully booked most nights and Nathan's stopped stressing about money since the investor came back on board. Personally, I would have told him to piss off after the way he treated us, but Nathan says that's not how business works – something about playing the long game.' I shrug. 'What do I know? But if things continue like this, Nathan says it'll be eight months until we break even. He's even talking about opening a second restaurant. And now there's extra cash, he's given me a job.' I put on a voice: 'Meet Muse's new *marketing director*.' A small laugh. 'I know, I know, *me*, on social media. Mind you, I

don't know how that's going to play out now with a baby
on the way and—'

My phone buzzes with a message. It's Nathan.

Can you do me a favour? ❤

'Sorry, Georgie, I have to go.'
I'm hit with another wave of guilt.
'But I'll be back tomorrow or the day after, I promise.
I'll bring a book next time and read to you and we can—'
I stop, studying my friend. Even with all the tubes and the
wires, she's still beautiful. She'll always be beautiful. I stand
up before it becomes impossible to leave.

On the way to the restaurant, I pass by Noordermarkt.
Every Saturday, the cobbled square outside the church
hosts a market, its stalls bursting with organic vegetables,
fruits, speciality breads and Dutch cheeses.

I lock up my bike and pull out my phone, ready to
film some quick content. After everything, I can't believe
I'm running Muse's TikTok channel. Flipping the camera
around, I stretch out a smile and press record.

'Lovelies, how you all doing? Come spend the day with
me! Starting off in Amsterdam's famous food market!
How incredible is this? As you know, Muse's spring
menu will be dropping very soon, so I'm getting ahead
of the game by checking out what organic treats we
can introduce into our new dishes. YUM!'

I zoom in on the crates stacked with seasonal vegetables
while the guy behind the stall gives me an awkward wave.

'Oh my God, it's stunning here! And after this I'm heading to the restaurant, where our star chef, Katya, is busy prepping for our set menu tonight. If you haven't made a reservation, sorry guys, it's all booked up. But we're releasing a few tables later this month and—'

I stop, breathless. Being this smiley is exhausting. How do people do it? I put my phone away and pick up a slice of Nathan's favourite gluten-free raspberry cake before jumping back on my bike and heading towards the restaurant.

It's a cold but clear day with only a few clouds scudding across the sky. The sun is shining brightly and the shop windows are filled with tulips. Finally, it feels like spring is on the way. I park my bike outside Muse and immediately I'm hit with a rush of butterflies. *I'm having a baby*, I tell myself again, *WE'RE HAVING A BABY!* It still doesn't feel real. It feels somehow wrong that everything is falling into place after so much tragedy. I'm nervous and excited as I pick up speed, walking through the dining area towards the kitchen. *We're having a baby, I'm going to be a mum!*

'Nathan!' I call out.

He appears from the stockroom clutching a tower of boxes and frowning.

'What's wrong?'

'The bloody wine hasn't arrived.' He heaves a sigh, dumping the boxes on the floor. Arching his back, he twists from side to side, stretching himself out.

'Is there enough for tonight?'

He comes over and kisses me on the lips. 'We're totally out of vino. I'm going to need you to go to the wholesaler, baby – that OK?'

I hide my disappointment with a weary smile; my news will have to wait.

'Where's Katya?'

'She's at the supermarket, we've also run out of cream and fennel. Ambroos has called in sick, everything's going to shit. Why?' He does a mock scream. 'Why today of all days?'

'It's OK, I'll go.'

'You're the best.'

My heart feels like it's about to burst. I'm desperate to tell Nathan about the baby but I want the moment to be perfect, not when he's feeling stressed and under pressure. I squeeze his arm. 'Just tell me what you need me to do.'

Nathan hands me a long list of organic wines. He's written the postcode on the back, and warns me the wholesaler's some distance out of town so I'll need to drive there. I bite into my cheek because I don't feel confident on the roads. The one-way system around the canals is a nightmare and leaves my head spinning.

'I'll do it now,' I say, hiding my anxiety.

'Hey.' He wraps his arms around me, pulling me into his warm body. 'How was it at the hospital? I'm sorry it's stressy here, I meant to ask.'

Tears fill my eyes and for a moment I can't speak.

He gives me a squeeze. 'I don't know what to say. It's so awful,' he says awkwardly.

'Why won't the police *do something*?' I blurt.

'Whoever's in charge should be fired. They've been utterly shit. How hard can it be to catch the people who did this? But you've got to stop blaming yourself.' He strokes my face. 'I can see how this is taking its toll.'

I hold up the list of wines, desperate to change the subject. 'I'd best get this to the wholesaler, pronto.'

'I love you,' he says, and kisses my nose.

I look back at him. He doesn't normally tell me that.

'Ditto,' I say, my lower lip quivering.

Jesus, these hormones! If I'm an emotional wreck now, what will I be like in a few months' time? I give Nathan a hug, holding onto my news even more tightly. I'll tell him later tonight. I'll light some candles, make it special.

Heading off, I swing past the security box. It's crammed full of keys except the ones to the company car. Nathan must have forgotten that Katya's taken it for the food run.

'Nathan?' I turn back, but he's already disappeared into the stockroom. *Great*. I'll have to take Betty, the ancient rust bucket of a van we squeezed our old lives into when we moved abroad.

Nathan's coat is hanging up by the door. I feel around in his pockets, finding tissues, chewing gum, crumpled receipts and eventually a key fob. Fishing the van keys out, I head back into the sunshine.

Betty's parked adjacent to the canal. I slide open the door, checking there will be room in the back for all the wine crates, and I'm shocked to find it's tidy inside. Uncharacteristically clean, in fact. I shrug off my surprise and jump behind the wheel, but in my hurry to get going, I drop the keys into the footwell. *Fuck's sake*, I mutter, grimacing as I fold double and reach around my feet.

Just my luck – they've got stuck beneath the seat. Heaving a frustrated sigh, I get out and use my phone torch to search for them among the litter of crisp packets and screwed-up pay-and-display tickets. I swipe my hand back and forth until my fingers knock into something hard and rectangular. What's that? I frown, angling the torch so it shines across what looks like . . .

I hesitate.

No, it can't be.

But it is, there's no mistaking it. I freeze, my heart racing as I stare at the candyfloss pink phone case like it's a bomb about to detonate.

Carefully I pick it up, cradling it in my palm as I ask myself, *Why would Nathan have Georgie's phone in his van?*

The battery's dead.

I waste no time plugging the phone into the charger powered through the cigarette lighter. I turn on the engine. And, within seconds, it comes alive. I swipe the screen and, to my surprise, it opens without needing a passcode.

Obscured behind the app icons is a photo of Georgie. She's stretched out across a sun lounger in a pastel blue bikini, her blonde hair shining under the midday sun. One arm is slung lazily above her head as she smiles suggestively from behind her sunglasses.

The WhatsApp icon is showing 107 unread messages. I tap it open, my eyes skimming across the *where are you?* messages from her friends. I refamiliarize myself with all the messages I've sent Georgie since the night she went missing, coming to a hard stop at her most recent WhatsApp with her dad.

Papa.

I click on it, expecting another confused *where are you*. My heart gets stuck in my throat as I scroll through the dozens of messages pleading for his daughter's life.

And there's a video.

With trembling hands, I press play.

It's Georgie. I watch her crying, I watch the knife being held to her throat by a man wearing a black mask, I watch my friend pleading for her life. I feel sick; I can't look at it a second longer. I hit pause, returning to the chat page, desperate to find something, anything to tear my thoughts away from the sickening torture; to reassure me that this is not happening, and there's a perfectly reasonable explanation why Georgie's phone, the same phone that was used for a ransom video, is in my husband's van.

THE FRIEND – BECCA

'That was quick!' Nathan looks at me in astonishment.

Without saying a word, I cross over to the other side of the restaurant. My hands are shaking as I place my phone on the bar, positioning it so it's angled at forty-five degrees. I leave it pointing towards me and then turn back to face my husband.

The skin across my arms is prickling. I'm tingling from head to toe. My body is on red alert, yet I'm struggling to make sense of what I should be feeling. Fear? Sadness? I look down at my trembling hands. Rage?

'Did the car run out of petrol?' he says, a note of irritation in his voice. 'Do you need me to fill it up?'

It feels like I'm delirious. I give my head a shake but it doesn't clear the thick fog that's moved in. Tears arrive and I swipe them away. Goddammit, now's not the time to crumble. I retrieve my anger before that disappears too.

Slipping into shock, I mumble the first thing that comes into my head: 'You said you'd never break my heart.'

Nathan looks up from what he's doing. 'You OK?'

'I guess there's just some promises you should never make.'

He frowns. 'Becca? What's going on?'

'Nathan . . . just stop.'

He eyes me uneasily.

'*I know*, OK.'

'Look, I'm not sure what's going on, but we're in a godawful rush. If you can't pick up the wine, I need to get hold of Katya—'

I take Georgie's phone from my pocket and he stops dead. His face instantly drains of colour.

My heart collapses with the confirmation. 'Oh God. What did you do?'

He stares at Georgie's mobile. It's like he's seen a ghost.

'I trusted you.'

Nathan looks up at me, his body completely still.

'I loved you.'

Silence.

'What happened, Nathan?' I ask.

The echoing silence spreads between us. For a second, I think he's about to speak, to reassure me it's not Georgie's phone, that he didn't take her hostage and blackmail her father for money. But he lowers his eyes. He won't look at me.

'You killed Jamie Finn, didn't you?'

His face crumples.

'Oh no. No, no, no.'

'I can explain – it was an accident.'

'Oh God.'

'I had to do something! He was stalking you; he was frightening you. And he was destroying our business. I was protecting you. It was only meant to be a warning, to tell him to stay the fuck away from you.'

I let out a gasp, clutching my hand over my mouth.

'Stop, stop,' he says, taking a step towards me. 'Please, listen.'

'You killed him.'

'I tried to reason with him. I knew about his scam with Georgie, I'd followed him the night before to the docklands—'

'Scam? What scam?'

'Yeah, it was all a scam.' Nathan shakes his head slowly. 'Your so-called best mate faked her disappearance. Those two were conning the public out of money.'

I shake my head. 'Georgie wouldn't do that.'

'Becca, wake up.'

'No. It doesn't make any sense—'

'Becca!' he shouts, louder this time. 'She's a washed-up druggie. A bitch liar who used you. Like she'd always used you.'

Bitch.

The word echoes and I'm hit with a flashback to New Year's Eve. I'm stumbling around, drunk, agitated and frightened. I throw an arm around Georgie to steady myself, hugging her too tightly. 'Please, let's go home now,' I beg. I remember the flash of irritation in her eyes and how she tried to shrug me off. She wanted to ditch me, but I clung on, refusing to let her go. Then I remember glancing down at my drink, just as she was slipping something into my champagne.

There was a moment of confusion where I looked up, catching her eyes. 'What have you done to me?'

'Twiggy,' she edged away.

'You drugged me!'

'Darling, I can explain . . .'

A fleeting moment of lucidity where I realized: Georgie's the reason I'm feeling so godawful. She must have spiked my drink earlier on.

'What have you given me?'

'I'm sorry.'

'You bitch!' I screamed. Then came the dark fury. And then I lunged at her.

'I tried to make you see what she was really like.' Nathan pulls me out of the past.

It was Georgie who drugged me. My God.

'But you didn't want to listen,' he continues.

I raise my gaze from the ground and stare back at him. 'But you killed someone,' I whisper.

'That bastard was ruining us! I gave him an ultimatum, tried to warn him off. I told him if he didn't stop with all the videos, I'd expose the pair of them as frauds. And that's when he lost it. He came at me like a madman. I don't know whether he was high, or drunk, or both, but he went for me, and I had no choice but to defend myself. It was self-defence – I pushed him away and he fell badly, and—' Nathan stops.

'Oh my God.' I stare at him.

'I didn't mean to; it was an accident.'

The photos of Jamie Finn's dead body crash into my head. The angry red marks from where he'd been throttled. As I imagine Nathan's hands closing around his neck, squeezing the life out of him, my knees start to give way.

'It just happened. He tripped and fell and banged his

head, I didn't mean to hurt him. Then I panicked, and rolled him into the canal.'

Liar.

'He was still alive,' I say.

'What?'

'The police said he died from drowning, not a bang to the head. You could have saved him.'

'I didn't know . . .'

'And then, after you murdered him, you decided to make the most of the situation. Oh God – you were the one who locked Georgie up and did those awful things to her.' I grimace, replaying the ransom video in my head. Black slits for eyes, the knife against her throat. I imagine the terror she must have felt and my stomach lurches.

'We were going to lose the business, Becca! When Brad Garcia pulled out, we were facing bankruptcy. After everything we'd sacrificed—'

'Georgie's in a coma. It's unlikely she'll ever wake up.'

'How was I supposed to know she was a diabetic? It was never my plan to hurt her – why would I do that? We needed the money and I knew her dad was good for it, that he'd pay up in the end.'

'And you let the police believe it was me!'

'No.' He shakes his head. 'Come on, I knew they wouldn't charge you. I thought we'd recoup the money we lost and it would all blow over.'

'You'd have seen me go to prison, all for your precious fucking restaurant!'

Nathan takes another step towards me. The expression in his eyes turns soft and tender.

'I love you, Becca.'

I edge away. 'You're sick.'

'I did this for you,' he says.

'You did it for YOU.'

'It was an accident. I was protecting you.'

'It's all been about *you*, about what you want, about *your* dreams.' I look around. 'I gave up everything for you. And you betrayed me!' I scream at him.

'Calm down, it wasn't like that. You have to listen to me.'

'I never want to listen to you again. On New Year's Eve, Georgie tried to warn me what you were really like, she wanted to remind me who I was before I met you.'

'Jesus!' He rakes his hands through his hair. 'She was using you!'

'She knew I deserved better.'

'She's a fucking prick-tease!' he yells. 'And she got what she deserved.'

We both fall quiet.

'What are you going to do now?' he murmurs.

My gaze flicks across the room. Nathan sees me anxiously eyeing the door. He steps in front of me, blocking my exit.

'Are you going to tell the police?' He moves closer. 'Think about it, what would be the point? They've dropped the case. We've got the money we need to finally buy a home. Things couldn't be better for us. We've a chance to start over. To be happy. What would be the point in sending me to jail?'

I stare at him. Holding onto my secret with both hands.

'Becca?' He eyes me nervously. 'I'm begging you. Please

think about us. Think about our future. I know you don't want to be without me.'

'Stop it. Please, stop.'

I try to shut out his words, but his voice tunnels into my thoughts.

'You'll destroy our lives. Do you want that? Because I don't, I love you so much.'

I feel my resolve weakening.

'I love you more than anything.'

He holds out a hand but I take a step back and give my head a little shake, trying to loosen his grip on me. My thoughts are spiralling. *Think, Becca, think.*

'It'll just be you and me,' he promises, fixing me with his gaze.

And the baby.

I can't let my baby grow up with a murderer for a father. *I can't pretend everything's OK.* The faces of Jamie and Georgie strobe behind my eyes. I shake myself out of my delirium. With a sudden burst of adrenaline, I lunge for the door.

'No, wait!' Nathan opens his arms wide and propels himself towards me.

In my panic, I stumble.

I reach out to break my fall. But then a weight lands on my back, pressing me into the cold marble floor.

'Get off me!' I scream as Nathan flips me over onto my back.

I stare up at my husband. Our eyes meet. And there's a moment of confusion where neither of us knows what to do.

Then the adrenaline kicks in again, like a rocket in my chest, and I start bucking and twisting. I scramble to get out from under him, but he's too heavy. He's too strong. Pinning me in place, Nathan uses his left arm to hold me down while he reaches up to the table above. I try to loosen his grip but, with his elbow jammed into my neck, it's all I can do to breathe.

'Let me go,' I wheeze. The room's blurring in and out of focus. Out of the corner of my eye, I see him blindly grasping around the table.

'You're hurting me . . .'

Plates and cutlery are shoved to one side. His hand wraps around a bottle of sparkling water. He brings it down, smashing the glass right next to my face. Water spills across the floor, seeping into my hair, ice-cold against my skull. Nathan raises his arm.

'Nathan, stop!' I scream.

His expression darkens as he holds the broken bottle above my head.

'I'm pregnant!'

His hand freezes.

'Please!' I wheeze. 'Don't hurt me.'

Blinking uncomprehendingly, his grip on my neck loosens. The pressure releases and oxygen rushes into my lungs. I take in great gulps of air while holding myself very still.

'You're lying.'

'I swear,' I cough, drinking in more air.

'You're fucking with me.'

'I did a pregnancy test this morning.'

A frown settles between his brows.

'I've still got it – I can show you. I wouldn't lie to you,' I whimper.

Nathan stares down at me as if contemplating his next move.

'Please. Think of us, think of the baby. It's what you wanted.'

He hesitates, and for a moment I think he's about to lower his weapon, but then his usually gentle blue eyes harden. With a look of determination, he raises the broken bottle, angling the jagged edges towards my throat.

Oh God, he's going to kill me.

I cover my face in an effort to block the attack. As his arm arcs through the air, I somehow manage to raise my knee and drive it into his chest. While he's off balance, I strike out with my foot and he stumbles backwards, his legs giving way. For a moment he pauses, giving me a look as if to say he's impressed by my unexpected strength. But then he scrambles to his feet, coming at me again.

'Stop!' I scream so loudly it feels like my throat's been ripped in two. 'You're on TikTok!'

Nathan falters.

With a shaky hand, I point to my phone sitting on the bar. I'd set up a live TikTok feed the moment I arrived.

He laughs hollowly. 'You're bluffing.'

In the distance, I can hear the faint sound of sirens.

'See for yourself,' I wheeze, rubbing my neck.

Keeping a wary eye on me, Nathan crosses the room. Three strides and he's at the bar. He peers into the screen, squinting.

'Oh fuck!' He recoils.

The wail of the sirens grows louder. Someone watching the live feed must have called the police.

'What have you done?' Nathan looks back at me in disbelief.

We stare at each other for what feels like an eternity, when really it's less than thirty seconds before the police cars screech to a stop outside. The flashing blue-and-white lights spill inside the room. Then all hell breaks loose.

There's yelling, followed by a stampede of officers with assault rifles at the ready. They storm towards Nathan and he drops the bottle, raising two shaky hands into the air.

Inspector Van den Berg appears shortly afterwards, calmly making her way into the restaurant while an officer snaps a pair of cuffs around my husband's wrists. She must have changed her mind about retiring. As she reads Nathan his rights, he doesn't take his eyes off me, not for a second. His gaze remains fixed on me as they frogmarch him towards the exit.

Even as they place him in a police car, he casts one final glance over his shoulder. The storm has cleared from his eyes and the darkness has been replaced with sadness. Nathan stares at me, misty-eyed, and for a split second he looks like a child again. A lost little boy in need of rescuing. The inspector lowers a hand to his head, guiding him into the back seat.

I can't bear it any longer, I tear my eyes away before he disappears altogether. Staring out across the canal, I let out a shaky breath. I tell myself it's safe to breathe again.

EPILOGUE

I've got butterflies in my stomach.

Stroking my hand over my baby bump in a gentle rhythmical back and forth motion soothes and calms me. My baby is helping with my anxiety, even before she's born. Although – I laugh to myself – I'm sure that feeling of peace will be ripped from me when I have a crying newborn on my hands.

But I can't wait.

Only two months to go. I smile, tilting my head back, reaching for the sunshine. Behind me there's a cacophony of shuffling feet, cutlery clanging, clinking of glass as tables are frantically laid in time for supper. Brad Garcia and I are hosting a special event in conjunction with the Rijksmuseum. In a matter of hours, the restaurant will be filled with some of the most influential people from the world of art and archaeology, celebrating the opening of the gallery's first Egyptian exhibition. The huge collection features ceramics, mummies, coffins, papyrus and stone-work, with one of the highlights being a dress dating back to 5000 BC.

When one door closes, another opens.

If you'd asked me this time last year whether I thought I'd be capable of managing one of Amsterdam's leading restaurants, I would have laughed in your face. But the strangest things happen when you're thrown in the deep end. It was either sink or swim after Nathan was arrested. I chose to swim.

I chose to live.

Taking over the restaurant has given me a purpose. I was feeling lonely and useless in Amsterdam because I'd been frozen out of the business. Back then, I didn't know where my life was going. But joining forces with Brad and buying Katya out of the restaurant has made me assertive. Finding a new head chef has proved I can be decisive. *I am confident.* And I'm not lonely any more. I'm too bloody busy to be lonely.

In fact, I'm so run off my feet, I barely have time to think about Nathan. Or maybe that's my body's way of protecting me from pain.

He's awaiting trial. He intends to plead not guilty but the evidence – his TikTok confession – is so damning, even his lawyer says he doesn't stand a chance.

What I did and the way I did it caused a media sensation – the first confession of its kind. Since it went viral, I've barely set foot outside my door without being photographed or having a microphone shoved under my nose by some journalist, podcaster or CrimeTokker.

It's exhausting.

But it's also a welcome distraction from thinking about Georgie, still lying in a coma, on life support. Or of Nathan and the web of lies he spun around me. With the help of a therapist, I'm beginning to understand and untangle the full extent of his manipulation. I'd been under his spell for *years*. He'd been gaslighting me for the best part of a decade, robbing me of my confidence, leaving me feeling weak and useless, convinced I couldn't survive without him. All so I wouldn't find the courage to leave.

Well, look at me now. I'm thriving.

I rub my hand over my stomach again. Me and my little boo are going to be just fine on our own.

Staring out across the canal, I take in its beauty. It's the most perfect autumn day. We're enjoying an Indian summer in Amsterdam, the sun hasn't stopped shining, which is great because all this vitamin D is doing wonders for the baby.

I breathe deeply through the next wave of butterflies. I suppose I am a little nervous – after all, I haven't seen him in months.

I thought I'd never hear from him again and then, last Monday, out of the blue, he messaged me on Instagram.

Rami finally confessed to me that he had stolen Georgie's handbag on New Year's Eve. But not for himself – for his sister. He'd been saving up for months to buy Samira a passport, putting the money he was earning at the parties aside, but it wasn't enough and time was running out. Then, when Georgie dropped her handbag during our fight, and when she didn't come back to collect it, Rami snuck it out of the house and took it home. He kept it hidden under the sink, anxiously waiting for the attention around Georgie's disappearance to die down. When I showed up at his place, he panicked. Desperate to get rid of anything linking him to Georgie, he arranged to meet the men in the Range Rover and sold the Chanel to them for 2,500 euros.

It was enough to buy his sister's freedom.

I wonder if he'll look any different. He'll be shocked when he sees me! And it starts me off thinking about a lot of things, including those feelings I was so afraid of allowing in.

Now I'm wondering, I'm thinking, I'm tangling myself up in knots . . . and then I look up.

I can stop wondering.

Rami smiles at me from the other side of the restaurant and his sister gives me a nervous wave. He's right, they don't look anything like each other.

I stand up and his eyes drop to my huge baby bump and he starts laughing and I start laughing and now we're both giggling. I don't think I've ever been so happy to see someone.

He comes towards me and the butterflies are back. And I'm wondering again, I'm asking myself, is he feeling them too?

ACKNOWLEDGEMENTS

The Afterparty was a dream to write, mostly because I was able to immerse myself in descriptions of my home city of Amsterdam, where I have lived for many years.

As always, a massive thank you to everyone at Pan Macmillan for the incredible job you do of publishing my books. An extra special thank you to my commissioning editors Alex Saunders and Raphaella Demetris, Chloe Davies for her PR wizardry and Kieryn Tyler for another absolutely stunning front cover. Thank you, editorial manager Melissa Bond, for navigating my edits, and thank you to Anne O'Brien, who always does a marvellous job of making my words sparkle in the copy-edit and unravelling my wonky timelines.

Thank you to my agent, Hattie Grünewald, and everyone at The Blair Partnership.

To Michael, thank you for everything, for our life together in Amsterdam.

A huge thank you to my friends, for all the laughter and giggles. A special shout-out to Allie Steemson for being the funniest, kindest and most supportive friend I could ever want. To the gang in Hungerford, especially Emma Milne-White who runs the best bookshop in the world, cheers to many more fun and silly evenings at the wine bar!

And, last but certainty not least, thank you to my wonderful readers. If it weren't for you, I wouldn't be able to spend my days thinking up devilish plots. Thank you for buying my books, reviewing them and talking about them in book clubs – your support means everything.

THE
VILLA

A Villa in Paradise
It's destined to be the ultimate reality TV show. Ten contestants. A luxurious villa on a private island. Every moment streamed live to a global audience who have total control over those competing for the cash prize.

A Journalist Undercover
Reporter Laura is told to get the inside scoop on her fellow contestants. But, once the games begin, she soon finds herself at the mercy of a ruthless producer willing to do anything to increase viewer numbers.

A Reality Show to Die For
There is more to every contestant than meets the eye, including Laura. They all have secrets they'd like to keep buried, and the pressure in paradise quickly reaches boiling point. How far will the contestants go to secure audience votes? And would somebody really kill to win?

THE ESCAPE

**The grander the house . . .
the darker the secrets.**

When struggling influencer couple Adele and Jack post
a crowdfunding video online, they're amazed when a
mysterious benefactor offers to buy them an idyllic
seventeenth-century French château. It's the lifeline
they need to leave all their troubles behind and patch
up their relationship after a rocky period.

The Influencer
For Adele, it's a dream come true. She will post videos
from the fairy-tale setting, renovating the grand building
as thousands of online subscribers follow their journey.
But the château is not all it seems and the local
community is far from welcoming.

The Sister
Then Adele's videos suddenly stop. Her sister Erin
travels to France to make sure she's OK, but the
couple have vanished. From the obsession of Adele's
fans to the unsettling history of the building and
the claustrophobic secrecy of the nearby town,
Erin must unravel the shocking truth behind
why the anonymous investor gifted Adele and
Jack their dream home in the first place . . .

THE ICE RETREAT

Healer?

Meet Hollie Jenson, presenter of Bad Medicine –
the smash-hit docuseries that exposes the perils of
extreme therapies. Her next target: a new retreat
run by wellness guru Ariel Rose, who claims
to have discovered the secret to healing pain
through her three-day ice rebirth treatment.

Liar?

Acting on the plea of a mother to find her son
who vanished soon after his stay at the retreat,
Hollie ventures into the Swiss mountains, where the
facility occupies a former observatory. There she
will search for the boy, while also hoping to expose
Ariel as the charlatan she believes her to be.

Killer?

As the isolation of the valley sets in, Hollie finds
herself in an increasingly dangerous situation.
There is much more to the retreat than meets the
eye and she must confront explosive secrets from
her own past if she is to make it out alive . . .